#17

BULLETS AND BEADS

A Miss Fortune Mystery

NEW YORK TIMES BESTSELLING AUTHOR

JANA DELEON

Art attribution: Design and derivative illustration by Janet Holmes using images from Shutterstock.

Created with Vellum

FOREWORD

Miss Fortune Series Information

If you've never read a Miss Fortune mystery, you can start with LOUISIANA LONGSHOT, the first book in the series. If you prefer to start with this book, here are a few things you need to know.

Fortune Redding – a CIA assassin with a price on her head from one of the world's most deadly arms dealers. Because her boss suspects that a leak at the CIA blew her cover, he sends her to hide out in Sinful, Louisiana, posing as his niece, a librarian and ex–beauty queen named Sandy-Sue Morrow. The situation was resolved in Change of Fortune and Fortune is now a full-time resident of Sinful and has opened her own detective agency.

Ida Belle and Gertie – served in the military in Vietnam as spies, but no one in the town is aware of that fact except Fortune and Deputy LeBlanc.

Sinful Ladies Society – local group founded by Ida Belle, Gertie, and deceased member Marge. In order to gain membership, women must never have married or if widowed, their husband must have been deceased for at least ten years.

Sinful Ladies Cough Syrup – sold as an herbal medicine in Sinful, which is dry, but it's actually moonshine manufactured by the Sinful Ladies Society.

CHAPTER ONE

I WALKED into Ida Belle's kitchen and stared at the hundreds of bright purple, gold, and green bottles covering every surface in the room. Gertie was at the sink, pouring liquid from a pitcher into a bottle, and Ida Belle was putting stickers on them. I stepped up to the counter and picked up one of the purple bottles and checked the label.

"This is all Sinful Ladies Cough Syrup?" I asked.

It wasn't really cough syrup, of course. It was moonshine. But as Sinful was a dry town and the Sinful Ladies were Southern Baptist, they had their own unique method of skirting the rules.

"Mardi Gras is our biggest sales time of the year," Ida Belle said.

"Even more than New Year's?" I asked.

Gertie nodded. "Most people host their own parties for New Year's, so they can bring in liquor from up the highway. But the Mardi Gras celebration is all downtown and that means everyone is on public display."

"So no obvious drinking for the Baptists," I concluded.

Gertie frowned. "But those Catholics get to live it up."

"Stop grousing," Ida Belle said. "They get to live it up for a couple of days before they have to give up something they love for forty."

"Baptists give up stuff they love year-round," Gertie said.

Ida Belle raised an eyebrow.

"Well, they're supposed to," Gertie said.

"Since this is a Catholic sort of thing, does that mean Celia's crew runs the festivities?" I asked, hoping that wasn't the case. Celia Arceneaux, our archenemy, could turn even the most fabulous of occasions into a dumpster fire. Sometimes a real fire. She'd single-handedly burned down the sleigh ride at Christmas.

"She tries to run everything," Ida Belle said. "But the mayor gets to decide committees, and we've never had one foolish enough to put Celia in charge of the whole shooting match, even when they were Catholic. So Celia represents her group. I represent the sane side of things. And everything has to be approved by the mayor and the sheriff."

Since the mayor, Marie, was a close friend of Ida Belle and Gertie's and the sheriff pretty much hated the sight of Celia, that was good news for Ida Belle's crew. No way Celia could stage a coup.

"So what all happens?" I asked. "I figured everyone headed to New Orleans for a big round of debauchery."

"Lord no," Ida Belle said. "Navigating Vietnam was easier than making it through Bourbon Street for Mardi Gras. But it was such a big hit that most every city and town in Louisiana has its own Mardi Gras celebration. Some are big enough to have krewes, which are groups put together specifically to throw down on Mardi Gras. Others that are smaller, like Sinful, just rely on some locals to put everything together."

"But our party is on Saturday night," Gertie said. "That way, anyone who wants to head to New Orleans for some of the big parades on Sunday and on through Tuesday can still do so without missing the local fun."

"So what happens in Sinful on Sunday then?" I asked.

"Mostly recovery and repentance from Saturday," Ida Belle said.

"There's funnel cake," Gertie said. "Between that and the cough syrup, there's a lot to repent for."

"Funnel cake?" I perked up.

"Assuming they got the stand put back together," Ida Belle said.

"What happened to the stand?" I asked.

"They set everything up today and were testing the equipment to make sure they're ready for tomorrow night when a squirrel decided he'd steal the product."

Gertie nodded. "Pulled a fly-by and snatched it right off the plate before the powdered sugar had even settled. Some people scrambled to catch him while others tried to jump on the table and climb the stand poles to avoid him, and the whole shooting match collapsed."

"I'm surprised everyone didn't just open fire," I said.

"Don't think they didn't want to," Ida Belle said. "But they're downtown. Can't just open fire on squirrels on Main Street."

"Unless they steal something valued at over a hundred dollars," Gertie said. "Then you're allowed as long as you don't hit people."

"Of course you are," I said. "So basically, it's a big party for the whole town?"

Ida Belle nodded. "Downtown is closed off and everyone gathers there. Everything kicks off with the parade. Different people build floats and they go through downtown and turn around in the neighborhood, then circle back. The most important float, built by the sheriff's department and Walter, holds the King and Queen of Mardi Gras."

"You're going to allow a parade after that sleigh ride fiasco?" I asked.

"Celia's been banned from the floats!" Gertie said and clapped her hands.

Ida Belle grinned. "There was an emergency vote of the Mardi Gras committee after Christmas. They decided—unanimously, I might add—that Celia was banned from floats for a year."

"I would have loved to have seen her face when they told her that," I said.

Gertie gave me a sad shake of her head. "I asked Marie to film it, but she said it wouldn't be professional as she was there in her capacity as mayor. Being professional gets in the way of a lot of cool stuff."

"Definitely," I agreed. I'd already run into several occasions when being professional interfered with the most expedient way to conduct an investigation. Things like breaking-and-entering being illegal and interfering with police investigations were a constant trial in my line of work.

Ida Belle snorted.

"So who are the king and queen?" I asked. "How are they picked?"

"Everyone in town who wants to, votes," Ida Belle said. "Walter has a ballot box down at the General Store. They have voting for a week in September. You were in DC when it happened."

"They do it that far in advance?" I asked.

Gertie nodded. "The king and queen have to get their costumes ready. And no one wants to go the simple route. Every year, the new king and queen try to outdo the year before. They've gotten very elaborate. Lots of sparkly stuff. Very pretty."

"So who was chosen for this year?" I asked.

"No one knows until they show up at the party," Ida Belle said. "Well, no one except Walter, Carter, the parade organizers, and the people chosen."

"Which means Ida Belle," Gertie said. "And because she won't keep a secret from me, that means I know as well."

"That's because you'll badger me until I either tell or shoot you," Ida Belle said.

"Well, don't keep me in suspense," I said.

"It's Ally and Deputy Breaux," Gertie said, doing her bouncing and clapping routine again.

"Cool!" I said. "Ally will be a beautiful queen. I'm a little surprised at Deputy Breaux, though."

"I think people wanted to give him a boost given how difficult things were around here last year," Gertie said. "He really had to step up to the plate and learn to handle things on his own. I think most of us worried that he'd never be able to make a decision without Carter telling him what it should be, but he did a great job considering everything he was up against."

"I can see that," I said.

The previous year in Sinful, a crime wave had sprung forth that started the day I stepped into town. Fortunately, none of the crime had actually been because of me, but there were some that still liked to point out that my arrival had appeared to be the catalyst that unearthed all of Sinful's sins. And as it appeared I'd made it a personal goal to get in the fat middle of every one of them, I had my detractors among the locals.

"Here." Ida Belle handed me a cup. "Try this and let me know what you think."

I hesitated a second because I never really knew which

direction they had gone with flavors or with proof. Some of their cough syrup could take salt corrosion off a pier. I smelled it first and got a waft of spicy.

"Cinnamon?" I asked.

Ida Belle nodded. "Red Hots. We needed a spicy one for the party but wanted to go the sweet route. I suggest a gulp and not a sip. Best if it misses your lips."

I should have known better, but I dumped the contents of the cup in my mouth, figuring I'd hold it for a couple seconds to take in the flavor, but that wasn't going to happen. It was sweet and the flavor might have been nice if it hadn't burned off my taste buds. I struggled to swallow but finally gave up and spit it out in the sink. If someone turned another stove burner on, I could probably ignite it.

I stuck my entire head under the faucet and let water run into my mouth and pour out.

"It's good," Ida Belle said to Gertie.

I attempted a glare, but as I could only get one watery eye open, it probably wasn't that effective. Finally, the burning went down a notch and I stood up.

"Don't give her any of the hot batch," Gertie said. "Otherwise, your water bill will be through the roof."

I stared. "Hot batch? What was that?" I managed to speak but had developed what I was certain was a second-degree-burn lisp.

"That was the mild version," Ida Belle said. "Hot is in the yellow bottle."

"You people have different genetics than the rest of the world," I said as I grabbed a piece of ice from the refrigerator and popped it on my tongue.

My cell phone went off and I pulled it out of my pocket. Carter. I answered with a somewhat muffled hello.

"Where are you?" he asked.

"Ida Belle's," I managed. "Why?"

"Shots were reported at your house," he said.

"Well, since I'm not there, that's not good."

I disconnected as he was starting to talk again and grabbed my keys off the counter. "Shots fired at my house!" I said.

Ida Belle sat down the bottles and covered the glue while Gertie turned off the stove, and we all ran out the front door. By the time we got into my Jeep, everyone had a gun out.

"What the heck is going on?" Gertie asked as I tore down the street toward my house.

"I was hoping you guys would know," I said. "Is it hunting season for something?"

"This is Louisiana," Ida Belle said. "There's always something being hunted. But not in the neighborhood."

"You don't think your former job has come back to haunt you, do you?" Gertie asked, and I could hear the concern in her voice.

I shook my head. "If this was anyone from my past, they would have made sure I was home and the entire house would have been blown to bits."

I sped into my driveway, jumping part of the curb as I went, and sure enough, two pistol shots rang out from behind the house as we leaped out of the Jeep. I rounded the house at a dead run, pistol drawn and ready to engage. When I reached the back of the house, I immediately spotted the problem. My insane neighbor, Ronald—who couldn't stand me—was in my backyard, firing his pistol at the alligator poised at the edge of the bayou. At least, I was pretty sure it was Ronald. He had his back to me but the pirate wardrobe definitely indicated it was him. Ronald lived for elaborate costumes, often of a questionable nature.

"Godzilla!" Gertie yelled and leveled her gun at Ronald.

Ida Belle grabbed her wrist as she squeezed off a shot and the bullet hit my grill.

I didn't have time to register my dismay—over the grill, not Gertie trying to shoot Ronald—because the idiot lifted his pistol and fired another shot. Fortunately for Godzilla, Ronald was an awful shot. Unfortunately for Carter, that shot went over the gator and straight into the sheriff department's boat, which was pulling up to the bank. Carter and Deputy Breaux both dived over the side and into the bayou.

"Drop it, Ronald!" I yelled. "Or I'll shoot you, and you know I won't miss."

Ronald flashed a look at me of pure hatred that quickly dissolved into fear. "That gator is stalking me."

"Drop it!" I ordered again.

"Please don't make me," Ronald pleaded. "As soon as he sees I'm unarmed, he'll come after me."

"You're certifiable!" I yelled. "And you're on my property waving and shooting a loaded gun. Think about the law and decide whose side it's on."

His shoulders slumped and the pistol slid out of his hand and onto the lawn. Carter and Deputy Breaux had surfaced and were dragging their now-sinking boat onto my bank. Carter was glaring at Ronald the entire time, but he must have figured I had the situation under control because he didn't bother to issue any of his own orders.

I *thought* I had everything in hand until Gertie lunged. She hit Ronald with a tackle that would have brought down an NFL linebacker and he screamed so loud it made my ears hurt. Then I heard a low rumbling growl, like something from *Jurassic Park*, and I whipped my head around in time to see Godzilla push up on all fours and start hauling butt straight for Gertie and Ronald.

I let out a whoop that made Ronald's screaming sound

puny and everyone turned toward Godzilla, pistols drawn. I knew no one wanted to kill the gator, but shots rang out. I saw them hit the ground around the charging beast but none of them pierced his hide. Unfortunately, our attempts to warn him off hadn't slowed him down in the least.

By this time, Gertie was straddling Ronald and strangling him with his lace collar. In the midst of gasping for air, Ronald must have heard all the yelling and turned his head to see Godzilla coming at them full speed. Adrenaline kicked in and he leaped up, sending Gertie sprawling to the ground next to him as he took off at a dead sprint for his house.

Godzilla didn't even pause next to Gertie. He kept running full speed for Ronald, who realized he wasn't going to make it to his house and opted for the magnolia tree on our property line instead. He scrambled up to the first branch and lay on it, clinging to it like a sloth. Godzilla stopped at the base of the tree and stared up at him. I figured he was silently wishing him to fall.

Ida Belle took off running for my house and I gave her a surprised glance before hurrying over to help Gertie up.

"Are you all right?" I asked.

"I'm going to kill that moron!" she yelled and took off for the tree.

Godzilla saw her coming and lowered himself back down, then he shook his head back and forth as though he was attempting to convey his displeasure. Carter, Deputy Breaux, and I crept closer to the tree, guns still in the ready position just in case the gator found any of us as offensive as he did Ronald. I heard my back door slam and looked back to see Ida Belle running across the backyard with a pie pan.

"Wait!" I yelled at Ida Belle as she approached. "Ally made that."

"Who cares who made it?" Ronald said. "Just give it to him so he'll leave."

"It's apple cinnamon crumble and I haven't even had a piece," I said.

Everyone except Ronald looked conflicted.

"I have a fresh bass thawing in the laundry room sink," I said. "Carter and I will just have to eat steak tonight instead."

"Works for me," Carter said. "But I'd like some of that pie now. He seems settled enough."

Meaning Godzilla, not Ronald.

"I'll make some coffee," Ida Belle said as we all started to walk away.

"What about me?" Ronald yelled. "You can't leave me here!"

"Sure I can," Carter said. "I'll see about getting you down when I'm done having pie. But then you're going straight to jail. And you're going to pay for the damage to my boat, for the expense to haul it back to the dock, and for my and Deputy Breaux's aggravation. When I'm done filling out all that paperwork, I'm going to charge you with discharging your weapon on private property, and I might even work up a case for alligator poaching."

Ronald's face flushed red. "I was defending myself!"

Godzilla looked up and hissed and Ronald tightened his grip on the limb.

"Really?" I said. "So Godzilla came into your house and you chased him out with your gun?"

"That's not important," Ronald said.

"Yes, it is," I said. "You know I have security cameras, right? I'll bet that when we pull up footage over that apple pie we're about to eat, we'll see you trespassing into my yard to shoot that gator. He was never a threat to you."

"What about Christmas?" Ronald raged. "He almost killed me. He ripped my costume off. Everyone saw me naked."

"Your birthday suit is not the worst thing we've seen you in," I said. "And since we didn't get full frontal, I'm good."

"I'm still kinda damaged by it all," Deputy Breaux said.

Carter nodded.

I looked down at Godzilla. "We'll be back later with a snack for you."

The gator rumbled a little and I shook my head. Nothing surprised me anymore.

Gertie pulled out her cell phone and took a picture of Ronald and Godzilla. "You're such an idiot," she said. "A pirate costume? Really?"

"Pirates are rugged and tough," Ronald argued.

"Ever heard of Captain Hook?" Gertie asked, and pointed to the gator.

We all laughed. It was time for pie.

CHAPTER TWO

I GOT Carter and Deputy Breaux some towels so they could at least dry off a bit and we sat down for pie and coffee. We took our time with the pie, which was excellent, of course. For the first ten minutes, we could still hear Ronald yelling, but after a while he gave up. We discussed the upcoming festivities, Ronald's penchant for wearing the worst thing possible for the occasion, and what devilment Celia would get up to at the Mardi Gras throw-down, but finally, we had to turn back to the business at hand.

"Something is going to have to be done about that gator," Carter said, looking directly at Gertie.

"He's *not* stalking Ronald," Gertie said.

"Of course he's not stalking Ronald," Carter said. "But he keeps turning up here because you've fed him here. And unfortunately for all of us, most of all Fortune, Ronald lives next door. It's only a matter of time before Godzilla wanders into the backyard of an owner who's a good shot. And I'm not going to be able to fault someone who pops him when people here have pets and children to consider."

Gertie's shoulders slumped. "I know. I figured he was smart

enough to stay away. I mean, look how he disappeared during alligator season. He might as well have been a ghost."

"Or maybe he wasn't interested in lines with bait," Carter said. "He might have been holding out for a chicken casserole. Regardless, he's back now and he's becoming a nuisance. I can avoid the paperwork on this one as far as Ronald being the victim because he was trespassing, but technically, that's two times Godzilla has gone after him in almost as many months. If the state gets wind of this, they'll send the game warden in to handle the situation."

"Will he relocate Godzilla to a preserve?" I asked.

"It's optimum," Carter said. "But it's not usually the way things go down. Especially with a gator that large."

"Gertie trapped him in a pair of pants," I said. "How hard can it possibly be?"

Carter stared at me. "*You* tried trapping him with an actual trap. How did that work out?"

"Maybe we should have used my pants," I said.

"I don't know what else to do," Gertie said.

Carter narrowed his eyes at her. "For starters, you can stop digging that hole in your backyard. You're not going to get that gator there and try to keep him as a pet."

"Oh, good Lord, woman," Ida Belle said. "Is that why you made us use my kitchen for the Sinful Ladies Cough Syrup? You didn't want me to see that hole?"

"I thought you said you were putting in a garden," I said.

"Well, that garden, so far, is three feet deep and twenty feet square," Carter said. "What exactly do you grow in that kind of space?"

"I thought maybe a koi pond?" Gertie suggested.

We all stared. Clearly, no one was buying it.

"What am I supposed to do?" Gertie said.

"Stop feeding him, for starters," Carter said. "And definitely stop feeding him here. Look at the facts—Ronald couldn't hit the broad side of a barn shooting a gun, but I have a better chance of asking that gator to comply and having it work than I do convincing Ronald that Godzilla isn't stalking him. Someone is going to get hurt."

"Someone already did," Ida Belle said. "Your boat isn't looking so good."

Gertie glared at Ida Belle. "Really?"

"Boats are people too," Ida Belle said.

Deputy Breaux rose from the table and peered out the window. "Looks like the big dude gave up. He's headed for the water."

"Then we're still having fish tonight," I said.

"Is Ronald still up the tree?" Carter asked.

"Yeah," Deputy Breaux said. "He probably won't come down until Godzilla disappears below the surface. I'll wait for him to de-tree and then cuff him. Technically, you were off the clock thirty minutes ago. I can grab a shower and change at the sheriff's department while Ronald takes a breather. He's going to need it after I make him walk all the way to town."

"I can give you a ride," Ida Belle said. "As long as Ronald doesn't sweat or cry in my SUV."

"Thanks, but he deserves to walk," Deputy Breaux said. "And I can work off the pie."

"Is the naked guy we arrested at the Swamp Bar still in jail?" Carter asked.

Deputy Breaux nodded. "Hasn't made bail. His friends claim they can't find his pants, and therefore they can't find his wallet. And apparently, none of them are willing to fund his streaking adventures."

Carter grinned. "Ronald will love him."

Ida Belle nodded. "Ronald thinks naked is crass."

"It isn't always," Carter said and winked at me.

Gertie fanned herself with her hand. "Stop it, you two. You're giving me a hot flash."

"You stopped having hot flashes back when Lincoln was president," Ida Belle said.

"Well, then I'm having a flash of jealousy," Gertie said. "It's been a while since I enjoyed naked company."

"Probably just as well, since the last one you tried that with was murdered and you were up for it," Ida Belle said.

Gertie sighed. "I didn't even get to sexytime with that guy. No, the last time—"

"We don't need to know," Carter interrupted as Deputy Breaux practically ran out the back door.

Ida Belle rose and motioned to Gertie. "Now that your adopted dinosaur has made his exit, we best get back to the cough syrup."

"Are you done burning my taste buds off?" I asked.

"Of course," Ida Belle said. "Besides, Carter's off the clock and he reeks of the bayou. I suggest a shower is in order."

She gave me a wink and headed out of the kitchen. Gertie cast a wistful glance back at us, then grinned before hurrying after her.

"I'm not sure what I'm going to do with those two," I said.

Carter held his hands up. "Don't look at me. I told you not to get involved with them right from the start."

"But then I wouldn't have all this fun."

He grinned. "There is that."

I hated to break the mood but I had been holding something in since the night before, waiting for the opportunity to tell him about it. Before he took his shower was probably best, so that way he could wash it all away and we could try to relax the rest of the afternoon.

"Director Morrow called me last night," I said.

The grin disappeared and he immediately shifted to serious mode.

Director Morrow had been my boss at the CIA. He was also the man who'd taken me in as a teen when my father was "killed in action" during a CIA mission. Except that I'd found out on Christmas Day that my father wasn't dead. He'd been spotted on a camera in Afghanistan, and facial recognition software that was constantly scanning the camera feed locked in on him. Then the alert system went crazy. Dwight Redding had been their number one guy. CIA operative extraordinaire. And apparently, they were as confused as I was as to how a dead man had crossed the street as if he were out for an evening stroll.

I had all kinds of questions myself, starting with why did my father abandon me and ending with did I have to return the life insurance money I'd collected. Director Morrow was supposed to be working on answers. Not necessarily to those exact questions, but there were plenty of others that needed covering. Besides, I figured I'd never get a satisfying answer to the first, and the HR department at the CIA wasn't going to be prompt with an answer on the second.

"Did he have more information?" Carter asked.

I nodded.

"Have you told Ida Belle and Gertie yet?"

"No. I wanted to tell you first."

Ida Belle and Gertie were my sisters, my mothers, and Gertie sometimes felt like my child, but I felt that this discussion was something that needed to happen with Carter first. I loved my girls but I was *in* love with Carter.

"So?" Carter asked.

"He said intelligence identified the building my father entered as one they suspected a high-ranking member of the

Taliban used when he was in the city. He wouldn't give me a name, of course."

"Of course. Not that it matters. Does he have any thoughts on that?"

"I'm sure he has plenty, but he's not sharing them with me. Come on, Carter. We both know how this looks. The man disappeared fourteen years ago and they returned what was supposedly left of him in a container the size of an engagement ring box."

"But there was a DNA match."

I nodded. "So either some other government faction stepped in and convinced him he was of more use as a dead man and made that happen, or he pulled a couple of his teeth for DNA testing and staged the explosion because he decided it was more convenient to become a ghost."

Carter's jaw flexed and I could tell that he didn't like either scenario and had already processed them himself. Either option meant my father had deliberately chosen to make me an orphan. The fact that he'd maintained that position for fourteen years was sobering and didn't exactly lean toward the idea that he was still "on our side" of the equation.

If my father was a traitor, it changed everything I'd ever known about him.

"So identification was based on the teeth," Carter said.

"That's what I was told. But the more interesting fact is that I attempted to locate the guys that made the identification. Two of them—both conveniently dead. And neither by natural causes."

"What happened to them?"

"One was lost in his boat on a fishing trip and the other, if you can believe it, was hit by a bus."

"Jesus. So what now? Are they going to dig up those remains to retest them?"

"They've already excavated the grave, but someone beat them to the punch. My guess is it happened shortly after that coffin containing teeth and some mementos went into the ground."

He blew out a breath. "This reeks of a cover-up."

I nodded. "The question is, of what? Is he a super-secret operative for the US, or did he jump sides and they don't want that to make the rounds?"

Carter reached over and took my hand in his. "I'm so sorry. I can't even imagine how hard this is. I hope Morrow gets you some answers soon."

I shrugged. "To what end? Is there an answer that's good enough to explain his choices?"

"No. Regardless of why, he's a piece of crap for what he did. I'm sorry to say that about your father, but that's how I feel and I want to be honest with you."

"I have a stronger word than 'crap.'"

"Yeah, I can think of a few. And I know it doesn't lessen what he did or how you had to grow up, but you have a family right here in Sinful. I love you. Walter loves you. Ally loves you. And God love 'em, those two meddling messes who just left here would lie down and die for you."

I smiled and squeezed his hand. "I know. And I wouldn't trade any of you for a shot at changing history. The reality is if my father hadn't done what he did, I might never have become an operative. And if I hadn't become an operative, then I would have never come to Sinful. And I truly believe this is where I'm meant to be."

"So do I. And right now, I believe you're meant to be in a shower with me, and then we're destined for a long nap in the hammock."

"Good thing it's warm outside."

He leaned over and kissed me. "It's about to be scorching inside."

I HURRIED UP THE SIDEWALK, following an awesome smell. Downtown was packed with Sinful residents, many wearing colorful masks and all with a huge lump of beads hanging around their necks.

"Slow down," Gertie said. "It's hard to go fast with this mask. It keeps slipping."

"So take it off," I said. "That's funnel cake. If they run out before I get some, I might have to open fire. That won't turn out well for anyone."

"I can't take it off," Gertie said. "I'm incognito."

I stopped short and pointed at her T-shirt, which read *Show Me Your Boots*.

"Do you really think anyone is in doubt after reading that?"

She grinned. "But it doesn't say 'boobs.'"

"I'm sure everyone is delighted at the difference," I said as I continued up the sidewalk.

Gertie waved a hand in dismissal as she jogged after me. "No one cares except Celia and she'll have a cow. Which will just make everyone else happy, so it's a win. Well, except for Celia, but who cares?"

"I don't. That's for sure."

I heard a whoop across the street and looked over to see several men, in what looked to be a large dog kennel, holding up their boots.

"Hey, Gertie!" they yelled. "Throw us some beads."

Gertie grinned and ran over to toss some beads over the fence panel, and the men scrambled for them and started arguing. I held back, still trying to figure out what the heck was going on as I'd just realized the men were locked up in one of three sets of pens, and the others had occupants as well.

"Why are those people in cages?" I asked as Gertie made her way back over.

"Temporary jail," she said. "There's not enough jail space to lock up the usual silliness and no way Carter wants to file that kind of paperwork. So they erect these temporary 'jails.' They toss people in there long enough to cool off and then they can get out and party again."

"There's a nun in that middle one."

"You can't take Catholics anywhere."

"Because Baptists are all the picture of decorum."

Gertie grinned. "Only if another Baptist is watching."

"Doesn't the hypocrisy ever bother you?"

"Hypocrisy is what keeps small towns intact. Now let's go get you that funnel cake."

"So if Deputy Breaux is all dressed up as king for the night, who's helping Carter put nuns in kennels?"

"Walter and Scooter help out. And Sheriff Lee, of course."

I nodded, not sure that Sheriff Lee counted much as help as I couldn't imagine him getting off his horse the number of times required to escort all the offenders to the makeshift clink, but apparently, they'd been making it work for years, so who was I to judge? I managed to get my funnel cake hot off the presses and we headed for the Sinful Ladies booth where they were hawking their "cough syrup."

"Must be flu season for Baptists," I said, pointing at the line at the booth. It was actually longer than the funnel cake line, which didn't seem right to me.

"Keeping things intact, remember?" Gertie said.

I shook my head and we stepped around the back of the booth where Ida Belle was handling a quickly diminishing inventory. I had helped unload all the cases of cough syrup earlier that day and I'd have bet only a third of what we'd stacked there was remaining.

"Wow!" I said. "You are going to run out."

"That's the plan," Ida Belle said. "Everyone knows to stock up early, then we can close up shop and enjoy the festivities. Give us another thirty minutes and this booth will be a ghost town."

"A ghost town with a stinking high profit," Gertie said.

Ida Belle nodded, looking extremely pleased. "Excellent profit. I see Fortune found the funnel cake."

Gertie and I had both finished eating our funnel cakes on the walk to the Sinful Ladies booth. Now I was just trying to brush the remnants of powdered sugar off my T-shirt.

"That's the one downside of funnel cake," Gertie said. "You can't hide the fact that you had one. That's why I always wear a white T-shirt when I know it's going to be available."

"Why would I want to hide that fact?" I asked. "I was thinking about getting another before they go the way of the cough syrup."

"You don't need to hide it," Ida Belle said. "But this town is full of people who are supposed to be avoiding all that fat and sugar. And since our local doctors are all in attendance, along with watchful spouses, there's lot of powdered sugar shaming that goes on at Mardi Gras."

"That sucks," I said.

"Don't worry," Gertie said. "Everyone's afraid to say anything to you. Besides, you don't need the admonishment. How you manage to stay in that shape with all the goodies you consume is a mystery to me, especially over the holiday. I automatically switch to everything elastic waist on November 1."

"Well, technically, I'm usually wearing yoga pants, so I'm already observing that rule," I said. "But I *have* had to up my workouts since I moved here. I thought CIA missions were tough, but they've got nothing on an attack of Sinful's baked goods."

"So you're running more?" Ida Belle asked.

I nodded. "Ten miles, five days a week, and I'm using Carter's weight set for lifting three times a week. And I throw in some squats, push-ups, lunges, and other stuff while I'm watching television."

Gertie waved a hand in dismissal. "I'll just stick with the elastic-waist pants. That sounds like entirely too much work. Although I will say that working up a sweat at Carter's house can't be all bad."

"You're impossible," Ida Belle said.

"It's been a while," Gertie said. "I'm living vicariously."

"You've been living vicariously since cable came to Sinful," Ida Belle said.

"I can't help it if there are no available men in this town who can keep up with me," Gertie said.

"I guess that's one way of putting it," Ida Belle said as she pointed to a crate of the mouth-on-fire cough syrup and motioned to me. "Can you and your finely honed muscles please haul that one to the front of the booth? They were running low."

"Sure." I hefted the crate up and wove my way through the Sinful Ladies who were busy peddling their wares and stuck it in an empty slot under the front counter. Ida Belle was close behind me with a second crate.

"People are buying them in bulk," she said. "This cinnamon flavor is a huge success. We might have to put it into regular rotation."

"Well, don't rotate any to my house," I said. "Me and my taste buds—assuming they ever return—will stick with the old boring one."

"Did I hear you say cinnamon?" A woman's voice sounded in front of us and I looked up to see two women approaching.

Speaking woman, midthirties. Five foot ten. Trim body and good muscle content. Facial features and accent indicated Russian heritage. Blond hair in ponytail. Threat level high if I had a man with a roving eye. She was a looker.

Friend also midthirties. Five foot nine. Slim but not as toned as her friend. Scar near her temple. Right arm broken previously. Same blond hair in ponytail. Might be related. Threat level low given that she was holding the hand of a child around five years old. However, jury was still out on the child. They were sneaky.

"I had a sip of something wonderful and tasting of cinnamon, and the lady said it was cough syrup." The woman winked. "So is this where I can get my prescription filled?"

Ida Belle smiled. "You must be related to Natalia."

"Not technically," the woman said. "I'm Katia, an old childhood friend, but we're like sisters. I surprised Natalia with a visit. And apparently, I came at the right time. This is so much fun."

"Nice to meet you," Ida Belle said. "I'm Ida Belle and this is Fortune."

I extended my hand to Katia, then to Natalia. "I don't think we've met yet, either."

"Not officially," she said, "but I've heard a lot about you."

"That's because you're Catholic and Celia is always flapping her gums over there," Ida Belle said. "You can't believe everything you hear."

Natalia frowned. "So you're not CIA?"

"Not anymore," I said. "Now I'm a small-town private detective and part-time illegal booze salesman."

Katia laughed.

"It's cough syrup," Ida Belle corrected. "Which is why it's not illegal."

"Of course," I said and smiled. "Hey, if you're Catholic, why aren't you toting around the real thing?"

"Because this had a great taste," Katia said. "Give me two bottles, please. I want to take some home with me. It's perfect for shots."

I nodded. "And probably for cleaning cancer out of your esophagus. Maybe removing a bit of stomach lining."

Katia laughed. "I take it you're not a fan."

"I'll let you know when my taste buds return," I said.

Ida Belle handed her two bottles of the death syrup and as I went to take her money, bursts of loud sound echoed around us.

"Is someone shooting, Mommy?" the little girl asked, clearly spooked.

"No, baby," Natalia said. "It's just fireworks."

"I don't see any fireworks," the little girl said.

"They're not close by," Natalia said.

"They have fireworks at this?" I asked Ida Belle. "I thought you said there were horses at the end of this parade. Has this town not learned anything about horses and fireworks?"

"The horses for the end of parade are selected based on their noise tolerance," Ida Belle said. "And the official fireworks are at the end of the parade and shot over the bayou, but some people like to do their own thing even though they're not supposed to."

"What is it with the South and fireworks?" I asked. "It's as big an obsession as fishing and hunting."

Ida Belle shook her head. "Fishing is religion. Fireworks are just addiction."

"Well, maybe you should stuff cotton in those horses' ears," I said. "Just in case."

"Sounds like you guys know how to party," Katia said. "And here I thought Natalia was crazy for giving up the whole career and big city thing to do the small-town mommy gig. But maybe she won't grow stagnant after all."

I saw the slight downturn of Natalia's lips and figured the subject was a sore one between the friends. Katia had every appearance of loving the fast-paced life. She probably wouldn't ever be able to wrap her mind around how her friend could prefer living in a place like Sinful. A year ago, I would have had the same disbelief. Until I moved here, I thought small towns were where everyone went when they'd given up on life. I had no idea just how much went on in tiny communities, but when you ruffled the pretty quilts that seemed to cover them, there were all sorts of things hiding beneath. Good and bad. The amount of bad had been somewhat eye-opening.

"It's impossible to stagnate when you're chasing a five-year-old all day long," Natalia said. "We should get back before the parade starts. Larry is holding us a spot up front so Lina will have a good view."

Katia rolled her eyes. "Wouldn't want to keep Larry waiting. Thanks, ladies. It was nice to meet you."

They headed off into the crowd and Gertie popped up beside me. "What's in those crates in front of you is the last of the hooch, and Walter wants it all if we can do it. I tried to convince Pastor Don to take a case but he still won't bite."

"Why Pastor Don?" I asked.

Ida Belle shook her head. "She wants him to use it for the Lord's Supper."

"Don't Baptists use grape juice to avoid the whole wine thing?" I asked.

"Boorrriiinnngggg," Gertie said. "I'm trying to give Southern Baptist an updated look."

"I'm not sure a drunken congregation is the look you should go for," I said.

"You might be right," Gertie said. "Some of the older

gentlemen like to run around in their boxers when they're relaxing at home with some cough syrup. I don't imagine the congregation or the Lord needs to witness that much of an individual."

"Especially when we all have to witness Celia's butt so much," I said, and we all laughed.

"Speak of the devil," Gertie said.

I turned around and saw our least favorite citizen stomping toward us.

"Look," Gertie said. "It's the Butt of Sinful. How will you be showing your rear tonight, Celia? Hope you wore your good drawers."

"I will not discuss my undergarments with you," Celia said as she stopped in front of us, hands on her hips.

"You don't have to," I said. "We usually get a full view at some point."

Ida Belle nodded. "One would think you'd have learned to wear pants instead of dresses."

"Ladies wear dresses," Celia said in her haughtiest voice.

"Good thing I'm not a lady," I said. "I hate dresses."

"I think a lot of problems in this town could be solved if we banned dresses and made everyone wear pants," Ida Belle said.

Celia's face flushed with anger. "The *only* problem this town has with too much exposure is a group of Baptist young adults who've taken up spots in front of the General Store."

"Are they standing there naked?" Gertie asked and pulled out her phone.

"Of course not," Celia said. "You're always so extreme. But they are causing a disturbance."

"Why are you telling us about it?" I said. "We're not their parents or the cops."

"You're Baptists," Celia said and pointed to Gertie. "And

this one is responsible for all the bad examples given to our youth in this town. Look at her shirt. Disgraceful."

"That's some odd logic you have," I said. "So what exactly are these arch-criminals doing?"

"The group of young adults—I can't refer to them as young ladies—are flashing the young men for beads," Celia said.

I glanced down the street but didn't see any sign of disturbance. I looked back at Celia and narrowed my eyes. "You're telling me there's college-aged boob-flashing going on down Main Street, and yet all the male members of Sinful aren't crowded around? I call foul."

Celia pulled herself board straight. "Every male in Sinful is not interested in such behavior."

"They are unless they're dead," Gertie said.

Celia stamped her feet. "I demand that you do something."

"What are they wearing?" I asked. "Because there's no way bare boobs are making an appearance or there would be a stampede."

"They're wearing their undergarments," Celia said.

"So they're flashing bras?" I asked.

Celia hesitated. "Bikini tops."

I stared. "The same bikini tops they wear on the bayou in the summer?"

"That's not the point," Celia said. "It's the principle of the matter."

"The principle of the matter being that if you wore one, the entire town would turn into a pillar of salt?" Gertie asked.

"This is not about me," Celia said.

"Sure it is," I said. "They're doing it to piss off you and other stiff necks like you, and it's working. Same as Gertie's T-shirt, which you keep glaring at. Why don't you drink a bottle of cough syrup and take a night off, Celia? For once in your life, try not to be a butthole."

"You'd like that, wouldn't you?" Celia said, sputtering.

"Everyone would like that," Ida Belle said. "Now get out of the way. We've got a booth to shut down. Go see your niece reign as queen. Maybe that will improve your attitude."

"As long as Ally insists on being tight with this one," Celia said and inclined her head toward me, "she's not my family."

"I'll let her know that," I said. "It will probably make her day. Bye, Celia."

I flicked my fingers at her in dismissal. She stood, open-mouthed for a couple seconds, then finally whirled around and stalked away.

"That woman is like a vacuum cleaner designed only to suck joy," Ida Belle said.

"That's because she's hasn't gotten lucky since she got pregnant with Pansy," Gertie said. "And since it was with that horrible husband of hers, I'm still sketchy on the 'lucky' aspect of it. She must be harboring resentment about the whole injustice of it."

"Injustice? Really?" Ida Belle asked.

Gertie nodded at her. "I mean, look at you. You haven't gotten lucky since fire was invented, but I don't see you marching around with a stick up your butt. Not most of the time. No resentment."

Ida Belle raised one eyebrow. "I think you and your calendar might be a bit surprised by my 'lucky' status."

I grinned. "Ida Belle and Walter on the sly. No white wedding."

"Premarital activity?" Gertie pretended to be outraged. "I'm shocked."

"I'm shocked you waited until you were engaged," I said.

"Who says we did?" Ida Belle grabbed some empty cartons and headed off, leaving Gertie and me standing there gaping.

"Am I reading that one correctly?" I asked. "Is Ida Belle

saying she and Walter have had a standing booty call prior to the engagement? I wonder how long? Back to the beginning?"

"Might be why he never stopped asking her to marry him," Gertie said. "What I'd like to know is how she managed that without anyone catching on. This is Sinful, after all."

"And I was a spy," Ida Belle said as she walked up behind us. "Are you two going to stand there and speculate about my potential love life all night or are we going to see the parade?"

"I'm thinking the whole love life discussion might be more interesting," I said.

I couldn't have been more wrong.

CHAPTER THREE

After closing up the cough syrup booth, Ida Belle, Gertie, and I wandered around downtown for a bit, checking out the other booths and chatting with people along the way. Eventually, we got separated and I spotted someone I never expected to see in the crowd.

Little Hebert.

He gave me a huge smile and a wave as soon as he saw me, and I crossed the street to greet him.

"I'm a bit surprised to see you here," I said. "I figured this sort of thing was outside of your decorum requirements."

Little smiled. "I *do* have my standards, but blood wins out when it comes to certain things. The Cajun part of me can no more fail to celebrate Mardi Gras than my Italian roots can ignore Columbus Day."

"Makes sense. What about your father? Is he here?"

"Of course. He never misses. The sheriff saves him a spot near the beginning of the parade route complete with a love seat. He's over there now and he'd love to see you. In fact, I was looking for you, hoping you could say hello before the parade got started."

"I'd love to!"

We headed toward the far end of Main Street and sure enough, on one side of the street was a love seat at the curb with Big resting on it, holding a funnel cake. Mannie stood off to the side, giving the "get lost" eye to anyone who might think about conducting business while the boss was relaxing. He gave me a nod as I approached.

"It's great to see you," I said as I stepped up.

Big gave me a huge smile and motioned to a folding chair next to the love seat. I pulled it around to face him and sat down.

"It's been a long time," Big said. "I haven't seen anything on YouTube. Haven't even heard a whisper of trouble with your name contained in it. Have you gone pedestrian on me?"

I laughed. "Heck, no. I'm not even sure that's possible. It's just been fairly quiet around here lately. I mean, when it comes to big issues. I've been doing small jobs—the usual sort of thing. Cheating husbands, missing cats, petty theft, and one particularly interesting case of a woman who claimed she was being haunted."

"And she thought a private investigator was the person to handle that?" Big asked.

"Well, the ghost was stealing."

"I'm guessing it wasn't a ghost at all," Big said.

"Nope. Just a nephew with a creative bent and drug habit. But the nephew is in rehab now and all her jewelry has been collected from the pawnshops, so another successful case closed."

"And this is interesting enough for you?" Big asked. "You're not going to get bored?"

I shrugged. "I like the figuring-stuff-out part. My previous job was a lot of action but not a lot of thinking. At least not about the target or the details."

He nodded. "I understand. Your energy was spent on the actual physical requirements and the mental acuity it took to pull off the mission. But now you're having to do a different kind of thinking than before so it balances out."

"The thrill factor is a lot less, but then so is the potential death end of things."

"I'm sure those who care about you consider that a good trade. I know that I do. But I wanted to make sure you're satisfied with your day-to-day journey. I don't think it's any secret that I enjoy having you around. Making sure you're happy serves my own selfish interest, but I make no apologies for attempting to arrange things the way that I want them. If you ever need a challenge or more of a thrill, let me know. There's always something in my line of work that needs looking into."

"Thanks."

It was one simple word but it conveyed a lot. I was touched that Big liked me so much he wanted to keep me around. The fact that he'd come right out and admitted it was surprising but it made my night. He was an important man in these parts —at least with the questionable legal element—and he had no use for most people. Being "in" with Big Hebert was not a position most could claim. And plenty wanted it.

"And how is your personal life going?" Big asked. "Have you and the good deputy made moves toward anything permanent?"

I laughed. "Lord, no. Until last year, the only thing consistent in my life was that nothing stayed the same. Now I've got a new job, I'm living in a tiny bayou town that's so far removed from DC I can't even begin to explain, and I own a house and a cat. I've had a huge influx of permanent in a short amount of time. I'm not interested in adding anything else to that list just yet."

"That's understandable. But your arrangement is to both your and the deputy's liking?"

"Oh yeah. We're both completely happy with the way things are." I tried not to make a face but I had to admit this line of talk seemed odd coming from Big. Why in the world would he care about my romantic entanglements? Of course, people didn't ask Big questions. He did all the asking. But then, I wasn't normal people, so I figured he couldn't hold me to normal standards.

"Why all the questions about my love life?" I asked. "I didn't take you for a romantic."

He smiled. "See—this is why I like you. Direct. You challenge what I ask rather than dancing around and hoping to provide the answer you think I'm looking for."

"I don't dance."

He laughed. "I don't imagine you do." He glanced over at Mannie, then looked back at me. "Let's just say that sometimes the things I think about would surprise you. And I believe good relationships make for strong, happy people. Single people are more of a wild card."

And then it hit me—Big was fishing around to see if I was available to get involved with Mannie.

Big noticed my expression and grinned as he leaned forward and lowered his voice. "You've figured me out. Ah well, forgive an old fool for wanting to see those important to him settled. Mannie is like a son to me and if I ever had a daughter, I'd want her to be just like you."

"I'm sure Mannie is perfectly capable of finding a lady friend if he decides he's in the market. Look at all the women walking by here and staring."

"Yes. But they don't hold his interest. I'm afraid the local fare might be too tame for him."

"Maybe tame is what he needs."

Big wagged his finger at me. "And I would likely agree with you on that point, but if Mannie doesn't think so, then it can never happen."

I smiled. "You're a good man. But don't spend too much energy worrying about Mannie. I have no doubt that when he's ready, he'll acquire a woman as efficiently as he does a target."

Big laughed. "I have no doubt you're right. And while I'm enjoying our conversation and the fact that I managed to make you just a tiny bit uncomfortable, I see your deputy across the street giving us the eye. Don't let me keep you any longer. But thank you for stopping by to chat with me."

"Of course. If I'm not wrapped up with a case next week, I might drop by your office just to shoot the breeze. Maybe tell you about some of my interesting missing cat cases. If you're going to be around, that is."

"I'm always around and you're always welcome. I look forward to our visit."

I said goodbye to Little and headed across the street where Carter was leaning against a light pole.

"Checking up on me?" I asked as I approached.

He shook his head. "As much as I'd prefer you weren't tight with the local mob connection, I don't think he'd do anything to get you into trouble. Not intentionally, anyway."

"Ha! Then you're giving him more credit than I do."

Carter smiled. "I think it would take someone far craftier than Big Hebert to get something over on you. And he's pretty crafty. So what's he up to this time?"

"Nothing that I could tell. He's enjoying the parade and wanted to make sure I wasn't bored with my new lot in life. He's afraid I'll leave. Apparently, he likes me and wants me to stick around."

"Can't fault the man for having good taste. So what did you tell him?"

"That I'm enjoying my new job. What it lacks in the physical aspects of my previous work, it makes up for in the mental portion. Even the simplest of cases still require poking around. I've learned that I'm naturally nosy and can't stand when I don't know the answer to things. Which is interesting, when you consider that before, I took a directive and made it happen."

He nodded. "Our service to our country was mostly as a weapon, not as a person. I sometimes struggle with that. But the reality is, there has to be people like us, with our ability to carry out jobs that most couldn't. But the longer you're out of the mindset, the harder it is to understand how you were ever there. You're a very intelligent woman. Sooner or later, you would have become unsatisfied with your job just like I did."

"I think I was already headed that way. If I hadn't been, then Sinful could have never grabbed hold of me like it did."

"You needed more than action. So did I. Finding lost cats and wayward husbands isn't the most exhilarating work, any more so than chasing down drunks and poachers, but it takes more out of us to do what appears to be less work even though it's not. And in so many ways, it's more satisfying."

He grinned. "Plus, I get to spend some nights with you, catching up on that physical activity thing."

I laughed. "That's definitely a high point of the career change. The food here is a close second, though. Just so you don't get an ego about things."

"I have no problem barely edging out Sinful cooking."

"Excuse me for interrupting." Mannie's voice sounded behind us and we turned around.

"If I could speak to the two of you for a moment?" He glanced around. "Maybe away from the crowd."

I frowned. Something was up. Mannie would never ask for a private conversation, especially with Carter and me both, unless something was wrong. Was there a problem with Big or Little? I hoped not. We headed to the far end of the street, some distance from the parade crowd.

"A former comrade of mine made contact this morning," Mannie said. "He overheard a bit of conversation between some superiors. Someone is conducting a discreet inquiry about Fortune. Quiet and not through official channels, but he suspects it's internal."

I immediately shifted into alert mode and Carter's expression went from curious to worried.

"Did he say what the inquiries entailed?" Carter asked.

"He couldn't hold position long enough to hear much," Mannie said. "There's some questions about Fortune's current location. That's all he managed to get. But he knows that I have contact with Fortune and he didn't like the way the exchange looked or was being handled, so he passed on the information."

Carter nodded. We both understood exactly what Mannie was saying. The intelligence community sensed something was off as if it were lit up in neon.

"He's going to keep his ears tuned," Mannie said. "If he hears anything else, he'll let me know. But I thought you might want to make some inquiries with your own connections."

"Definitely," Carter said. "Thank you for letting us know."

Mannie gave us a nod and headed off. I shook my head as he walked away.

"A former comrade, huh?" Carter said. "What do you think Mannie's previous employment consisted of?"

"Similar to yours except with the navy."

"I figured as much. Which means the information is credible."

"Would you be happier if it had come from dubious sources?"

"Hell, yeah. You know what this means as well as I do."

"Someone's trying to determine if I'm still active."

"I find the timing particularly suspect given the situation with your father."

"Yeah, that's no coincidence."

"I'm going to make some calls tomorrow. Touch base with a couple of guys who might be able to add some more information to our tiny pile."

"And I'll check in with Morrow again."

"I know I don't have to tell you to watch your back."

"I'm not sure I know how to function without doing so." I blew out a breath. "I think I'm going to tell Mannie about my father."

"Do you think that's wise?"

"You mean can I trust him? Yeah. And if he understands what's going on, he'll know better what information to go looking for. Rest assured, he's not going to leave this at that phone call from his comrade any more than you and I are."

Carter gave me a small smile. "You inspire loyalty in people like no one I've ever met before. If you'd been military, you'd be running the Pentagon."

"Ha! I'm too honest to be political."

"There is that." He leaned over and gave me a kiss. "Let's table this for tonight. There's nothing to be done right now but I hear there's a parade to enjoy. Maybe this one will manage to occur without incident."

I raised my eyebrows.

"Okay, without anyone getting seriously hurt," he said.

"Probably a safer bet."

I LEFT Carter to handle his deputy business and located Ida

Belle and Gertie in the place they'd pointed out to meet up for the parade. They were surrounded by members of the Sinful Ladies Society, some of whom I was told had been squatting in that spot since lunchtime. I thanked them for their dedication, but most were so jolly on cough syrup that they probably wouldn't even remember having spoken to me the next day.

Gertie had retrieved a backpack at some point during our separation, and I gave it the serious side-eye as she pulled it in front of her lawn chair and went for the zipper. I looked over at Ida Belle, who nodded.

"I inspected it before we left the house," Ida Belle said.

"The trust among us is epic," Gertie said.

"Trust and verify," I said.

Gertie shook her head. "We all worked for the government for too long."

Ida Belle snorted. "No. We've known *you* for too long."

"I haven't known her that long," I said. "I'm just a quick study."

Gertie pulled a pair of kneepads from the backpack, followed by elbow pads, and looked up at me. "Are these okay with you?"

"I'm not sure," I said. "Why do you need them?"

"Because you have to be a bit aggressive to get beads," Gertie said.

"Can't you just buy a bag of them?" I asked.

"Sure, just like you can buy a bag of candy for Halloween instead of going trick-or-treating, but what's the fun in that?"

"Not risking a situation that calls for kneepads?" I suggested.

Gertie waved a hand in dismissal. "They're just a precaution. I'll be fine."

Ida Belle shook her head. "Ask her about last year."

"That was a fluke," Gertie said.

"Everything with you is a fluke," Ida Belle said. "I'm convinced you don't know the definition of the word."

"I'm almost afraid to ask," I said.

"The long and short," Ida Belle said, "is there was a scramble for beads that Gertie had no business being in the middle of, and the end result was a totaled truck, the glass window broken out of the General Store, and one Mardi Gras gown up in flames."

"We got her out before it burned past her knees," Gertie said. "I don't know why everyone makes a big deal out of it."

"I assume the gown didn't belong to Celia then?" I asked.

Ida Belle shook her head. "Not sure people would have helped her out of it. The woman in question is a former resident. She decided Sinful was too dangerous and retired to Florida."

Gertie grinned. "Where she got struck by lightning her first trip to the beach."

"It's really disturbing the things that bring you joy," Ida Belle said.

Gertie waved a hand in dismissal. "All she lost was a couple inches of hair. And she was a miserable cow anyway. Fortune, you would have hated her. If Celia had an evil twin, that would have been her."

"Well, it does seem as if Satan keeps trying to bring her back into the fold with all that firepower directed her way," I said.

A foghorn sounded and I tensed. Ida Belle put her hand on my arm.

"It's signaling the start of the parade," she said.

I relaxed. "I hope I stop this reactionary thing at some point."

"I don't," Ida Belle said. "Not until we're sure everything is good."

"Speaking of which, I'm having a sleepover with Carter tonight but we need to meet tomorrow morning," I said.

Ida Belle raised one eyebrow. "A sleepover? Is that what it's called now?"

"Makes sense," Gertie said. "When it's over, they sleep."

I laughed and even Ida Belle grinned.

"Woman," Ida Belle said to Gertie, "you are going to be the death of me."

"Probably," Gertie said. "But I promise to wear something sensible to your funeral."

"It would be the first time," Ida Belle said.

I heard the sound of big truck engines firing and soon, I could hear the crowd roaring up the street. We were positioned at the end of the route. Gertie had explained that this was a strategic decision. Most of the parade participants tended to scrimp early on with the bead flinging, but apparently, when they got close to the end and realized they had plenty of stock, they really let the goodies fly.

I have to admit, the parade was interesting. Of course, we'd recently survived Gertie and her parrot Francis taking down the house at the Christmas gala, so the bar had been set rather high. But from just a regional interest sort of perspective, I thought Sinful was rather creative.

I'd figured there would be a line of four-wheelers with scantily clad women on deer racks, a couple of pickups with a passel of drunks in the bed, and maybe a few flatbed trailers decorated up with some streamers. But Sinful went a whole different direction.

There was the occasional pickup of drunks, but most had elected to pull their bass boats. And they were beyond festive. Decorations ranged from simple green, gold, and purple streamers to elaborate drapes that covered the sides of the boats and the seats. The people were all in various degrees of costume—some with beautifully sequined gowns and others opting for a T-shirt in Mardi Gras colors and a mask. Some were representing local businesses and others were just individuals who wanted to get in on the fun.

All of them were throwing doubloons and beads.

Which had Gertie and every other citizen of Sinful except me, Ida Belle, and the sheriff's department employees scrambling into the street, racing for the goods.

Unfortunately, Gertie wasn't the only one who'd figured out the end-of-the-line strategy, and a hefty crowd was gathered around us. When the first beads hit the air, the rush to grab them had me ducking and moving back. I jumped up onto a bench and watched as grown men and women moved like NFL linebackers, scrambling for a fumble. A couple seconds later, Ida Belle hopped up beside me. Gertie rushed in for a clump of beads near the curb and caught an elbow to the side. She countered by leaping headfirst toward him and catching him in the face with her backpack. He stumbled sideways, taking out two women, four men, a trash can, and the nun. Gertie practically dived for the beads and came up triumphant, holding her wares above her head, gloating.

"Maybe she should have worn a helmet," I said.

"She'd have been arrested for spearing," Ida Belle said.

"That's illegal?"

"It is during the Mardi Gras parade and weddings."

I stared. "There's spearing at weddings?"

"Catching the bouquet is serious business in a place like Sinful."

"I'll remember to be in the restroom when we get to that part of your wedding."

"Gertie will be there with her crab net and a gun. No one will stand a chance."

"Gertie doesn't want to get married."

"No. She just hates to lose."

Shouting began down the street and I strained to see what was going on.

"That should be the king and queen," Ida Belle said.

"Awesome!" I pulled out my cell phone so I could get a pic of Ally and Deputy Breaux.

A couple minutes later, their float came into full view. It was the only flatbed trailer that I'd seen so far, but it made sense that a boat wouldn't have worked for this one. The trailer was completely decked out in gold, purple, and green streamers and drapes and had a platform with fancy thrones on it in the center.

Ally and Deputy Breaux sat on their thrones, both grinning and waving at the crowd. They looked great. Deputy Breaux had on a black tux and didn't at all resemble the rumpled, somewhat shy cop that was his norm. Ally was simply gorgeous. Her gown was mermaid style and completely covered with green lace and sequins. It sparkled like gemstones and Ally was radiant.

"She's so pretty!" I said as I took pictures.

Ida Belle nodded as she snapped her own shots. "She was the prettiest baby. Managed to hold on to that. A lot don't."

Ally spotted Ida Belle and me on the park bench and gave us a huge grin and wave. She poked Deputy Breaux and he looked over and gave us a big smile and a thumbs-up.

"They make a cute couple," Ida Belle said.

I stiffened slightly. "You don't think..."

"What? No. Not that kind of couple. Deputy Breaux wouldn't make it a day with someone like Ally."

"Why not? I mean, I don't see them as a match either, but they're both super nice."

"Exactly. Put them together and it's so much sweet we'd all have a toothache. Deputy Breaux is a good guy but I have a feeling that Ally will end up with a man who's not afraid to poke the bear."

"Why do you say that?"

"Because she took up with you. I think she likes the excitement, but she's not the sort of person to go looking for it herself."

"So you're saying she wants a man she has to worry about?"

"Just a little. Makes things exciting."

"I suppose there's plenty to worry about with Sinful men, but most of it doesn't fall into the exciting realm."

Ida Belle nodded. "Mostly, the worry is over having enough money for beer *and* the electric bill."

A battle cry went up toward the beginning of the street again, but this one sounded more frantic and intense than the cheering for the king and queen.

"What's going on?" I asked.

"Must be the float for the Swamp Bar. Some of their doubloons have a stamp for a free beer on them."

"Good Lord, are they trying to cause a riot?"

"Celia thinks so. She petitions every year to ban them from the parade."

"Of course she does. I'm surprised she hasn't gotten her way."

"The Swamp Bar produces more volunteers for cleanup than the Catholic church, so they get to stay."

"How do they manage that? More free beer?"

"You got it. When the Catholics are only offering to light a candle, you can see why the bar gets the bigger draw." She pointed at a shiny new black metallic bass boat, all done up with Mardi Gras decorations. "Here they come. Looks like Buck finally got a new boat."

I nodded. Buck was a friend of Whiskey's, the owner of the Swamp Bar. In one of our many investigations, Gertie had managed to total Buck's boat, although he never knew who the culprit was. The new one looked much spiffier and I imagined Buck was no longer grousing over the loss of his old one. A couple of guys I recognized as Swamp Bar regulars were on the boat seats, holding beers in one hand and tossing doubloons with the other. I wondered how many of those free beer coins they already had stuffed in their pockets.

"Who's that behind them?" I asked.

There was a somewhat beat-up truck pulling an even more beat-up boat behind the Swamp Bar entry. A guy in overalls and no shirt was driving the pickup. The woman in the boat was every bit of seventy and had on an outfit that would rival some of Gertie's—leopard tights and a halter. She had no business wearing either, and the halter top must have thought so as well because it appeared to be straining against its cargo to get away.

"That's Dolores Cormier and her boobs," Ida Belle said.

"Was she supposed to leave them at home? I mean, her top thinks so, but I'm not sure how that would work as they sort of come attached."

"They weren't attached until a year ago. She's seventy-two years old and those are double-Ds. Show me anything on your body that hasn't succumbed to gravity by age seventy-two and I'll sign over my retirement to you."

"Wow! A boob job at seventy-two? That's really progressive for Sinful. I'm surprised Gertie hasn't collected the name of her surgeon."

"She can't stand Dolores. The woman has a bad habit of batting her eyes at other women's husbands. Fortunately for the wives, the husbands are either young enough to be grossed out or too old to see her doing it."

The roar went up in front of us as the Swamp Bar float pulled up and Gertie yelled, "I'm going in!"

I cringed as she launched into the fray, shoving and stumbling her way toward the coins. She was bested every time until the boat was almost past, then she managed to snag a coin by putting a hockey check on the nun.

But the nun was not ready to leave the game.

CHAPTER FOUR

I COULD SEE the nun's red Nike running shoes glowing under her habit and knew it was on. She hopped up from the ground and ran straight at Gertie, grabbed her wrist, and attempted to wrestle the coin from her hand. Gertie pulled a spin move and stumbled backward into one of the local fishermen, who lost control of his beer can and sent it flying right at the truck hauling Dolores and her boobs.

As if guided by remote control, the beer can went right through the driver's open window and hit him square in the middle of his eyes. The driver yelped and involuntarily yanked the steering wheel toward the crowd while simultaneously pressing the accelerator. The truck launched forward and the crowd scrambled to get out of the way. Ida Belle and I dived off the bench just before the truck ran it over.

I hopped up in time to see the truck careen into the funnel cake booth and strike the vat of batter. I watched in dismay as the impact sent the heavenly batter into the air and onto Celia and her minions, who had been standing nearby. A squirrel shot out from under the collapsed booth and ran straight up

Celia's dress. She screamed as if she had the starring role in a horror movie and spun around as though she'd been possessed.

"Stop, drop, and roll!" a man yelled.

Another man whacked him on the back of the head. "She's got a squirrel in her drawers, you idiot. She's not on fire!"

"She should change her drawers more often then, if squirrels have moved in."

The squirrel must have realized he'd miscalculated his risk factor and climbed out of Celia's dress and ran straight up the front, using her head as a launch pad into a nearby tree. Celia collapsed and I turned my attention back to the truck, which was still out of control.

The driver had finally corrected the steering somewhat but was still skirting the side of the street. Unfortunately, he hadn't corrected his speed.

Then amid the roar of the crowd I heard his frantic cry—no brakes.

Ida Belle and I ran for the truck, which was now headed straight for the bayou, but there was no way we were going to catch it before it hit the water. And even if we managed to catch up, I had no idea how to stop it from a downhill roll with no brakes unless Celia was handy to throw in front of it. The truck took a bounce through a dip in the grass and the bass boat took an even bigger one. Dolores and her boobs went careening off the seat and into the bottom of the boat. I was about twenty feet from the boat when the truck flew off the embankment and into the water.

I ran up to the edge of the embankment, a crowd of people only steps behind me. The bass boat was now floating and had disconnected from the trailer. Dolores crawled her way up from the bottom and the crowd gasped.

"Wardrobe malfunction!" someone yelled. "My eyes! My eyes!"

The halter had officially fallen down on the job.

Or ripped in two on the job.

"She's no Janet Jackson!"

"For Christ's sake, someone throw her a tarp!"

"Or someone hotter offer her your shirt!"

Dolores either heard the crowd's comments or the breeze had finally gotten through the scar tissue, and she grabbed a life jacket and pulled it over her head. It stuck out a mile but at least all the things that could get her arrested were covered. Then she hopped into the driver's seat, started the boat, and took off down the bayou. A couple of people cheered and threw beads at her as she left.

The driver of the truck had finally managed to crawl out the window of his sinking vehicle and stared in dismay as he watched his boat disappear.

"She's stealing my boat," he yelled.

Carter and Walter stepped up beside me.

"You know where to find her," Carter said.

The driver looked over at us. "Aren't you going to help me out of here?"

Walter shook his head. "Scooter told you those brakes were shot a month ago. You shouldn't have even been driving that thing. I suggest you start swimming."

"And pray there's not a lawsuit forthcoming," Gertie said. "Everyone who saw that halter malfunction might sue for damages."

"I'm more upset over the funnel cake," I said.

A low rumble of agreement went through the crowd.

"I want that woman arrested!" Celia stomped up, covered with funnel cake batter and pointing at Gertie.

Carter rolled his eyes. "Of course you do. And I don't care any more this time than I have the last ten thousand times you've made that declaration."

"She caused all of this," Celia continued to rant. "Running into the street like a hoodlum. Shoving people like this is some sort of wrestling event."

"Or a Black Friday sale," one lady said. "There's some serious shoving then. People don't get arrested there either, though. It's a thing called 'fair play.' You should get a clue, Celia."

People nodded and Celia's face turned red. "You have ignored her shenanigans for far too long. She's making a mockery of this town."

"No," Carter said. "You're doing a fine job of that all on your own."

"He's right," the nun said. "Put a sock in it, Celia. You're ruining my buzz."

Celia gasped. "How in the world can you side with this... this woman-child?"

"Because she's not the one flashing her goods, for one," the nun said. "The woman with the unfortunate halter incident is Catholic, if I'm not mistaken. So maybe we should clean up our own doorstep before we just pin all the problems in this town on the Baptists."

Carter raised his hands. "The Lord has spoken through his servant. And since he has more clout than the sheriff, I'm going back to the parade."

Celia stood there, slack-jawed and staring at the nun, clearly dumbfounded that her religion had forsaken her. I really hoped someone bothered to explain that it was because she was a joy-sucking butthole. But then, I also didn't figure it would do any good.

Carter turned to the crowd. "Show's over. Here, anyway. Let's all head back to the parade route and I'll radio Sheriff Lee to let the parade continue."

"What about me?" the driver yelled as we all started walking away.

"Should have fixed your brakes, you cheapwad," a woman yelled.

"I can't believe there's no more funnel cake," another man groused.

"Should we do anything?" I asked as we started to walk away.

"Heck no," Ida Belle said. "He can swim just like everyone else. Not like he's far from the bank, and all that racket likely sent the gators away. They'll tow his truck out tomorrow but I'm sure it's totaled."

"The boat trailer is probably good though," Gertie said. "And his boat."

I laughed. "Well, since a boat appears to be the most important mode of transportation in Sinful, I guess he'll be fine."

We all collected back on Main Street and the parade started again. Only five or so more floats remained, and they were mostly locals who had done up their boats so their friends or wife and kids could have some fun flinging beads to the excited crowd. The last float contained Sinful's mayor, Marie Chicoron, who was also one of Ida Belle and Gertie's best friends.

Marie looked smart in her purple suit and mask and thrilled the crowd by throwing doubloons with interesting options like dismissal of a parking ticket or one drunk-and-disorderly excused. I assumed Carter and the sheriff had been in on the design of the offerings, as they would be the ones to implement them if anyone cashed in. And I had a feeling that every single one of those doubloons would be cashed in before summer even hit. This *was* Sinful, after all.

As soon as Marie's float got through downtown, everyone shuffled a bit toward the bayou at the beginning of Main Street where Walter and Scooter were ready to go with the fireworks display. When the first shot went off, Ida Belle looked over at me, probably waiting for me to dive behind the nearest structure with my weapon drawn, but I was firmly planted.

"See? You're improving," she said.

"Fireworks sound different," I said. "God knows, I've heard enough of them since I've been in Sinful. And it helps when I know they're coming and I'm looking directly at them. But it would be the ideal time to commit a crime, the noise level is so high."

"Let's not give anyone ideas," Ida Belle said.

I laughed as a huge shower of green, gold, and purple spread out over the sky. It really was pretty. Sometimes, I had moments when I was surprised with myself, like standing there with a bunch of other people, on a grassy bank, late at night, watching fireworks explode over a large swatch of mostly dirty water.

And I was enjoying the heck out of it.

If anyone had told me this would be my life a year ago, I would have had them sent up for mental assessment. But there I was, wearing jeans, T-shirt, and tennis shoes, and only a single weapon on my body. Well, besides my actual body, which was a pretty darn good weapon. But still. I had come a long, long way from the day I'd arrived in this patch of marsh.

"The finale is coming," Gertie said and clapped.

And then it started. Shot after shot, a split second apart, lighting up the entire bayou with their showers of color. Then a couple of men pulled out their pistols and fired a few shots over the water. My hand twitched when the first shot went off, but I managed to keep myself in check and cheered along with everyone else when the last of the burning embers disappeared from the night sky.

And that's when I heard screaming.

I pulled out my pistol and ran straight for the sound. It was almost an involuntary reaction and obviously the popular one as I wasn't the only person running with a drawn weapon. It was rather scary when you thought about it, especially as most of them were probably drunk. Even the nun had gotten in on the action and had hauled a shotgun out from under her habit.

I'd have to process that one later.

A small crowd had already formed at the source of the screaming, and I pushed through them and saw Katia, the woman who'd bought the hot cough syrup, lying on the ground with a pool of red running down her side. Natalia was bent over her, pressing a small jacket against the center of her chest, and it was clear where the blood was coming from. She was yelling for someone to call 911 and to help, and I ran over and dropped down next to her, then lifted the edge of the jacket and took a look at the wound.

It was a single bullet hole, right through the center of her chest, which explained all the blood loss. I felt my heart drop. There was no way she would survive this. Her eyes flew open and she stared up at us, her expression filled with confusion and fear. She tried to talk but it was only a gurgle, then a couple seconds later, she went limp and her eyes went vacant, staring up into the night sky.

Natalia let out a choked cry and collapsed, sobbing. A second later, an older man ran up and gazed wildly around.

Early fifties. Six feet even. A hundred seventy-five pounds. Lean build. Huge widow's peak. Wire-rimmed glasses with fairly thick lenses. Zero threat as soon as I kicked the glasses off.

"Where's Lina?" he yelled, completely panicked.

A woman standing in the crowd came forward, holding the

little girl I'd seen with Natalia earlier. She had her face buried in the woman's neck and was weeping loudly. The man gathered the girl in his arms and stared, dumbfounded, at the situation in front of him.

Carter burst through the crowd and dropped down next to me, took one glance at the dead woman, and his expression immediately tightened. He rose and waved his arms for attention and the crowd quieted.

"What the hell happened?" the man holding the child demanded. "Katia was standing here with my daughter. Did she see this happen? Someone answer me! Natalia?"

The woman who'd been holding Lina stepped forward and I recognized her as one of the locals who frequented Francine's Café.

"I heard Lina scream," she said. "I turned around and the lady was on the ground with blood coming out of her chest. Natalia ran up and tried to help her, and I picked up Lina and backed away so she wouldn't see what was happening."

"You didn't see the shot?" Carter asked.

"No," the woman said. "They were standing a bit behind the rest of us."

Carter eased over to Natalia and squatted next to her. "Can you tell me what happened?"

She looked up at him, her eyes red and swollen from crying, her expression full of fear. "I don't know," she said. "Lina left her jacket on Main Street so I went back to look for it. When I returned, I saw Katia..."

Her voice broke and she started sobbing again.

"I've lost everyone," she cried.

The man holding Lina, who I now assumed was Natalia's husband, reached down with his free hand and helped his wife stand. He wrapped his arm around her, pulling her close.

"You have your family," he said. "I'm so sorry about Katia."

If I hadn't been watching closely, I might have missed the flash of anger that passed over his face. It was so quick, but I knew I'd seen it correctly. The man was upset and he'd been panicked when he couldn't find Lina. But something about Katia's death also made him mad and that was odd.

"I'm sorry, Larry," Carter said to the man. "But I'm going to have to get statements from all three of you."

"Can it wait until tomorrow?" Larry asked, casting concerned looks at his wife and daughter.

"That will be fine," Carter said. "But I'll need your cell number in case I have to reach you about anything tonight. I'm sorry, but once the forensics team is here, I might need answers right away."

"Of course," Larry said and gave Carter his number.

"I'll contact you tomorrow morning," Carter said. "Do you need medical attention or can I call anyone to come help you?"

"No," Larry said. "We'll be fine. We've dealt with worse."

I looked over at Ida Belle and she shook her head. Apparently, she didn't know what Larry was talking about. It was just as well. The situation in front of us was far more pressing than something that had happened in the past.

Carter motioned to Walter, who'd been standing nearby, and he and Scooter began moving the crowd away. People shuffled off, mostly in shock and almost completely silent. This was not the way a festive occasion was supposed to end.

"Do you think it was a stray bullet?" Gertie asked. "Several people were firing during the finale."

I squatted next to the body and leaned over to get a closer look at the entry wound. "I don't suppose I could lift her shirt for a better look."

"No." Carter's voice sounded over me. "I don't suppose you could. I need you ladies to clear the crime scene."

I sighed. I hadn't expected that Carter would ask us to get

in the middle of his investigation, but I had hoped I wouldn't be dismissed along with the rest of the Sinful residents. But Carter took his job and the law seriously, and in a case of a death in the middle of a public event, he couldn't afford to be accused of not handling the scene correctly.

I rose from the ground and we shuffled off, some distance behind the crowd.

"My place?" I asked.

"Definitely," Ida Belle said.

I might not have gotten the look at that bullet wound that I would have liked, but I'd gotten a good enough one.

Our discussion couldn't wait.

CHAPTER FIVE

IDA BELLE immediately went for the coffeepot when we got to my house, and Gertie pulled leftover blueberry pie out of the refrigerator and started cutting pieces to heat. I had to smile. These girls really knew me. I headed to my office to shed my tennis shoes and bra and grab my laptop. By the time I got back to the kitchen, we were all set up at the table and ready for a meeting of the investigative minds.

Gertie stabbed a big piece of pie and started talking with her mouth full. "Spill. I know that look."

Ida Belle nodded. "Yep. Get to talking. You would have left basic curiosity until tomorrow, which means you saw something."

"We can start with, that shot wasn't an accident," I said.

Gertie's eyes widened. "Seriously? I thought it was an accident and you figured out which one of those yahoos fired in the wrong direction. I mean, no one in Sinful even knows Natalia's friend. Why would someone shoot her?"

"You're assuming it was someone from Sinful," Ida Belle said, then looked back at me. "What makes you sure it wasn't an accident? Trajectory?"

I nodded. "I would have liked a closer look without the shirt but since Carter was in professional mode, I have to go with my basic assessment. The angle wasn't right. Not for a bullet shot into the air and descending."

"You think she was shot point-blank?" Gertie asked. "Jesus, I know most people were drunk and there was a ton of noise and milling around, but wouldn't someone have noticed?"

"It wasn't point-blank or the damage would have been different," I said. "And yeah, one would assume that Katia, at the very least, would have noticed someone approaching her with a handgun pointed at her chest."

"So where did the shot come from?" Gertie asked.

"My opinion—and this is based on a very cursory look at that entry wound—is that it came from above."

"So roof height?" Ida Belle asked.

"Or a pole or tree," I said. "Even on top of the cab of one of those ridiculous pickups some drive would probably have given enough clearance."

"But it wouldn't have given them the skill set," Ida Belle said.

"No," I agreed. "And either someone with decent ability took a heck of a chance..."

"Or someone with excellent ability took advantage of an opportunity," Ida Belle finished.

"Katia has never visited Sinful that I'm aware of," Gertie said. "So whoever killed her must have followed her here. Maybe that's why she pulled a surprise visit. She was on the run from the Russian mob."

"Or she wasn't the intended target," I said.

Ida Belle and Gertie both froze and stared at me.

"Why would you say that?" Gertie asked.

"Because Katia and Natalia look very similar. Ida Belle thought they were related when we first met Katia. And when

Katia was shot, she was wearing a black jacket, just like Natalia. She wasn't wearing it when we were at the booth. She had it tied around her waist."

"But the wind picked up before the fireworks, especially down by the bank," Ida Belle said.

I nodded. "So a tall, fit woman with a blond ponytail, wearing a black jacket, holding Lina's hand, and standing in questionable light would look like...?"

Gertie gasped. "It would look like Natalia. But who would want to kill her?"

"That's something you guys would have to tell me," I said. "I don't know anything about her. I only officially met her tonight."

Ida Belle frowned. "I don't think anyone knows much about her. She keeps to herself. Hasn't taken up with the local mommies with kids Lina's age, but then, she also homeschools the girl, so that's part of it, I suppose."

"Homeschools? In Sinful?" I asked. "I figured that was for cities where the schools were sketchy or the kids were picked on or whatever."

"And that's often the case," Gertie said. "But not here. Sinful has a really good school system and teachers who want to teach and have been dedicating their lives to it for years, sometimes decades. I haven't been around Lina much, but she seems to be a normal child, just a bit shy."

"So you can't see any problem with her mixing with the other kids?" I asked.

Gertie shook her head. "I've seen her talking to other children downtown in the General Store while her mother shopped. Lina was smiling and appeared to be having a good time."

"What about church?" I asked. "Don't tell me there's a family of atheists in Sinful."

"Probably plenty of them," Ida Belle said. "But they're still sitting in church on Sunday."

"Larry is Catholic," Gertie said. "They go to church but I've never seen Natalia volunteering at any of the joint functions we do. Of course, I can't speak to the Catholic-only functions. For all we know, she might be really active in those."

"I don't think so," Ida Belle said. "But Beatrice will know."

Beatrice Paulson was a member of Celia's group, God's Wives, and Ida Belle's secret spy within the competing organization. She would be able to provide the insider Catholic view on the situation, at least.

"So why does Natalia keep to herself so much?" I asked. "I mean, I noticed the Russian accent, of course. Is there prejudice here about that kind of thing?"

"I wouldn't think her country of origin is as much a talking point as the age difference between her and Larry," Gertie said.

"What's he got—fifteen, twenty years on her?" I asked.

"I'd guess somewhere in that range," Ida Belle said. "It also doesn't help that Natalia is a looker and Larry is a geeky, balding bore."

"He's in good shape, though," Gertie said. "I was in the park last week working on some tricks with Francis and saw him running. He was wearing baggy sweats—he never wears things very fitted—but he pulled up the bottom of his shirt to get something out of his eye and he has abs."

"We all have abs," Ida Belle said.

"Yeah, but I could see his," Gertie said. "And I wasn't standing all that close."

"And since she hasn't updated her prescription glasses in about a hundred years, that means dude is better built than most guys his age," I said.

"Especially in Sinful," Gertie said. "Beer tends to catch up quickly around here."

"While the abs are somewhat interesting," I said, "I still don't think it's a good reason to hook up with a guy. What else can you tell me about Larry?"

"Not as much as you'd like," Ida Belle said. "He's not a Sinful native. He inherited the house from a great-aunt of his and moved here about three years ago. Claims he's semiretired."

"Why do you say 'claims'?" I asked.

"Because he leaves town most weeks and is usually gone for several days," Ida Belle said. "Sometimes even a week or two at a time."

"And you know this how?" I asked.

"Phyllis LaFont lives next door," Ida Belle said. "She's convinced he's got another family somewhere—an older first wife. Grown children."

"That's a very specific idea," I said.

Ida Belle shrugged. "Phyllis's first husband left her for a much younger woman so there's a bit of personalization in her assessment."

"You think?" Gertie said. "If I see Phyllis coming when I'm downtown, I'll duck in anywhere to avoid another comprehensive review of all her ex's sins. Last week, the only option was the porta-john they'd brought in for the parade. I was stuck in that thing for ten minutes while she bent Marie's ear about that man."

"You voluntarily spent ten minutes in a porta-john?" I asked, cringing.

"You've never met Phyllis," Gertie said. "Trust me, it was the better alternative."

Ida Belle shook her head. "Mind you, her first husband set out of here twenty years ago. It amazes me that in two decades the woman hasn't found something else to complain about, even though she remarried after he left. But there you have it. If you want to know the comings and goings of Larry Guillory, Phyllis can tell you."

"So what kind of work is he supposed to have done?" I asked. "He's sorta young for retirement."

"Government, which accounts for the early retirement age," Gertie said. "Supposed to be some kind of computer guy. That's the buzz, anyway. I've never asked. Honestly, I'm not sure I've exchanged much more than pleasantries with the man in all the time he's been here. He's not much for talking."

Ida Belle nodded. "Walter says the same thing and if Walter can't get something out of a person, no one else in Sinful stands a chance."

"Interesting," I said.

The lack of general information on a family who'd lived in Sinful for three years had my spidey sense going off. People could hide the fact that they were a serial killer for an entire lifetime in a city, but it was hard to hide a hangnail in a place like Sinful, unless they were exceptionally crafty.

"I don't buy into the starter-family conspiracy," Ida Belle said, "but if he was really a techie guy, then he might be doing some government contracting, especially if he had anything to do with security. Likely, it's all innocuous. But given Phyllis's particular bent, she would create drama around it."

"If it was internet security, it's definitely a great skill set for postretirement work," I said. "So he could be contracting for the government or making ten times that working for the security companies that former military special forces have started. It seems a popular work choice when they're done with the service."

"Well, they're not exactly trained to do your taxes," Gertie said.

"There is that," I said. "So if we assume Larry doesn't have another wife who is also an Olympic-level sharpshooter, then what else do we have? Anyone know how he met his wife? Where they moved from? And why Sinful since his ties to the town were slim at best?"

"My guess is because he's cheap," Ida Belle said. "He inherited the house free and clear, and it's not a big place so it can't be expensive to maintain. But Walter says every time Larry comes in the General Store, he complains about the upcharge on the items in the store."

"Then he could hike his happy butt up the highway to the big-box stores," I said.

"Which is exactly what Walter tells him," Ida Belle said. "But he tells Walter he doesn't want to put more miles on his car—also inherited. Natalia has an econobox. Probably can barely fit a child seat in it."

Gertie nodded. "Phyllis also said he replaced most of his backyard grass with deck and a rock garden. He told her he was appalled at the watering costs to keep up the lawn so he just left a little spot for Lina to play in. Phyllis scored some good bushes out of the deal, though. Apparently, shrubbery uses too much water as well."

"Walter said Larry told him one day that the only reason he was willing to pay the upcharge for the box of tinfoil he was buying was that the gas to buy one item would outweigh the savings and he needed the tinfoil that day," Ida Belle said. "Larry also said that he wouldn't be needing another for a while as he washes and reuses it."

"Alrighty then," I said. "He moved his family here because a free house and car dropped in his lap. So far, I see a couple reasons why people might want *Larry* to disappear, but I don't see anything sinister about his wife."

"Maybe she eats too much or uses too much toilet paper," Gertie said.

I shook my head. "You know, in any other place, I'd take that as a joke, but in Sinful..."

"Looks like we're going to have to go back to basics on this one," Gertie said.

"What one?" Ida Belle asked. "This isn't our case. In fact, Carter is probably at the crime scene right now fuming because he knows we're here discussing official police business. He's not going to let us stroll into his investigation."

"She's right," I said. "And since I can't see cheap Larry hiring us to work for him, I think we might have to stay on the sidelines speculating."

Gertie's disappointment was obvious. "Then why are we talking about it at all?"

I stared. "Because we're all nosy and like a puzzle."

"Oh yeah." She nodded. "That makes sense. But I still don't see any reason why we can't take a casserole to their house tomorrow and if we happen to, chat a bit. That's just the proper Southern thing to do."

"That comment Larry made—'we've dealt with worse'—I would love to know what that meant," I said.

"Me too," Ida Belle said. "And Gertie's right. Carter can't complain about people following good manners. We won't be the only people delivering food there tomorrow."

I grinned. "You mean we're not the only nosy ones in town?"

"No," Ida Belle said. "We're just the best at it."

CHAPTER SIX

IT WAS WELL after 2:00 a.m. before Ida Belle and Gertie headed out and I went up to bed. I hadn't heard a peep from Carter but I hadn't really expected to. I knew he'd be working the crime scene for hours and he had to get his observations down while they were fresh. Not to mention that he knew making contact with me would prompt questions he couldn't answer, and he probably didn't want to revisit the same tired old ground even though he knew it was bound to happen again unless one of us died.

I hadn't told Ida Belle and Gertie about Mannie's information, either. We'd had entirely too much stimulus already and I wanted to go over everything when we weren't as tired and drunk on sugar. I figured I'd hit that bit of news the next morning when we met up. I knew it would worry them and they'd both be ready to play bodyguard. At least waiting gave them and me one more night of decent sleep before they insisted on being with me 24-7. We'd all already decided to forgo church, figuring Gertie was going to be stiff as heck and no one was going to be in the mood for joyful singing. Besides, with all the baking the café did for the parade, there wouldn't be any banana pudding this week, which was the real reason I got out on Sunday mornings.

I had just finished showering and put on my Carter's-not-staying-over sleepwear when I heard a sound downstairs. Merlin was already sound asleep on my pillow so it couldn't be him and really, unless he'd figured out how to pop the tab on a beer, he wasn't the best bet, anyway. Carter wasn't foolish enough to come enter my house without announcing himself. But there was one person who was brave enough to plop down in my kitchen with a beer and wait for me to show up.

Mannie.

I pulled on clothes appropriate for viewing, checked my weapon for readiness, just in case someone who wasn't welcome had developed a steel backbone or had gone temporarily insane, and headed downstairs. As soon as my feet hit the first-floor hardwood, I heard a chair scrape across my kitchen floor. I headed in, gun drawn, and spotted a smiling Mannie sitting at the table.

"Took you long enough to get down here," he said. "Were you naked?"

"At some point," I said. "Most people are when they shower. How did you get past my alarm system?"

"Magic?"

I raised one eyebrow.

"You didn't turn it on," he said and frowned. "That's really careless given the circumstances."

"Crap! I knew I was forgetting something."

"Too much to drink?"

"More like too many things to ponder. Were you still downtown when the shooting happened?"

"No. Mr. Hebert doesn't find fireworks entertaining and he finds standing in a crowd of people even less so. We packed up and left after the runaway-truck, chest-flashing part of the night."

"But you heard about it."

"Of course. Why do you think I'm here?"

"Oh!" I stared for a moment. This was totally unexpected. "Do you have information?"

He smiled. "I wouldn't be here otherwise. I try not to make breaking into women's homes a habit. Yours comes with even more concerns than most."

"So what do you know? Is that first-family speculation about Larry true?"

"I hadn't heard that rumor and to the best of my knowledge, it has no validity. What I do know is that Larry claims to be a retired government keyboard jockey but he's neither retired nor a simple computer tech."

"Really? So what does Larry do?"

"According to my sources—intel."

I perked up. That put an entirely different slant on things.

"So is he working in an office out of New Orleans?" I asked.

"No. Larry leaves New Orleans on military transport, usually bound for DC."

"Why all the cloak-and-dagger then? I asked. "Why doesn't he just live in DC and go into the office every day like a good little government soldier?"

"That's the sixty-four-thousand-dollar question, isn't it?"

"I'll bet the answer is really good."

"So do I, which is why I'm hoping you can ferret it out. I'm afraid business has been rather tame lately and Big has latched onto this bit of intrigue. He's hoping, since you were there, that you have some theories on the matter."

"Well, I can tell you what I think about that bullet hole. It wasn't a random shot in the air by one of the locals that took her out."

I filled him in on the trajectory, as best as I could determine, and what it would take to make that kind of shot. He nodded when I finished.

"So it was murder," he said. "I thought Big was probably making drama out of par for the course for Sinful but I shouldn't have been so skeptical. That man has a sixth sense about things. He zeroed in on it as being out of balance, so to speak. Any theories on why someone would want to murder this friend of the wife's?"

"All I know is that the friend paid a surprise visit and based on accent, both she and Larry's wife are Russian. Maybe the friend was into something and thought she'd lie low in Sinful for a bit."

"But trouble followed her here."

I nodded. "Something about her death irritated Larry. There was this expression—only for a second—but I caught it."

"So maybe the friend was trouble and Larry knew it. Then he wouldn't have been happy about the visit or the subsequent fallout, assuming this woman was using them to hide out."

"Exactly. But there's another potential explanation—the friend looks like and was dressed like Larry's wife. And was, in fact, standing there with the couple's daughter."

Mannie raised one eyebrow. "That *is* interesting."

"Yes, but even if Larry is still on the intel books, why would someone want to kill his wife?"

"I don't know. Sending a message, maybe? If we knew exactly what Larry worked on then we might have a better guess. Based on Mr. Hebert's gut, I made a few phone calls and kicked up some information on Larry but nothing on the wife or the friend. Given your observations, there's probably no simple explanation behind the shooting. And I can tell by your expression that you don't think so either."

"Is there ever? Good Lord, assassinations were less complicated than this civilian stuff."

"If it *is* civilian stuff."

"And there's the big unknown."

He nodded. "I did find the military simpler in many ways. But the sleeping arrangements and the food are much better on the civilian side."

"Definitely."

"So are you going to be poking your nose into police business?"

"Not officially. We don't have a client and I don't think the Heberts can stretch to cover this one for me."

"Probably not, but you have an interest."

"Of course I'm interested, which you already knew. You didn't come here in the middle of the night for my beer."

He grinned. "I'll bet the good deputy has dropped in late for more than the beer."

"You'd be correct. Sometimes, it's for a roast beef sandwich."

He laughed. "If that were the only reason, it would truly be a shame. You're an interesting woman, Fortune. I'm sure you're giving Carter plenty of reasons to keep you on his radar."

"Why do I get the impression that my relationship amuses you?"

"'Amuses' isn't really the correct term as I believe it implies a certain level of disdain. I'm simply impressed that someone with your history can venture so well into normal romantic and domestic pursuits. Let's just say it gives me hope for myself someday and leave it at that."

I smiled. "You know, if you want to go the sabertooth

route, Gertie has been checking you out since the first moment she saw you."

He cringed. "I haven't had enough beer for that comment."

I laughed. "One of these days...the right woman will hit you just the right way and you'll see things differently."

"Maybe. It's an interesting thought, anyway."

I spent another couple seconds imagining Mannie in domestic bliss but it wasn't all that simple. He was a man of action, and picturing him in a recliner watching a football game wasn't all that easy an image to formulate.

"You know," I said, shifting gears, "when I saw you here, I thought it was about the other situation."

He shook his head. "I've shared all the intel I have on that for the moment. But I'm still making inquiries."

"And I appreciate it. But there's something I need to tell you."

He straightened a bit in his chair and gave me a nod.

"You know my father was in the same line of work as me and he was really good at it."

"I've heard as much."

"Then you also heard he was killed during a mission when I was a teenager."

"Yes. The Heberts had me do a thorough check on you before they ever became involved."

"Wouldn't want to sully their reputation by association?"

He smiled. "Something like that."

"Well, I learned a couple months ago that my father is still alive."

I don't know what Mannie had been expecting to hear, but that clearly wasn't it. His eyes widened in surprise and he set his beer down so hard on the table that some sloshed out. I'd never seen him do anything so dramatic and it was slightly unnerving.

"You're certain?" he asked.

"I'm certain that Director Morrow believes it's the case. And I'm equally certain that he's not happy about it."

Mannie nodded and I knew he'd immediately understood all the implications—mostly negative—if it proved to be factual.

"Tell me what you know," he said.

I explained about the camera and the Taliban connection, and Mannie asked a few questions about his remains. It didn't take long to bring him up to speed because there wasn't a whole lot to tell. What we knew was far outweighed by what we wanted to know.

"So you think the inquiries made about you have something to do with your father's return from the dead?" he asked.

I shrugged. "I don't know, but you have to admit that the timing is suspicious."

He frowned and I could tell he didn't like it any more than I did.

"You have to be on alert," he said. "And that means no more forgetting your alarm. If the enemy thinks you can lead them to your father, they won't hesitate to make a move."

"If the enemy knows anything at all, then they'll know I have no idea where my father is and that I'm probably just as pissed as they are to find out he's still alive."

"I get that, but while *I* know you're telling the truth, the enemy will simply think you're protecting an active operative."

I sighed. "And they'll think I'm still active as well. I know. I covered all of this with Carter after you told us about the inquiries."

"I know you're more than capable of handling a man, even an assassin, and probably far more than one. But if the enemy is after your father, they're not going to send just anyone.

They'll send the best *team* they can put together. In certain circles, both of your reputations precede you."

"Yeah."

I stared out the kitchen window into the backyard. The window that probably should have had the blinds drawn as soon as the sun went down. The window that I'd just had sensors put on because I was no longer safe in my home, in the town where people often forgot to lock their doors.

Mannie rose from his chair and gave me a sympathetic look. "I'm sorry. I know you had different ideas about how your future was going to look."

"It can still look that way. I just have to figure this out first."

"I know Carter is standing right next to you on this and those two crazy women won't let you out of their sight for very long. But I'll be looking into things myself. And I'm certain that the Heberts will be anxious to help in any way possible. I won't tell them anything because that's your call. But if there's anything you need that you can't put your hands on, let me know. Their connections sometimes put military intelligence to shame."

"Thanks. I really appreciate it."

He gave me a nod, then headed out the back door. "Lock it and turn on that alarm," I heard him say as he walked away.

I did as instructed and closed the blind, noticing that he was walking the perimeter of my backyard as I snapped it shut. I cut myself a slice of pie and flopped down at the table. This was bad. When people like Mannie got worried, it was well beyond your typical emergency. I knew that, of course. I'd known that since that first phone call from Morrow. But with every passing week, the noose seemed to tighten.

I was unofficially back in the game.

CHAPTER SEVEN

DESPITE THE EXCITEMENT of the parade, the murder, the news that someone in the intelligence community was trying to locate me, and the ongoing drama surrounding my father's return from the dead, I actually slept decently. Which was likely due to the pie, the beers, and the shots of Sinful Ladies Cough Syrup I'd had before finally trudging upstairs and collapsing in my bed.

It wasn't a very long sleep, however. I hadn't made the trek from the kitchen until almost 3:00 a.m., and since Merlin considered anything past 7:00 a.m. slacking, he was standing on my chest at 7:01 treating me to his rendition of opera. I'd never been a huge fan of opera, and Merlin wasn't improving that situation any. I knew that if I kicked him out of the room, he'd either sit outside the door and sing louder or be extraordinarily quiet all day while plotting his revenge. The second option was the one that had me climbing out of bed and heading downstairs to give him his breakfast.

It was just as well. Gertie and Ida Belle arrived ten minutes later, Gertie looking like the Michelin Man. Most of her body was wrapped in what looked like ice packs. Her arms were forced out so wide that she had to turn sideways to get in my front door.

"Should I even ask?" I asked as I closed the door.

"You should ice injuries for the first twenty-four hours," Gertie said. "Then you switch to heat."

"So you're telling me that tomorrow, you're going to show up wrapped in heating pads like a burrito and expecting me to find you twenty extension cords?"

"Probably," Ida Belle said. "You might want to have a spare breaker on hand just in case she shorts out the whole shooting match. In fact, I might call the power company and warn them. Does this house have a backup generator?"

"You're hilarious," Gertie said. "And since you forced me out of the house in the middle of my second round of icing and before I could manage a first cup of coffee, I think we should move this barage of insults into the kitchen."

"Will she fit down the hallway?" Ida Belle asked. "Maybe we should have her walk around and come in the back door."

I grinned as Gertie managed to lift one arm and give Ida Belle the finger, then had to have help putting it back down before she could traverse the hallway. Once in the kitchen, we each grabbed an arm and got her into a chair. Given all the extra weight and the extreme bulk, she swayed back and forth a bit until Ida Belle yanked my tablecloth off the table and tied her to the chair.

"I feel like that woman in Florida," Gertie said. "The crazy bird lady. Remember?"

"How could we forget?" Ida Belle said. "It's not every day that you get chased around a buffet with a plastic flamingo."

"Which, when you think about it, is really a shame," I said. "It was one of the less dangerous of the situations Gertie has managed to get into."

"Not for the dessert table," Ida Belle said.

"That was a big loss," I agreed.

"If either of you would like to stop with the recollection of that very unfortunate incident, I'd love a cup of coffee," Gertie said.

"You're the one who brought it up," Ida Belle said as she poured a double serving of coffee into a thermos and passed it over to Gertie. Then she poured herself a cup and refilled mine before taking a seat across from me.

"I'm sorta surprised to see you up and at 'em already," Ida Belle said. "Merlin?"

"You know it," I said. "I was afraid to sleep in even though I barely got four hours."

Gertie sighed. "If only I had a hunky man to take away my sleep."

"Oh, Carter never made it here last night," I said. "In fact, I haven't even heard from him this morning. But then I figure he's avoiding me as long as he can, given what he does for a living and who I am as a person."

Gertie and Ida Belle glanced at each other.

"Then since Carter isn't the reason for your lack of rest, what's going on?" Ida Belle asked. "Because as interesting as the situation last night was, I don't think it kept you awake."

"The wardrobe malfunction might have," Gertie said. "Gave me nightmares."

"Good point," Ida Belle said and gave me an expectant look.

"As much as it pains me to admit it, seeing inappropriate body parts on people I never wanted to see them on has become sort of common since I moved here," I said.

"Then there is something else bothering you," Ida Belle said.

"A couple of things, actually," I said. "I was going to tell you part of it last night. Then the murder took center stage, and since it was far less personal, I sort of put it off again."

Gertie immediately clued into my use of the word "personal."

"It's about your father," she said.

I nodded and brought them up to date on the latest news from Morrow and the information Mannie had given Carter and me the night before. They listened intently, never uttering a word, and even when I finished, they just sat staring at each other with a level of concern in their expressions that I hadn't seen since my showdown with Ahmad.

"So what's the plan?" Ida Belle asked finally.

I smiled, my chest clenching a bit. Not even a hint that they might need to step back. Not even a flicker of fear that some of the best-trained assassins in the world might be gunning for me. I knew that would be the case with them, but there was something so totally empowering about experiencing it firsthand.

"Not much at the moment," I said. "Morrow, Carter, and Mannie are all working their resources and I am on high alert."

"What about Harrison?" Gertie asked, referring to my former partner at the CIA.

"Morrow has already worked him into the loop," I said. "He'll utilize any resources he has, but he's been out as long as I have."

"But he's on alert as well," Ida Belle said.

"Yeah," I said. "He's taking extra precautions. I'm sure anyone interested in me and what I'm up to already knows who he is and what our relationship was. Harrison is prepared. We know these sorts of things can happen when we take the job."

"But you don't necessarily plan on it," Gertie said.

"No," I said.

I'd already done a couple rounds of guilty feelings for the position Harrison was in. He'd left the CIA and gone into private security because he wanted to start a family and do the whole normal-life thing. This was a complication that he didn't need. And even though I knew he didn't blame me for it, I couldn't help feeling responsible.

"This isn't on you," Ida Belle said.

Jeez, the woman was a mind reader.

"I know that," I said.

"But you still feel guilty because it's your father causing it," Gertie said.

I didn't say anything.

Ida Belle leaned forward in her chair. "Remember this—the person most wronged by that man is you. And there's nothing you could have done to change the actions he decided to take all those years ago. You were a child when he went off to do whatever it is he's been doing. So there's nothing you could have done to prevent what's happening now. It is all precipitated by his choices."

Gertie nodded. "Even if you'd never become an operative, and you were a hairstylist with six kids and living in Idaho, people who wanted to find your father would have still come looking for you now."

"Yeah, but they would have been a lot less armed," I said.

"You've taken the necessary precautions," Ida Belle said. "But Mannie is right—that alarm does no good if it's not engaged."

"It probably doesn't do a whole lot of good when it is engaged," I said. "At least, not against the kind of people who would come gunning for me. I could disable this in seconds and it's military grade."

"You're special, Fortune," Ida Belle said. "And I have no

doubt that people who might show up here would be special as well, but special has all kinds of levels."

"My money's still on you in a gunfight," Gertie said. "Unless you give Ida Belle a second on the draw. She's still lethal."

Ida Belle waved a hand in dismissal but I could tell the compliment pleased her. "I'm years past drawing on someone like Fortune and thinking I'd come out of it unscathed, but Gertie makes a valid point. Of all the people I've ever met, you're probably the most capable of taking care of yourself, but even you can benefit from a little warning."

"I promise, I will have the alarm on as soon as I'm in for the night. And the shades drawn. I'll even put tacks on the stairs if you think I should."

"Merlin would love that," Gertie said.

"You're right," I said. "Scratch the tacks."

"What about nailing your windows shut?" Gertie asked.

"They wouldn't lift the window," I said. "They'd cut the glass and crawl through."

"Which means you need to do a walk-around every time you leave the house and then again when you return," Gertie said. "People could get to your backyard from the bayou and with all the bushes and trees, no one could see someone coming in a back window, even in the middle of the day."

"She's right," Ida Belle said. "And instead of someone in your kitchen drinking beer, they could just leave a bomb that goes off when you walk inside."

"I'm pretty sure if someone is in my backyard during the day, my industrious neighbor, Ronald, will see them," I said. "He seems to spend a lot of time watching my lawn."

"Yeah, but would he call the cops if he sees someone breaking in?" Gertie asked.

"Hmm. Probably not," I said. "But at this point, there's no reason to presume that anyone wants me dead. More likely, they want to know if I'm working with my father, because apparently, he has something they want. If I'm dead, I can't give it to them."

"Okay, so kidnapping is more likely than death from a distance," Ida Belle said. "So how do you plan on getting out of the house if someone comes inside in the middle of the night?"

"Can't come out the bedroom window," Gertie said. "She could easily make the drop into the yard from the front porch roof but someone would be standing there waiting on her."

"There's something upstairs I need to show you guys." I felt something cold on my feet and looked down. "Gertie, you're melting."

Ida Belle looked under the table and shook her head. "You're going to need a Shop-Vac to clean this up. Maybe even a new kitchen floor."

"Well, untie me and help me get these things off and into the sink," Gertie said.

"I don't think they're going to fit in the sink," Ida Belle said as she untied the tablecloth. "A bathtub maybe."

"Start with the sink," I said as I unwrapped a pack from Gertie's arm. "We can carry over onto the back porch if needed."

Ten minutes later, we'd tossed the last of the packs outside and Ida Belle had Gertie standing in front of a floor fan.

"On the plus side, I don't have to mop the kitchen floor," I said.

Gertie pulled a dishrag over her hair. "Is this absolutely necessary? I figured I'd be too sore to roll my hair this morning, so I did it last night. It might be days before I can manage rollers again."

I shook my head at the bruises on her arms and wondered what the rest of her looked like. "I still don't understand why you don't just buy a bag of beads. I'm doing that next year."

"I've tried it already so don't bother," Ida Belle said. "It's the thrill of the chase."

"It looks more like she played a rugby game than thrilled in a chase," I said. "But if this is your idea of fun, who am I to stand in the way?"

"Am I dry enough to go upstairs yet?" Gertie asked.

"I suppose since you've stopped dripping you'll do," Ida Belle said. "But you're not getting in my SUV until your clothes are dry."

Gertie waved a hand at her. "I'll just take them off."

I grimaced. "That's a discussion that can wait. Maybe forever. Follow me."

We headed upstairs to my bedroom and I motioned them into the closet.

"Oh, you did a built-in shoe rack," Gertie said as she studied the shelving on the back wall of the closet. She ran her finger over a couple pairs of tennis shoes and shook her head. "We really need a shopping trip. All you have here are tennis shoes and sandals."

"You brought us up here to show us a shoe rack?" Ida Belle stared at me as if I'd lost my mind.

"Of course not, although I'm not tripping every morning, so there's that. But remember the secret weapon storage Marge put in a bedroom closet? Well, I did something similar." I pulled the shoe rack and it swung away from the wall, revealing a cubby with a ladder into the attic behind it.

"There was dead space behind this wall so Carter and I worked on this," I said. "If someone breaches, then I can climb through here and exit the side window in the attic into the oak tree. A quick jaunt across Ronald's roof and down another tree and I'm one house away from trouble."

"Ha!" Ida Belle said. "You're one house away from doubling back for retaliation. And that's *if* you use this ladder at all."

"She said she would," Gertie said.

Ida Belle shook her head. "She said she 'can.' That doesn't mean she will."

"If a situation arises that might precipitate the usage of the escape route, then I'll do an assessment and make a call," I said.

"I bet that's not what you told Carter," Ida Belle said.

"It's like I said before," Gertie said. "The trust is overwhelming."

"She's not entirely wrong," I said. "But if this ladder ever becomes a necessary option, then I figure Carter will have more to worry about than me doing what I normally do."

"Which means whatever you want," Gertie said. "Good girl."

Ida Belle frowned and I studied her for a moment. Usually, if there was an instant for a woman to take care of herself and avoid the white knight, she was waving her flag higher than anyone. But this time, I sensed a change.

"You all right?" I asked her.

She looked directly at me and I could see the worry behind her usual stoic expression. "This is different from Ahmad," she said. "With that situation, you had time to prepare a sting operation. You had a facility ready to go with backup in place."

"And none of it went according to plan," I reminded her. "Look, despite my levity, rest assured that I'm taking this very seriously. I know all the risks and potential pitfalls. I'm going to pay Ally a visit this morning and explain to her why girls' nights are on permanent hold until this is resolved. I know you, Gertie, and Carter have different feelings about proximity but you're also trained. Ally isn't. I won't risk her. And I won't risk myself. I've worked too hard to get a life to throw it away by trying to be Superwoman."

"Except you sort of are Superwoman," Gertie said. "But we're glad to know that you have contingency plans."

Ida Belle nodded, her shoulders relaxing some. "And I think it's a good call keeping Ally at some distance. She's going to fight you on that one, you know. She's loyal to a fault and she cares about you."

"I'm not going to hedge things with her," I said. "By the time I'm done, she won't even wave at me if she sees me crossing the street downtown."

"I'm sorry you're in this position," Gertie said and sighed. "I really wanted your permanent move to Sinful to be like a baptism—ridding yourself of the old life and starting a new one."

"I know," I said. "And it is. There's just this one last hurdle."

But even as I said the words, I wondered if they were true. What if my father disappeared again? He'd been a ghost for fourteen years. I had no doubt he could manage it again. And his enemies would never believe that I didn't know his whereabouts. For that matter, my former employer probably wouldn't believe it either, even though it was fully aware of the fact that he'd abandoned me to do whatever it was he was doing.

Unless someone got their hands on Dwight Redding, I'd spend the rest of my life looking over my shoulder.

CHAPTER EIGHT

Gertie grunted and clutched the casserole dish in her lap. "Can you take it easy on the potholes?" she complained. "You're giving my bruises bruises."

"I told you to sit on a pillow," Ida Belle said.

"I wouldn't need a pillow if you drove like a normal person," Gertie said. "But you insist on doing warp speed and hitting every hole in the street like it's some vehicle version of Whac-a-Mole."

"I'm driving in a straight line in my own lane," Ida Belle said. "If I'm hitting too many potholes for your taste, take it up with the mayor's office."

"Like that makes a difference," Gertie said.

"Why wouldn't it?" I asked. "The mayor is one of your best friends."

"Yes. But unless she's developed the ability to create money from air, there's no budget for repaving the streets," Gertie said. "Which is why we have these potholes. That filling stuff doesn't work worth a crap. One day, someone's going to lose a toddler in one of those holes. Or a moped."

"Well, depending on the quality of the moped, we might get a fundraiser then," Ida Belle said.

"What about the toddler?" I asked.

"No one minds losing a toddler," Gertie said.

I laughed. "I would have loved to see you teach. Did you have a moat between the chalkboard and your students?"

"I taught high school," Gertie said. "I just wore a big silver cross."

I grinned as Ida Belle pulled to the curb and nodded toward a white clapboard house with peeling paint and a slightly sloped porch roof. Phyllis hadn't been lying about the grass thing. A few trees and a couple of patches of grass remained, but the bulk of the tiny front lawn had been paved with a circular drive. It was lumpy and even I could tell the grade on it was completely wrong.

"Let me guess," I said. "Larry poured his own driveway."

"Unfortunately, there wasn't a rule against it," Gertie said.

I stared. "Seriously? There's something in Sinful that doesn't have a rule?"

"Oh, there's a rule *now*," Gertie said. "But his driveway was grandfathered in, so despite it looking like the kindergarten class constructed it, nothing can be done. His neighbors are fit to be tied."

"Another good downpour and they'll all get their wish granted," Ida Belle said. "Because that drive is going to slide right off the lawn and into the street."

"Maybe it will fill the potholes," I said.

Gertie laughed and glanced over at the house. "How do you want to play this?"

"You do your usual food-death-Southern requirement thing and get us in the door. Information-wise, I'd like to know about his wife and her friend—where are they from, how did he and Natalia meet. Basically, anything we can learn about

Natalia and Katia would help us form a picture of why this might have happened. And if possible, I'd love to know what Larry meant about them having dealt with worse."

"You're thinking it might have something to do with Katia?" Gertie said.

"I don't know," I said. "I just know her death irritated him as much as it worried him and that's not exactly a normal reaction. I'd like to know why he was angry but I doubt he'll just come right out and tell us."

But I'd been wrong before. And I was wrong again.

We were on our way up the steps when the front door opened and Carter stepped outside.

Crap!

I scanned the street, but his truck was nowhere in sight. He took one look at us and frowned, then began a hasty approach.

"I suggest you get back in your vehicle and leave," he said.

"I suggest you remember the manners you were raised with or I'll call your mother," Ida Belle said.

Gertie held up a casserole. "Since it's after noon, I'm going to guess this won't be the only tray sitting on their kitchen counter. So unless you can come up with a good reason why we shouldn't do what we do every time someone dies in this town, we'll be completely ignoring your advice."

Carter gave me a pained look but I ignored him completely and walked by. What did he expect? The caveman routine was outdated as it was, but it would have never worked on the three of us. I glanced back when we walked up on the porch and saw him stomping off down the street.

"Somebody's pitching a five-year-old fit," Gertie said. "Looks like you're going to be sleeping alone for a while."

"Good," I said. "I've been short on parents for a long time. I'm not in the market for someone to tell me what to do."

"I'm pretty sure you never have been," Gertie said.

"And Carter knows that better than anyone," I said. "He can get over it, or not. But I'm not having this discussion with him every time there's a crime in Sinful."

Ida Belle turned back to look at him and frowned. "He does seem a bit more sensitive than usual. Makes me wonder why."

"Probably because this is a mare's nest and he's mad that it landed on Sinful's doorstep," Gertie said.

"Maybe," Ida Belle said, but she didn't look convinced, which had me wondering about it too. Carter had been a little quick on the draw this time.

"Or maybe he's upset that something is taking his attention away from the situation with Fortune," Gertie suggested. "He does have a lot on his mind."

"So you're saying we should give him a break?" I asked.

"A break, yes. What he wants, no," Gertie said.

"I suppose I could manage that," I said. "Well, since we're already in trouble, ring the doorbell and let's see if we can get into deeper hot water."

As Gertie lifted her hand to press the button, I heard raised voices inside and stopped her. I pressed my ear against the glass section of the door but I couldn't make out the words. Just the tone, which wasn't pleasant.

"Should we come back later?" Gertie asked.

"Heck no," Ida Belle said. "People say more when they're slightly out of control."

"I have to agree with her," I said. "If they're off-balance, they might let things slip that they normally wouldn't."

Gertie pressed the bell and we waited. It took a bit, but finally the door swung back and Larry looked out at us, his face still flushed. He blinked once and it was clear he was trying to get focus back to what was in front of him. Then he gave us a nod and stood back and waved us in, apparently resigned to Southern mourning requirements.

We followed him to the back of the house to the kitchen. Unlike most of the homes I'd seen in Sinful, this one had not been updated. The cabinets were thin, cheap wood and most of them drooped. The laminate countertops were a strange shade of green and had cracks and pieces missing. The stove was something right out of the Old Testament and I wondered if it even worked. Even the curtains looked as though if they had one more washing, they'd turn into dust. Boy, no one had been exaggerating that cheap thing.

On the plus side, the place was neat and clean, and cheap people didn't collect a bunch of useless stuff, so it wasn't cluttered with coffee mugs or thimbles or whatever else people got up to collecting. Well, except for the collection of covered dishes on the counter. Gertie had called that one correctly. We weren't the first to turn up bearing food and wouldn't be the last. Hence Larry's look of resignation. It was probably a double-edged sword. He didn't strike me as much of a people person, but then there was free food involved.

Free had won out.

"Please have a seat, ladies," he said. "Can I offer you something to drink? Natalia just went to check on Lina. She'll be right back. She made a pot of coffee when Deputy LeBlanc was here. We also have sweet tea if you prefer that."

We all voted for sweet tea and took a seat as Larry started filling glasses.

"How is Lina doing?" Gertie asked.

"Okay, I hope," Larry said. "To be honest, I'm not sure. She's always been a quiet child. We keep trying to get her to talk but she's trying to act like everything is fine. She woke up screaming twice last night but we couldn't get her to tell us why either time."

"Nightmares, I would assume," Gertie said.

Larry nodded and set the glasses of tea on the table before taking a seat. "That's what I figure. I just wish she'd tell us. We let her sleep in our bed, thinking that would help her feel more secure, and she did go right to sleep. But I guess when her subconscious came out to play, it wasn't kind."

"Was she close to Katia?" I asked.

"Not at all," Larry said. "Katia had never met Lina until now. Katia was closer to Natalia's sister than Natalia. I suppose that's a blessing the way things turned out. If Lina had been attached..."

"Katia and Natalia are Russian, right?" I asked.

He stared at me for a moment and then nodded. "I guess the accent still gives her away although Natalia has worked hard to get rid of hers. Katia never bothered."

"Her clients were mostly Russian," Natalia said as she stepped into the kitchen. "She had better sales than any other associate because of her accent. No reason to lose it."

"Certainly," Larry agreed. "I'm sure it served her well."

"We're really sorry for your loss," Ida Belle said to Natalia. "Is Lina okay?"

Natalia nodded and took a seat next to Larry. "She's restless but sleeping. Finally. Last night was rough. I wish I knew what to do."

"I'm sure you're doing everything you can," Gertie said. "Just be there so she feels secure. There's really nothing else to be done right now."

Natalia nodded but I got the impression that she'd only half heard what Gertie said. Her skin was pale and had that haggard look that came with intense stress. There were dark circles under her eyes and I noticed her hands shook as she lifted her coffee mug. She'd probably benefit from less caffeine but I wasn't about to say so. People had been shot for less.

"I assume Katia lived in the US," Ida Belle said. "Did she have family here? Is there anyone we can help you contact?"

Natalia shook her head. "She had no family. When she left Russia, they disowned her just as my family disowned me."

"What about your sister?" I asked. "Larry said Katia was friends with her. Did she stay behind as well?"

A flash of pain crossed Natalia's face and she jumped up from her chair. "I'm sorry but I'm not feeling well. Please excuse me."

She practically ran out of the room and I looked over at Larry, feeling responsible.

"I'm sorry," I said. "I didn't realize her sister was a bad subject."

Larry glanced down the hall and his jaw flexed. "How could you?"

"I don't understand how people can do that," Gertie said. "Just write off family like that over a lifestyle choice."

"Natalia's sister didn't write her off," Larry said, and I could tell he was starting to get worked up again. "She was killed in New Orleans three years ago. Natalia was almost killed as well."

"Oh, wow," I said. "That's horrible. I wouldn't have said anything—"

Larry waved a hand. "You couldn't have known. It was a mugging gone wrong and Natalia was still dealing with the aftereffects when we moved to Sinful. We never talk about it."

I glanced at Ida Belle. We'd found out what Larry had meant about dealing with worse. But that bit of information had only yielded more questions. I wondered how many we could get answered before his mood went from surly to outright pissed.

Gertie, however, dived right in. She shook her head and gave Larry a sympathetic look. "The crime down there has gotten so bad. I used to love for Ida Belle and me to take a shopping trip to the French Quarter, but we really limit them these days. It's just not a safe place for two senior ladies to be walking around."

I held in a smile. If Ida Belle and Gertie went walking around the French Quarter, my money was on them scaring the muggers.

Larry nodded but his expression went almost blank, which was interesting. Clearly, he had strong feelings about what had happened to his wife and her sister, but he wasn't about to give details.

"If Katia had no family to tend to her, would you like us to help you with arrangements?" Ida Belle asked. "You've already been through enough. If we can take something off your plate..."

"I appreciate it," Larry said. "Deputy LeBlanc said he called the emergency contact in Katia's phone, but it was a coworker so I doubt he'll be taking charge of things. Natalia and I haven't discussed it yet but I'm sure she'll want to make the arrangements. If you could provide me with some names and phone numbers for the businesses we'll need, that would be a big help."

"Of course," Ida Belle said. "I can email them if you'd like. I have your address from the charity auction last year."

"Thank you," he said, and rose. "I'm sorry, but if you'll excuse me, I need to check on my wife."

We stood and headed to the front door.

"Please let us know if we can help in any other way," Gertie said.

He gave us a nod and we headed down the sidewalk and climbed into Ida Belle's SUV.

"Well, that was weird," I said as Ida Belle pulled away.

"You think?" Gertie said. "I was looking for a hidden camera thinking we'd crossed over into the *Twilight Zone*."

"I will admit, I almost feel like we left knowing less than we went in with even though that's not exactly true," Ida Belle said.

"In a way it is," I said. "We got information, but that information created more holes so net, we're in the negative."

"So what now?" Gertie asked. "We don't even know Katia's last name, so it will be hard to track down any information on her until we can manage that much, at least."

"But we do have Natalia's last name," I said. "And that mugging happened in New Orleans so we might be able to find something on that."

"'Might' is the optimal word," Ida Belle said. "A mugging in New Orleans isn't exactly front-page news."

"But this one resulted in a death," Gertie said. "Surely that rates at least an online write-up."

"Maybe," Ida Belle agreed. "But even if we had a police report, what would it tell us? That two women were attacked and one of them died? What does it matter? Katia wasn't there."

"But Katia might not have been the target, remember?" I said. "If the attack in New Orleans wasn't random, then Natalia might have been the intended and her sister got it instead."

"If the killer is really after Natalia, he's either incompetent or she has nine lives," Gertie said. "If I had blond hair, I wouldn't want to hang out with her. You might want to keep your distance."

"I'm going to hazard a guess that Natalia and I have little in common," I said. "The old dude for a husband and the little kid sort of clinch it. And while I do share their aversion to casual mingling, I'm not about do-it-lousy-yourself in order to save money."

"If Natalia *is* the target, their aversion to mingling might explain why it's been three years between attempts," Gertie said. "If you don't make friends, there's no one to leave a forwarding address with. And knowing Larry, he took his time changing it over because of the fees required."

"Except that they didn't live in New Orleans," Ida Belle said. "That much, I do know. They moved here from up north —Virginia, I think."

I smiled at the thought of Virginia being "up north," but Louisiana residents had strict opinions about the definition of Yankees, so I wasn't about to disagree.

"So why were the sisters in New Orleans?" Gertie asked.

"Girls' trip?" I said. "But if that's the case, it complicates our theory. Why would someone go to the trouble to follow Natalia to another state when they could have mugged her in her hometown? Seems like a lot of unnecessary effort."

"The whole thing is a mangled mess," Ida Belle said. "We don't have enough information. Not on Larry, Natalia, her sister, or Katia."

"And given Mannie's information about Larry working government intel," I said, "I don't think information on him or his family is going to be easy to come by. There's a reason he has them all on lockdown."

"Do you think Natalia knows what he does?" Gertie asked.

I shrugged. "Hard to say. She might just think he's a private person or a bit odd. For all we know, she might be just as happy with the silent, no-close-friends arrangement as he is."

"That's true," Ida Belle said. "Women who look like Natalia don't usually marry men like Larry without a good reason. And it usually has nothing to do with love. But without knowing her background, it's impossible to say what that reason was. Maybe her past in Russia was bad and she fled and latched onto the first man who could take care of her. The fact that he prefers them keeping to themselves was probably all the more attractive to her, assuming she didn't want to constantly address her past."

"Maybe he didn't like Katia because she reminded Natalia of that past," Gertie said.

"Could be," Ida Belle said as she pulled into my driveway. "Especially since Katia still had ties with Russia through her job."

We headed inside to the kitchen on autopilot. Gertie sliced pie and started heating it up. Ida Belle filled glasses with ice and pulled sweet tea out of the refrigerator. I headed to my office to grab my laptop. Minutes later, we were all in our designated spots at my kitchen table, but no one had even lifted a fork.

I opened the laptop and did a search for Natalia and New Orleans and located a few sentences in a news report.

"It's not much," I said as I repeated the basics. "New Orleans Detective Sean Reynolds, spokesperson for the police department, reports two women were mugged in the French Quarter Saturday night. Annika Baskin, a visitor from Moscow, died at the scene. Her sister, Natalia Guillory, is in critical condition. The police have no leads and are asking anyone with information to contact them."

I did more searches for Annika Baskin, Natalia Guillory, Natalia Baskin, and Larry Guillory but came up empty. It wasn't really surprising. Larry being intel, and thereby suspicious full time, meant he would attempt to keep his and his family's presence off the internet. Social media would be out of the question.

I slumped back in my chair and blew out a breath. "So

where do we go to get more information on a couple who doesn't talk on a social basis?"

Gertie shrugged. "Seems like the only place to get information is from the source."

"We were just at the source," I said. "Now we have more questions than before we went in. And I don't think Larry is going to be forthcoming if we just show up and launch the Spanish Inquisition. He's government intel, not a fisherman. He'd know in a second what we were doing."

"So we don't talk," Gertie said. "We listen."

"I am so confused," I said.

"Don't look at me," Ida Belle said. "I don't understand half of what she says."

"You two are a disgrace to women everywhere," Gertie said. "What's the oldest method of getting information?"

"Torture?" I asked.

Gertie sighed. "Eavesdropping. Women throughout history have kept themselves safe and in control by eavesdropping. Remember how Larry and Natalia were arguing when we walked up to the front door? I seriously doubt that's the last time that's going to happen, and I doubt it was over redecorating that hideous kitchen, although it should have been. So all we need to do is listen to their private conversations."

"I think people might notice if we're standing on the front porch leaned against the door," I said. "Besides, we couldn't make out anything anyway and I don't think we can request they only argue in the living room."

"Sometimes, I can't believe you were CIA," Gertie said. "You people are supposed to be the underhanded, sneaky ones. You're called spooks, for Christ's sake. All that illegal wiretapping and bugging hotels and such."

"That's political stuff," I said. "My missions involved less unsavory targets."

Ida Belle snorted.

"I assume you're suggesting we bug their house?" I asked.

"Of course," Gertie said. "What did you think I was suggesting—that we hide behind their sofa? This isn't Cold War Russia."

"It's Sinful, so I'm never sure what's appropriate," I said.

"Lurking behind sofas is only acceptable if you're playing hide-and-seek or spying on your teen daughter and her boyfriend," Gertie said.

"Well, since we don't have any kids and we're too old for hide-and-seek, I guess those options are out," I said.

"Speak for yourself on the hide-and-seek thing," Gertie said.

Ida Belle waved her hand. "We're off topic. Exactly how is it you think we can bug their house? It's not like we can masquerade as the cable guy. And if Larry even smells a hint of a service charge, anyone we put up to it won't make it through the front door."

"Couldn't we ask Mannie to do it?" Gertie asked. "He could claim he's with the gas company and there's a leak. Mannie has the expertise to get the equipment set up and the sneakiness to do it without anyone noticing."

"Maybe regular people," I said. "But Larry is intel. He's automatically suspicious. Trust me on that one. They don't get into that line of work and then become all paranoid. They're already paranoid, which is what attracts them to that line of work. It wouldn't surprise me if he does a regular sweep of his house for bugs."

Ida Belle frowned. "She's right. We've known some of those type. Larry would be on alert on a normal basis but now he's going to be at DEFCON 1."

I nodded. "And it's not like the paranoia is without merit. Intel employees have to be very careful."

"I get it, but why at home?" Gertie asked. "It's not like he'd be talking shop with his wife. What does the enemy think they're going to overhear? A discussion about what's for dinner?"

"Oh, I didn't say the enemy would be the one listening," I said. "It would be far more likely that his employer was keeping tabs on him."

Gertie shook her head. "There is so much wrong with that statement. So if bugging his house is out, maybe we should just lurk around the bedroom window tonight."

"That's a good way to get arrested," Ida Belle said. "Or shot."

I looked at Gertie, a bit surprised. "Did you not notice the camera on his front porch? It was tracking us the whole time we approached. Cheap Larry didn't scrimp on his security system inside either, and I doubt all that expense is to protect that 1970s glassware."

Ida Belle nodded. "He's either paranoid or he knows something people would like to have."

Gertie threw her hands in the air. "Then you two come up with something. Since you think all my ideas are bad."

"Don't you think if I had an idea I would have stopped you already?" Ida Belle asked.

Gertie's eyes widened and she clapped. "I've got it! What about one of those listening antennas? You know, the kind with that umbrella thingie that you can hear from far away."

"A parabolic microphone?" I asked.

"If that's the umbrella thing, then yes," Gertie said.

"Because that wouldn't be noticeable at all," Ida Belle said. "Us standing in the yard holding a satellite dish. Between the neighbors and Larry's camera, we might as well go for hiding behind the couch. We'd have a better chance of not being discovered."

"I'm not suggesting we stand on the sidewalk," Gertie said. "We could use it in their backyard."

"You mean the yard that Phyllis LaFont is monitoring?" I asked.

"And probably another camera," Ida Belle said.

"We can disable the camera," Gertie said.

"Can't disable Phyllis," Ida Belle said.

"Sure we can," Gertie said.

I wasn't about to ask her what she had in store for the nosy and unfortunate Phyllis. And ultimately, it didn't matter.

"That won't work anyway. A parabolic microphone can't listen through walls," I said.

Gertie slumped, her excitement replaced with disappointment. "You know, our government should really spend some money developing better surveillance equipment."

"The government spends quite enough and they already have more information than they can handle," Ida Belle said.

I drummed my fingers on the table.

"What?" Gertie asked me. "You have that look."

"What look?" I asked.

"That look where you have an idea but haven't quite figured out how to make it happen," Gertie said.

Ida Belle nodded. "Lay it on us. Maybe we can help."

"I was just thinking that we might be able to hear some conversations with a long-range laser," I said. "I've had some success directing them at a window and hearing what's going on inside even when I didn't have line of sight to the speakers."

"Awesome!" Gertie said. "Problem solved."

"Except for one small thing," I said.

"The camera?"

"Phyllis?"

"The lasers start at thirty thousand dollars," I said.

Gertie spit her sweet tea all over Ida Belle and Merlin,

who'd been lounging in the corner. Both of them gave her the stink eye, but only one of them would be paying me back for it later tonight.

"Good Lord!" Gertie said. "I could buy a new Caddy for that. New to me, anyway."

"I could put turbos on my SUV," Ida Belle said.

"You two are missing the important part of this discussion," I said.

"What's that?" Gertie asked.

"Is it tax-deductible if it's illegal to use?" I asked.

"But is it illegal to just listen or only to record?" Ida Belle asked.

"That's an interesting point," I said. "I'm not sure."

"Why the heck not?" Gertie asked. "You were CIA. They specialize in listening."

"But we didn't care about the whole legal or not legal part," I said.

"Should have seen that one coming," Gertie said.

"It doesn't matter anyway," Ida Belle said. "We don't have thirty grand to buy a fancy laser."

"I do," I said. "I mean, if they make me pay back the life insurance for my not-so-dead father, things could get tight since I've paid cash for everything here. But my expenses are low—Merlin doesn't eat much and Gertie, Ally, and Carter keep me in food a lot. Francine's and microwave dinners aren't expensive, so alcohol is probably my biggest outlay. As it stands right now, I have some money to invest in the business and nothing else I need to buy."

Gertie gave me a sad shake of her head. "Where did I go wrong with you? There's not a stitch of furniture in this house that's not older than you are. Your entire wardrobe came from Amazon and you have fewer pairs of shoes than Francis."

"Why does Francis have— You know what, never mind." I

looked at Ida Belle. "Do you have any thoughts on how I should be spending my money?"

"Well, there's always engine upgrades," Ida Belle said. "But you can't get much out of that Jeep so I don't see the point. And since you can't wear more than one outfit or pair of shoes at a time and you have a perfectly good washer and dryer, I don't see the urgency there, either. Furniture is stuff you sit on or sit things on. Unless it collapses, it's good."

"You and Larry have more in common than you think," Gertie said.

"Heck, buy the darn thing," Ida Belle said.

"Really?" I said. "You think I should?"

"Why not?" Ida Belle said. "Like you said, it's a tax deduction. And it gives Gertie a reason to lurk around someone's backyard uninvited, so everyone wins."

"What do you get out of it?" I asked.

Ida Belle grinned. "I'm the getaway driver. The payoff is always the same for me."

"I wonder if they'll confiscate the equipment if we get caught," I said.

"When have we ever gotten caught?" Ida Belle said. "I mean, yeah, Carter might know stuff, but knowing and proving are two different things."

"We still have logistics to work out," Gertie said. "We can't stand in the front yard pointing a laser at a window, and if we're standing in the backyard then there's Phyllis and the potential camera to consider."

"The camera is easy enough," I said. "I simply walk into the backyard wearing black hoodie and ski mask and disable it. Unless Larry's watching a screen 24-7, he won't know it's down until he goes to check."

"And Phyllis?" Gertie asked. "Unfortunately, she doesn't have wires you can cut."

"You said her first husband took off," I said. "Is the second one still in residence."

"Gone as well," Ida Belle said.

"Then I have an idea," I said.

"Sleeping pills? Brownies with Ex-Lax?" Gertie asked.

"That's just mean," I said. "Mean is plan B."

"So what's plan A?" Gertie asked.

I grinned. "Letting her help."

CHAPTER NINE

GERTIE LOOKED at Ida Belle and shook her head. "She's lost the plot."

"Maybe not," Ida Belle said. "Phyllis already suspects Larry is up to no good. If we pitch it as someone else has suspicions and has hired us to check up on him, then she'd be more than willing to prove to everyone that she's not the crazy one."

"But she *is* the crazy one," Gertie said.

"Which is why she'll help us," I said. "And she'll keep her mouth shut until we have enough evidence to out Larry as the cheater he is."

A slow smile spread across Gertie's face. "That's kinda genius," she said.

"I think so," I said. "But before we get Phyllis all excited, I have to acquire the laser, and that's going to take more than an Amazon delivery."

"Can Morrow help you?" Ida Belle asked.

"Sure, but he won't," I said. "Not as long as he's still getting paychecks for the CIA and wants to draw his pension. But I know someone who can probably get what I need."

"Who?" Gertie asked.

"Mannie," I said.

"Ohhhhh!" Gertie's eyes widened. "I really love that guy. Really love him."

"We know," Ida Belle said. "You're going to say if only you were twenty years younger, then I'll say you'd still be old enough to be his great-grandmother, then you'll give me the finger, then we can get on with business. So now that I've done the play-by-play, we can just move to the getting on with business part."

"If only I were twenty years younger," Gertie said.

Ida Belle groaned and I had to laugh.

"That whole 'love is in the air in spring' thing must be true," I said. "At the parade, Big Hebert asked me about Carter and I finally realized he was fishing to see if I was available to be set up with Mannie."

Ida Belle and Gertie both looked a little surprised.

"Really?" Gertie asked. "I never took Big as one for having an interest in the romantic entanglements of other people."

"I think he wants Mannie happy," I said.

"And he thinks a woman is the answer?" Ida Belle said. "He should just give him a raise and a really cool new firearm. That's a much safer bet."

"Probably accurate," I said. "The whole relationship thing is a crapshoot. I've got a good one and even I can see that. But anyway, back to business. I think with Mannie's former military connections, he can probably acquire the laser."

"Great!" Ida Belle said. "So the laser is now part of the plan, but what do we do in the meantime?"

"Well, the only personal thing we know about Natalia is the attack on her in New Orleans," I said.

"Yeah, but that news article didn't tell us much," Gertie said. "And my guess is a police report wouldn't tell much more, assuming you could even get your hands on it. That crap is so common down there, they probably fill in the blanks and it becomes yet another unsolved tragedy."

"I might be able to get the police report," I said.

"This I've got to hear," Ida Belle said. "Because no way is Carter going to indulge you and I know you're not crazy enough to try to steal it from the New Orleans Police Department. If it was Gertie, sure, but you're not that crazy."

"I prefer whimsical," Gertie said.

"No breaking into police departments," I said. "But I think the Heberts might have a connection there. The case was probably shelved as unsolved ages ago and since it didn't involve people important to the city, I'll bet any contact they have there wouldn't blink at getting them a copy."

"For cash, of course," Gertie said.

"I have no idea what kind of arrangements the Heberts have with the people they get information from and I'm pretty sure I don't want to know," I said.

"So all of these big-ticket requests probably rate a personal visit rather than a phone call," Ida Belle said.

"Agreed," I said. "So pack a bag."

They both stared.

"Why?" Gertie asked.

"Because whether or not we get that police report, the next place to go poking around for information is New Orleans," I said. "Maybe we can luck out and find an ER nurse who cared for Natalia. Maybe Natalia talks in her sleep."

They both continued to stare.

"What?" I asked. "I know it's thin but if you want to move on this, then we have to work with what we have. They can't all be as simple as missing cats and fake ghosts."

"But you want to go to New Orleans?" Ida Belle asked. "Today?"

"Yeah," I said, not getting the problem. Then it hit me.

Mardi Gras!

Okay, so maybe it wasn't the smartest idea to descend on NOLA on the busiest weekend of the year. But then, on the other hand, maybe it wasn't the worst idea. If we could actually run down someone who dealt with Natalia after the mugging, they might be so distracted or possibly drunk that they'd offer up more than they otherwise would.

"I assume there's no hope of acquiring a place to stay anywhere near the French Quarter," I said.

"Does sleeping under a bridge count?" Gertie asked.

"Depends on how nice the bridge is," I said. "I've slept in worse places."

"This isn't the sandbox," Ida Belle said. "We don't sleep on the ground here. But I do agree that tracking down info on the mugging is the only thing we have to go on at the moment."

"Okay, so pack a bag just in case we can find somewhere to stay," I said. "If not, then we'll just drive back to Sinful. It will be a long night of coffee and Red Bull."

Gertie started clapping. "Road trip! And Mardi Gras! The last time I was at Mardi Gras in New Orleans, I met the hottest sailor with the most incredible stamina."

Ida Belle grimaced. "If that sailor is still alive, I'm sure his stamina isn't what it used to be."

"Oh, I'd find me a much younger one," Gertie said.

"That would make sense if *your* stamina was what it used to be," Ida Belle said. "Besides, this is a business trip. No hot sailors. No talk of stamina. And no running in the street for beads. If you get run over, they'll leave you right there until the end of the parade."

"We can't have just a little bit of fun?" Gertie asked.

"Only if we finish up the business," I said. "And only if the fun isn't life-threatening. Unless you're talking to Carter. Then we're headed down there to party until we can't walk straight."

"Ha!" Ida Belle said. "Poking your nose into his investigation and going to NOLA for Mardi Gras are probably a close match as far as things Carter won't be thrilled with you doing are concerned."

"Well, he can get over it," I said.

"Anyone home?" Carter's voice sounded from the front door.

"Speak of the devil," Gertie said.

Ida Belle rose from the table. "Let's head out and pack a bag."

"You always want to leave when things are going to get interesting," Gertie pouted.

"Back here," I called out as Ida Belle ushered Gertie down the hall. A couple seconds later, Carter walked in.

"Where were the troublesome twosome off to in such a hurry?" he asked.

"They're off to pack their bags."

"Are they taking a vacation?" His voice contained way too much excitement over the thought.

"No. The three of us are taking a short girls' trip, though."

His excitement instantly waned. "A trip where?"

"New Orleans." I leaned back in my chair and waited for the explosion.

"You're going to Mardi Gras? Have you lost your mind?"

"I'm a newly minted Louisiana resident. I'm pretty sure attending at least one New Orleans Mardi Gras during your lifetime is required."

He shook his head. "Do you have any idea how dangerous it can be?"

"I was a CIA assassin in the sandbox."

"The French Quarter during Mardi Gras has a lot more variables and way more alcohol."

"I'm taking backup."

"Those two are *not* backup. They're accelerant."

I smiled. "I just figured you're going to be busy for a while with this murder case and you'd actually appreciate us not being here trying to get in your business."

He frowned and I could tell he was weighing the benefits of our being gone against the potential dangers of a big party night in the French Quarter. I also noted that he didn't even bother to deny that Katia's death was a murder, which meant the medical examiner had already confirmed what I'd observed. But then, my guess was Carter had known it as well, which was why he moved people away from the crime scene so quickly.

"It is a murder, isn't it?" I couldn't help goading him just a tiny bit.

"You know I can't talk about an active investigation."

"You don't have to. I know a thing or two about trajectory."

He sighed. "Can you please keep this to yourself? And the other two, who I'm sure already know your thoughts on the matter."

"We're detectives, not gossips. I mean, at least when it comes to crime. I mean, serious crime. Not illegal booze or breaking one of Sinful's many oddball laws like you can't wear black ball caps in August."

"Too many people were passing out from the heat."

I shook my head. "And you really think a parade and a bunch of bead-flinging drunks are a bigger threat than living here for decades? The mental stress of trying to remember all those stupid laws is enough to send anyone over the edge."

His lower lip quivered and finally he smiled. "Stop pretending you even bother to try following the rules."

"I do the important ones."

"Like what?"

"I'm a big fan of the no-public-nudity rule. I wish everyone else was."

"Yeah, there's been a lot of that over the past year. More than I recall happening before."

I put my hands up. "That's not on me. You seem to have a problem with your aging population and their ability to purchase clothes that remain in place."

"I think the real problem is that our aging population is refusing to age and do things cute little old ladies are supposed to do—like sit pleasantly and knit."

"Gertie knits."

"Not full time, or things would be easier around here."

"But not nearly as interesting."

"You're really going to do this—go to that party zone with those two?"

"It sounds like fun. I want to see it and I'm bored here. I don't have any cases and you know what happens when I'm bored."

He sighed. "I thought I'd fallen in love with a nice librarian."

"Did you really? I mean, come on. Before the great reveal, you had to know that there was more than met the eye with me. No use playing dumb now when we both know better."

He shrugged. "Maybe it was wishful thinking."

"You'd be bored out of your mind with some normal woman who shuffled books all day long. What would you talk about at night—the Dewey decimal system?"

He pulled me up from my chair and gave me a kiss. "I don't have to tell you to be careful, right? And you'll be armed."

"I'm armed in the shower."

He grinned. "Not when you're in there with me. Then I'm the one who's armed."

"No. Actually, I am then as well. Marge had this sneaky secret tile fixed up. Fits a nine-millimeter behind it perfectly."

"How in the world did you find it?"

"Merlin came running into the bathroom to complain about his breakfast being late and jumped on the toilet. He had a little too much speed and shot off the seat and into the shower with me. Chaos ensued and it all ended with scratches on my legs, the tile dislodged, and the urgent need for a new shower curtain."

"So that's why you changed it. I thought for a minute you'd had a domestic twinge."

"You should have known better. Hey, speaking of domestics, will you feed Merlin while I'm gone? Ally would do it but I don't want her here alone, not even for a minute."

"Sure, but I'm not hanging out with him. He's a butthole." He kissed me again. "I have to go. Call me when you get there. Send me a text often so I know you're still alive."

"You're being very dramatic."

"I'm just taking history into account. Do you have a place to stay?"

"No. If we can't find something close to the city, we'll probably end up driving back after the festivities tonight and then you're off cat-feeding duty. Don't worry. I don't plan on drinking. It slows my reaction time. Ida Belle is the same way."

"Can you get Gertie so drunk it stops her reaction time completely?"

"Probably not. Gertie is all about collecting those beads that cost a penny and that you can buy online by the boxful. There should be a psychological study done on that, you know."

"I'm sure plenty have studied it. I'm just not so sure they came up with answers. Text me."

I could tell his worry was genuine and I had to admit, it

felt good. Carter was a great guy and, in some ways, being my boyfriend was probably the hardest thing he'd ever done. God knows, I didn't make it any easier on him but that wasn't likely to change. I had to do me. It had taken me a long time to figure out exactly who I was and then a little longer to accept it. Now that I was perfectly happy with the fine balance I'd established between regular joe and trained killer, I wasn't willing to attempt a gear shift.

I followed him to the front door and as he stepped out onto the porch, a car I didn't recognize pulled up to the curb. A man got out and started walking our direction.

Midthirties. Six foot two. A hundred ninety pounds. Excellent muscle tone. Dark sunglasses. Black suit. Suit wasn't off the rack. Definitely not a Fed.

"Deputy LeBlanc?" the man asked as he approached.

"Yes," Carter said, looking as confused as I was.

"I'm Vitali Fedorov," the man said, and extended his hand. "We spoke this morning concerning Katia Grekov."

"Yes, of course. Katia's emergency contact. You got here fast."

"My employer was upset about the situation," Vitali said. "He arranged for the use of the company jet."

"He must have really valued Katia as an employee," Carter said. "Can't be cheap to fly here from New York even if you own the plane."

Vitali smiled and it made my skin crawl. "Katia was a very important and highly regarded member of an elite marketing team. I imagine her loss will be felt for years to come."

"Were you and Katia..." Carter's voice trailed off.

"Involved?" Vitali asked. "No. But we were friends."

Carter nodded. "I'm very sorry for your loss."

Vitali nodded. "Can you tell me anything about her death?

Is there anything I can assist with? My employer has authorized me to remain here as long as needed."

Carter glanced at me, then looked back at Vitali. "Let's go back to the sheriff's department, if you don't mind."

"Of course," Vitali said. "I'm sorry to have interrupted you but your deputy told me I could find you here. I would have waited but he thought you had other business outside of the office and I'm not good at sitting around. I truly apologize for the inconvenience."

"It's no problem at all," Carter said. "Small-town people don't see interruptions at the same level of rudeness as big-city folk do."

I nodded. "Interruption in a small town is the only way to get a word in. I'm sorry for your loss, Mr. Fedorov."

"Thank you, Ms. Redding. Enjoy the rest of your day."

Vitali headed back to his car and Carter turned back to look at me.

"I don't like him," I said.

"You don't even know him," Carter said.

"Doesn't matter. Take my word on this—don't trust a thing he says."

Carter watched as Vitali pulled away and frowned. He gave me a nod and a quick kiss, then hurried off to his truck. I watched until Vitali's car disappeared and shook my head. I had no idea why Katia had him down as her emergency contact, but Vitali Fedorov was not being truthful.

I stepped back inside, locked the door, and pulled the dead bolt behind me. At least this trip would accomplish a couple things—I wouldn't be as easy to locate, and hopefully, we'd track down someone who could shed more light on what happened to Natalia's sister. I ran upstairs to pack an overnight bag, happy that all my clothes were designed to stay in place, no matter what kind of nonsense I got up to.

I CALLED Mannie once we hit the highway and told him I needed a quick consultation about something important. He put me on hold for a second, then told me to stop by whenever I could. He didn't so much as raise an eyebrow when he opened the door and let us inside. I wasn't sure how he managed that completely uninterested look. I would be practically hopping, wanting to know what was going on.

"Mr. Hebert is happy to speak with you, as always," Mannie said. "He's on a call and as soon as he finishes, he'll make himself available."

"That's great," I said. "But actually, I needed to talk business with you first."

He raised one eyebrow before waving us across the lobby. I assumed that was as much of a show of interest as I was going to get out of him. We headed to a small room on the back side of the first floor that contained a table and four chairs and we all took a seat. Then I explained the situation with Larry and our inability to gain information through the regular gossip train.

He nodded. "Given his profession, his dedication to privacy isn't surprising. And it sounds like his wife is on board with the whole hermit thing. So what did you have in mind? I don't know that we could get away with a listening device. If Larry isn't sweeping for them, his employer might be. Assuming they aren't already listening."

Gertie shook her head. "Does the government listen in on all their employees?"

"If they're intel, probably," I said. "My apartment in DC was bugged. I knew the location of all of them but didn't bother taking them out. Sometimes, when I was bored, I'd pretend to let someone in, say something sketchy, then crank up the music really loud. Before a neighbor could even lodge a complaint, I'd get a call from headquarters with some lame question."

"So you'd turn the music down," Mannie said.

"Exactly," I said. "If I was feeling especially punchy, I'd crank it back up, then refuse to answer the phone."

"And did that get rid of them?" Gertie asked.

"No. Then they started texting, requesting I call. We didn't exactly have the option of being out of reach unless we were at a critical point in a mission. Anyway, eventually, I'd get bored and just leave the apartment."

"What exactly are they listening for?" Gertie asked.

I shrugged. "Relaying confidential information, talking trash about your boss, Aunt Sharon's lemon pie recipe? Who the heck knows? They're paranoid."

"So what did you have in mind for Larry then?" Mannie asked.

"Long-range laser," I said.

He whistled. "Great hardware but major bucks."

"It's a tax deduction," I said.

He smiled. "That it is. So I'm assuming you'd like me to acquire one for you."

"You seemed like the most likely person to handle something like that," I said.

He nodded. "I can probably hook you up. Might take a day or two, though."

"No worries," I said. "Do you have an account that I can wire the money to?"

"I'll collect when I deliver. Do you have a maximum amount to spend?"

"Will thirty-five thousand work?"

"It should. I'll let you know if that's not the case. So what lucky city are you off to terrorize?"

"How do you know we're going anywhere?" Gertie asked.

"Because the camera system here is excellent," Mannie said. "I spotted the overnight bags in the back of Ida Belle's SUV when you opened the door."

"These ladies are taking me to my first official Mardi Gras in New Orleans," I said.

Mannie raised one eyebrow and I wondered if he was about to go down the same road as Carter. But instead he smiled.

"Are you sure Mardi Gras is ready for the three of you?" he asked.

"We're about to find out," I said.

"How did you find a place last-minute?" he asked.

"We didn't," Gertie said. "We're going to wing it. Or sleep in the truck. Or drive back tonight. We'll figure it out."

Mannie frowned. "Give me a second."

He pulled out his phone and sent a text, then motioned to us. "Mr. Hebert is ready to see you now if that works for you."

I almost laughed at the politeness of the request.

"Has anyone ever said it doesn't work for them?" I asked.

"Once," Mannie said.

He walked off without elaborating and based on his expression, I wasn't sure I wanted him to. We followed him to the elevator and then to Big's office where the head man was in his usual spot at his desk. But this time Little wasn't there. Big gave apologies from Little but he had urgent business handling a supply delay. With words like "urgent" and "supply delay" coming from Big Hebert, it probably paid to know as little as possible.

"Ladies," Big said once we were seated. "Please tell me how I can help you. Are you on a case?"

"Not officially," I said.

He grinned. "That's the best kind. So can I assume you're

interested in what happened to Ms. Guillory's unfortunate friend?"

I nodded. "But with Larry being intel, they're locked up tighter than Fort Knox. We can't get the scoop on them through the regular gossip channels and since they've only been in Sinful a few years, there's no background to be had from that source, either."

"It's so rare these days for people to not have their lives all over social media that when one doesn't, it's automatically suspect," Big said.

"Are you on social media?" Gertie asked.

"Of course," Big said. "The way to avoid being suspect is to blend."

I wasn't sure that Big Hebert could effectively accomplish blending, but it wasn't the worst idea I'd heard. Still, I had zero intention of signing up for the parade of idiocy I'd seen online, and if anyone tried to make a cute combination of my name and Carter's, I was pretty sure someone would have to post bail.

"I'll have to friend you on Facebook," Gertie said.

"I look forward to accepting your friend request," Big said.

I considered this for a minute and then wondered if maybe Gertie wasn't onto something. If anyone checked her friends and saw Big Hebert there, it might change the way they acted. In a good way. At least, I considered people avoiding me a good thing. And wouldn't Carter be thrilled if I not only set up a Facebook account but friended Big Hebert? I could just picture his expression. In fact, it might be worth doing just to see his reaction.

"So what can I help you with?" Big asked.

"Natalia Guillory had a sister who was killed in New Orleans three years ago during a mugging," I said. "Natalia was seriously injured. We found a bare-minimum news story online, but I was wondering if there was any way you could get us a police report."

"Do you think the two incidences are related?" Big asked.

"I don't have anything concrete, but two murders surrounding one person is suspect at least. And since there's so little information available on the family or Katia, we're going to track down any potential source we can find. Knowing the people involved in a crime is often just as revealing as the details of the crime itself."

"Very perceptive," Big said. "And accurate. I do a full background on everyone I do business with. It's quite interesting what people hide."

"It is," I said. "And I have no doubt that the Guillorys—Natalia, at least—could be hiding something about the incident in New Orleans. Whether it's related to Katia's murder remains to be seen."

"I think this is a smart angle to take," Big said. "I know someone who can probably help. Let me make a call and see what I can do."

"We really appreciate it," I said. "At the moment, this is the only angle we have to work."

"It's hard to get a feel for someone when their job is secrecy," Big said. "If you can get me a last name for Katia, I can run her through my own channels."

"That would be great," I said. "It's Grekov. And there's another guy—Vitali Fedorov. He's Katia's emergency contact. Apparently Carter notified him this morning and he's already in Sinful. Showed up at my house earlier looking for Carter. He claims to just be a friend and coworker and said their boss lent him the company jet because he was so upset about the situation."

"Your tone says Mr. Fedorov did not pass muster," Big said.

I shrugged. "I didn't like him. Not the custom-made black

suit or the dark sunglasses or the way he seemed so businesslike about the entire thing. Like he was there to handle a shipping mistake or something. Too slick."

"It sounds like the Men in Black to me," Gertie said.

"I don't think aliens killed Katia," I said. "But it wouldn't surprise me if he was here to cover things up."

Big made some notes on a pad. "I will see what I can find on our friend Mr. Fedorov." He looked back at us and smiled. "So I understand that in addition to business, you ladies are off to NOLA for a bit of Mardi Gras fun."

Since we hadn't offered that information during our chat, I assumed that was the content of the text Mannie had sent earlier.

"That's right," I said. "I figure you can't really claim citizenship here unless you've been to Mardi Gras in the French Quarter."

"Absolutely true," Big said. "In my younger, fitter days, I never missed. Now I prefer quieter pursuits with smaller crowds."

Gertie nodded. "Fewer witnesses."

I inwardly cringed, but Big laughed and I relaxed again, trying to imagine a younger, fitter Big. But the image eluded me.

He reached into his desk and pushed a set of keys across to me. "These are the keys to an apartment I own. Here's the address." He passed me a piece of paper to join the keys.

Ida Belle picked up the paper and her jaw dropped. "This is on Saint Charles Avenue. Right on the parade route and just blocks from the French Quarter."

"Yes," Big said. "I picked it up for a song from a man who liked to create debt but wasn't as interested in paying it."

"We won't even have to leave the apartment," Ida Belle said. "We can watch the whole thing from the window. Praise the Lord! We might actually get out of New Orleans without visiting the emergency room."

"Where's the fun in that?" Gertie asked.

Big chuckled. "I have the utmost faith in you ladies to produce something on YouTube before your visit is over."

"We're attempting a YouTube hiatus," I said.

"You can attempt it," Big said and looked at Gertie, "but I wouldn't bet on it. I've already seen the video of the Sinful parade. Nice work blocking the nun. A little aggressive, but since you're not Catholic, I suppose that gives you a pass."

"The resulting fallout wasn't as nice," Ida Belle said.

"Actually, the runaway truck was quite fun, especially when it sent the funnel cake batter all over that horrible woman that you people insist on keeping alive," Big said. "The squirrel was just icing on the cake, although I imagine the poor thing will need therapy after being up that woman's dress. I will say I could have done without the topless finale. That woman needs to remain clothed at all times. Maybe even in the shower."

"Really?" Gertie asked. "She's had work done."

"Not enough," Big said.

"Interesting," Gertie said. "I figured all the guys would be celebrating a peek at the goods."

Big grimaced. "That wasn't a peek. It was an assault. There's something to be said for leaving a little mystery in one's romance."

Gertie nodded. "That's why I want to get a tattoo—a sexy tattoo."

Ida Belle shook her head. "No one wants to think about you in relation to tattoos and definitely not sexy ones. Mr. Hebert, your offer of the absolutely incredible apartment is highly appreciated."

"Definitely," I agreed. "Can we pay you something, at least?

These two told me that places are rented years in advance and get ten times the usual price for Mardi Gras."

Big shook his head. "It's not like I'm giving up profit in order to lend you my place. I only ask that you leave it in the same manner you found it." He glanced at Gertie. "And if for any reason that isn't possible, then you can reimburse for damages."

"Deal," I said, and rose. "We best get on the road. I have a feeling we're going to be in for a hike once we find a place to park."

"I have a reserved parking space in a nearby garage," Big said. "The address and space number are on the back of the paper."

"That's awesome!" I said.

"As long as someone hasn't already parked in it," Ida Belle said. "People don't exactly observe the rules during Mardi Gras, and parking is one of the first ignored."

Big smiled. "The space has a sign that clearly indicates the owner."

Ida Belle brightened. "Then we should be fine."

I had a feeling that even if someone who wasn't familiar with the Heberts attempted to park in Big's space, their car would be quickly relocated. Big seemed to have people indebted to him in most places and people who were afraid of him in all places.

"This whole trip has really picked up," Gertie said as we headed out. "A super awesome apartment right on the parade route, a parking space that only someone with a death wish would attempt to occupy, and I can catch beads without even getting off the balcony."

I nodded. I had to admit it all sounded perfect.

Which always worried me.

CHAPTER TEN

As Ida Belle directed her SUV from the service road and onto the highway, a car sped by in the fast lane that looked familiar. I frowned as I recalled where I'd seen it.

"Follow that car," I said. "But not so close he suspects anything."

Ida Belle looked a bit surprised but increased speed in order to keep the vehicle in sight.

"Who is it?" Gertie asked.

"I'm pretty sure it's Fedorov," I said. "Unless someone has a car just like his and is coming from Sinful."

"Unlikely," Ida Belle said. "I assume the car is a rental since he's from out of state, but most people in Sinful don't drive a Lexus."

He continued down the highway at a good clip, then suddenly changed lanes to exit. Ida Belle slowed until he disappeared onto the service road, then followed suit. I recognized the exit as one that housed one of the somewhat seedy motels between Sinful and New Orleans. Surely someone with custom suits and driving a Lexus wasn't staying in such a sketchy place. But then I remembered it was Mardi Gras. Still, seemed like a decent place could be found closer to New Orleans even if the best hotels were taken.

Ida Belle pointed as he turned under the interstate. "That road only goes to the motel."

"That Lexus is going to stand out like new money in that parking lot," Gertie said.

"I know," I agreed. "I don't understand why someone with his obvious expensive taste and the means to indulge it would stay somewhere like this. I know New Orleans is pretty booked, but surely he could have found something nicer than this."

"Maybe he wanted to be close by in case he was needed," Gertie said.

"Or he wanted to be close by because he's up to no good," Ida Belle said.

I nodded. "I have this gut feeling that's it."

Ida Belle turned under the interstate and headed for the motel. "I know better than to go against your gut."

When we got to the motel, we spotted the Lexus parked in front of a unit at the end of the building.

"What now?" Gertie asked. "We can't exactly knock on the door and ask him what he's up to."

"No," I agreed. "It's definitely better if he thinks everyone bought his act, so I can't afford for him to see me."

Ida Belle parked in front of the office and opened her door. "Then let me go see what I can find out. He's never seen me. You duck down if he comes out of his room."

I nodded and Gertie and I kept our eyes glued on the room in front of the Lexus. A couple minutes later, Ida Belle came back out looking like the cat that had swallowed the canary.

"I take it you got something?" I asked.

She started the SUV and left the parking lot. "It's amazing what a business card with a detective agency logo, a story about a cheating husband, and fifty bucks will get out of a middle-aged, divorced, man-hating clerk."

"Jackpot," Gertie said.

"There wasn't much to tell," Ida Belle said. "The clerk said he was abrupt and rude and paid with cash."

Gertie looked disappointed. "That's it?"

Ida Belle grinned. "He paid with cash *yesterday*."

"Oh!" I said. "Now, that *is* interesting."

"Looks like your gut is batting a thousand," Ida Belle said.

"Are you going to tell Carter?" Gertie asked.

"Tell him that we segued on our girls' trip to interfere with his investigation?" I asked. "Not a chance. I told Carter after Fedorov left this morning not to trust him."

"Good enough then," Ida Belle said. "If he chooses to ignore that then it's his own fault."

"So what do we do with that information?" Gertie asked.

"Nothing yet," I said. "Let's wait and see what Big can dig up on Fedorov and Katia. In the meantime, we'll see what we can find in New Orleans. And we find something to eat. That whole light lunch thing sounds like a good idea until it's going to be several hours until food is available again."

"New Orleans definitely has plenty of food," Gertie said. "I'm almost as excited to eat as I am to see the parade. I can't believe we're going to be right on the parade route."

"The first hurdle is getting parked," Ida Belle said. "If we can manage that, then everything else should be easy."

I nodded, but my thoughts were far away from the parking situation.

Who was Vitali Fedorov? And had he killed Katia? Or was he here to kill Natalia and that's why he remained?

THANKFULLY, there was no issue with the parking space. In fact, Big must have called ahead because as we pulled up to the garage, the attendant jumped up and practically ran over to the SUV, ready to assist us with everything from locating the space to removing our bags. His anxiety was a bit funny, but then I had to remind myself that the Big Hebert I knew was a totally different person from the one most people knew. And I didn't presume that our relationship couldn't be altered, so a certain level of respect was due if I wanted to maintain my status. I knew my cavalier attitude amused Big, but that was only because it was never at his expense.

It was a bit of a hike from the garage to the apartment, but the garage attendant knew a guy, and before we'd even gotten the last bag out of the SUV, a car had pulled up with a driver who looked like an extra from *The Sopranos* who said he'd be honored to take us as close to the apartment as he could manage and then carry the bags the rest of the way.

A couple minutes later, we were hiking the one block left to Big's apartment while Mr. Soprano cleared the sidewalk in front of us, carrying all three bags. I'd tried to handle my own but had received a look that told me no way was I touching my bag until I got to the apartment. He was probably afraid that word would get back to Big that he hadn't followed instructions.

"I could get used to this level of service," Gertie said as we walked. "Maybe I should go into the godfather business."

"You looking to be the godmother?" Ida Belle asked and laughed.

Gertie nodded. "If it gets me cool apartments, parking spaces, and baggage hauling everywhere I go, then heck yeah. Sign me up."

"I don't know that you're necessarily suited for that kind of business," I said. "While Ida Belle and I are distinctly aware of just how threatened our mortality is by proximity to you, others will not necessarily recognize the danger."

"I could shave my head," Gertie said. "Get one of those scalp tattoos."

"It would itch," Ida Belle said. "And unless you kept it shaved all the time, no one would see the tattoo. And before you ask, I am not shaving your head. Not now and not in a maintenance capacity."

"Maybe I could just dye it black and wear that dark eyeliner," Gertie said.

"Are you planning on competing for that girl in *Twilight?*" Ida Belle said.

"Not like a vampire!" Gertie argued, then frowned. "Okay, maybe it would look a bit like a vampire. Never mind, I'll figure it out."

Fortunately, we arrived at the apartment before Gertie could come up with another ill-advised fashion deviation. I was prepared to hike up the stairs when Soprano grunted and led us into a small courtyard. He headed to a door on a side wall and gestured with his head. I unlocked the door and found a small entry with a service elevator.

"That explains a lot," Ida Belle said.

I nodded as Soprano put our bags on the elevator, then gave us a nod and headed off. I'd been wondering how Big had managed to navigate the stairs on the building. First off, I'd never seen him stand for more than a minute, much less walk, and I wasn't completely certain that his large frame would have even fit on the narrow, historical ironwork. I locked the door behind us and hopped in the elevator. A couple seconds later, the door opened into a large open area with living room, dining room, and kitchen.

"Good God!" Gertie said, her head bobbing around, trying

to take it all in. "He must have bought two apartments and combined them."

"More likely he owns the entire building," Ida Belle said.

I gazed around in deep appreciation. The walls were exposed brick, and a huge fireplace with a giant mantel stood at the far end of the living room. The kitchen, while not my thing as I had an allergy to cooking, was a beautiful display of white cabinets, white marble countertops, and backsplash with a hint of sparkle. An enormous balcony, the length of the entire living area, stretched across the front of the building.

"This place is seriously gorgeous," I said.

Ida Belle nodded. "You know I'm into serviceable rather than appearance, but dang, this makes me want to remodel."

"You'd have to deal with contractors," Gertie pointed out. "In your space. For God knows how long, because...contractors."

"Never mind," Ida Belle said. "The moment has passed."

She picked up her bag and headed toward a hallway on the wall with the fireplace. Gertie and I followed and were pleased to find two bedrooms with a shared bath. The first bedroom had twin beds and the second a queen. The bathroom was accessible from each bedroom as well as the hallway. At the end of the hallway, I opened a door and saw the biggest bed I'd ever laid eyes on.

"That has to be custom," Gertie said. "Good Lord, it's as big as my entire bedroom."

Ida Belle had wandered by and peeked into what I assumed was the master bath and whistled. "You have to see this walk-in shower. It's got a bench and a television in it."

We all headed into the bathroom, and all three of us stood in the shower, admiring the size and the options of sprayers and showerheads.

"This is bigger than the men's locker room showers at the gym up the highway," Gertie said.

"And just how would you know that?" Ida Belle asked.

"Remember, I joined before that cruise I took to get my bikini body ready," Gertie said.

"That still doesn't explain why you know about the men's locker room showers," I said.

"It was an honest mistake," Gertie said. "I sat in the steam room after I worked out and my glasses were still fogged when I went to change."

Ida Belle gave her the side-eye and I laughed. Clearly, she was as convinced as I was about the honesty of the mistake.

"Let's get out and find some food," I said. "I figure we can take the rooms in the hallway and leave the master shut."

"Probably wise," Ida Belle said.

Gertie glanced wistfully at the giant bed as we closed the door but even she was smart enough not to argue with the plan. Since Gertie snored the loudest, we gave her the room with the queen bed and Ida Belle and I took the twins. There was no point in unpacking as we weren't going to be there long, so we tossed our bags onto the beds and headed back to the front rooms.

Gertie ran out onto the balcony and stuck her head back in to yell, "You've got to come see this! The view is perfect. And there's even chairs and a huge bench."

I grinned. Of course there was.

Ida Belle and I headed onto the balcony and I had to admit, the view of Saint Charles Avenue wasn't remotely lacking. We'd be able to see the parade and if people were ambitious with their throwing, Gertie might even add to her cheap bead collection.

A knock on the door of the apartment had us all freezing in place.

"I'll get it," Gertie finally said and popped back inside. Ida Belle and I both checked our firearms and followed.

The door to the apartment was on the same wall as the elevator but nearer the kitchen. Gertie swung the door open and her jaw dropped when she saw a New Orleans policeman standing there.

"I haven't even done anything yet," she said.

"Are you implying that you intend to?" the cop asked.

"No," Gertie said. "Of course not. The 'intend' part anyway."

He looked a bit apprehensive but lifted his hand to show an envelope. "I have a package for a Ms. Redding."

Ah! Big had already come through with the police report.

"That's me," I said.

The cop gave me a once-over and I could tell he was confused as to why someone of Big Hebert's status had called in a request for police documents to be delivered to the likes of us. We didn't exactly look like his usual employees. But then we were in Big's apartment and it didn't look as if we'd broken in, so I could see where he might have trouble balancing it all out.

He handed me the envelope and took off without asking a single question. He probably figured he was better off not knowing. Given that he'd just provided a perfect stranger an official police document on an open investigation, I didn't blame him. You can't be compelled to tell what you don't know.

I headed to the kitchen island with the envelope and hopped onto a barstool. Ida Belle and Gertie took a seat on each side of me and eagerly leaned in as I pulled the one measly page out.

"Wow," Ida Belle said. "That's not much longer than the news article."

There were the usual notes of location, time, victims, and other required information at the top of the page, then the statement taken from Natalia at the hospital, which amounted to one paragraph. After that were a couple more notes about the workup of the crime scene and the search for any potential camera footage available—there wasn't any—and that was it.

I dropped the paper on the counter. "So the two sisters were jumped in a parking lot by two men in hoodies. Natalia heard footsteps behind them but before she could turn around, one of the men had hit Annika across the head with something long and she fell. The other man raised a pipe to strike Natalia but she ducked and he caught her in the arm instead."

"Which explains the arm injury you noticed," Gertie said.

I nodded. "He struck her again in the side and then again in the head as she fell, and she lost consciousness. Both assailants wore masks. Two college students heard them screaming and ran to help. They saw the two men running away but could not offer any help with identification as it was night and they were too far away and with their backs to the students. The police found Natalia's handbag next to a car in the direction the students had indicated the men ran. No prints were found, suggesting the men probably wore gloves. And that's it."

"That's disappointing but not unexpected," Ida Belle said. "We knew if it was unsolved, they had little to go on, and I'm going to guess that's usually the case with these types of things. How do you launch a credible investigation with such minimal facts?"

I shook my head. "I wouldn't even know where to start. If the victim and the witnesses can't identify them, and nothing was caught on camera, where would you even begin?"

I stared at the disappointing police report and noticed a

slight lift in the corner of the envelope. "What is that?" I asked, and I picked the envelope up and shook it to empty whatever was in the bottom.

Two pictures of Natalia fell out onto the counter. One with heavy makeup and short hair and another without the makeup and with longer hair.

"I guess they needed pictures to advertise for more witnesses?" Gertie said. "Probably couldn't get one of her sister. Natalia looks a little younger there, though."

I frowned and reached for the photos, then flipped them both over. "These *are* photos of Natalia and her sister. Look, the names are on the back."

I turned the photos back over and we stared at them again. The heavily made-up woman with the short hair was Annika.

"Twins?" Ida Belle asked.

"If not, that's some seriously strong DNA," I said.

Ida Belle frowned. "This lends more credibility to your theory that Natalia was the target. The men went after both but the one they meant to get lived."

"If this was a hit," Gertie said, "I'd be asking for a discount. Nothing like getting it wrong twice to call unnecessary attention to your intended victim."

"Natalia does seem to have nine lives," I said. "But all of this is so strange. So let's assume for a minute that someone is after Natalia. They must have had a lock on her at her home, then followed her to New Orleans when she met her sister. But why wait?"

"New Orleans would offer an easy way to kill someone and make it look like a local crime rather than a targeted victim."

"Unless the wrong woman died," I said. "And look at the date on the police report. This happened just a month before they relocated to Sinful. Larry said they moved to Sinful after it happened but I didn't think he meant right after."

"So they moved and the killer couldn't find her," Gertie said.

"Until now," Ida Belle said. "Where again, the wrong woman died. It's still convoluted, but in a fantastic way, it does make some sense."

"If we're right, then that means someone is still gunning for Natalia," I said.

"Fedorov?" Ida Belle asked.

"Anything is possible," I said. "But if Fedorov is the guy then why was he Katia's emergency contact?"

"Because we're wrong about the Natalia angle and Katia was the intended victim all along," Ida Belle said. "It's just as viable. Maybe more so given Fedorov's appearance and lies. And it's just as possible that Natalia and Annika were attacked by strangers. It's hardly an uncommon occurrence."

"Should we tell Carter our suspicions?" Gertie asked.

"And have him jump all over us for getting into his business?" Ida Belle asked. "And besides, what proof do we have except that Fedorov lied about when he arrived here? It's just theories at this point. There's not even enough here to get a protective detail on Natalia. And Carter and Deputy Breaux can't spend all their time sitting there, either."

"If Natalia is the intended victim, how fast do you think they'll make another move?" Gertie asked.

"I don't know," I said. "That can go two different ways. One, they're patient and careful and they back off until the right opportunity presents itself again. Or two, they're panicked and desperate and they jump at the first opportunity."

"Do you think we should warn Natalia?" Gertie asked.

"No," I said. "If people are trying to kill her, then there's a reason. And if there's a reason, then Natalia would know it."

"Unless it got knocked out of her when she was attacked in

New Orleans," Ida Belle said. "We need to find out the extent of her injuries."

"You'd think there would have been more online," I said. "I mean, there's a reason you couldn't find information about someone like me on the internet, but is it normal to find next to nothing about a regular person?"

"I don't think it's necessarily abnormal," Ida Belle said. "I know we think everyone is online but I imagine people manage to stay off if they keep to themselves. No mention by organizations if you're not involved. No school pictures if your kid is homeschooled. No work mentions if you don't work or if you work for the government."

"I suppose you're right, but you'd think there would be something somewhere," I said.

"We don't know what her situation was when she lived in Russia," Ida Belle said. "She might not have had access. And we don't know when she met Larry. If it was shortly after arriving in the US, she would have adopted his standards, which were to maintain privacy."

"Let's face it," I said, "we don't know much of anything about her past or her marriage."

"And I don't see any way of finding out without it coming from the horse's mouth," Gertie said. "I guarantee you no one in Sinful can tell us, and I'd bet it was the same where they lived before."

"I'm sure you're right," I said, and picked up the paper. "Okay, then we need to try to run down Detectives Bishop and Thompson."

Ida Belle groaned. "You got a first name on that Thompson?"

I scanned the sheet again. "Unfortunately, no. I guess we can't call up and ask for them by badge number, right?"

"That might seem a bit suspicious," Ida Belle said. "But if we can find Bishop then maybe he will tell us."

I pulled out my cell phone and dialed the NOLA PD.

"Hi," I said when a man answered. "I'd like to speak to Detective Bishop. I might have some information on an old case of his."

"Bishop is working Saint Charles today. Not sure what blocks he's covering."

I thanked him and disconnected. "They have detectives working the parade?"

"They probably have the janitor working the parade," Gertie said.

"So why don't criminals take that opportunity to commit crime all over the city since all of the police force is on the parade route?" I asked.

"Because everyone not at the parade is sitting home with loaded firearms," Ida Belle said.

"That's right," I said. "I keep forgetting...Louisiana."

"I guess this means we have to brave Saint Charles Avenue," Gertie said.

Ida Belle rolled her eyes. "Stop acting like it's some big sacrifice. You know you've been dying to get down in the middle of that mess ever since we got here."

Gertie grinned. "Maybe a little."

"The big parade starts in about an hour and it's a fairly long route," Ida Belle said. "If we don't locate him before it starts, we probably have no chance. Not in that mess."

"I agree," I said. "So let's make sure we're prepared before we head out. Is everyone wearing comfortable clothes with at least one pocket and good running shoes?"

"I bought a new sports bra," Gertie said. "Was really hoping to run and try it out."

"Why didn't you run in it at home?" Ida Belle asked.

"No one was chasing me there," Gertie said.

"We're going to hope no one chases you here," I said. "But just in case, I'd like to have our bases covered as well as possible. Does everyone have a charged phone?"

They both nodded.

I hesitated for a moment, then finally asked, "Loaded weapon?"

"I'm wearing clothes, aren't I?" Ida Belle said.

"I have a couple in my purse," Gertie said. "I'm sure something will fit in this new bra."

"Do me a favor and don't make it hot," I said.

"My boob is not going to pull the trigger," Gertie argued.

Ida Belle shook her head. "You say that..."

"Humor me," I said.

"Fine," Gertie said. "But you lose precious firing time chambering a round. I hope I don't need that extra second."

"Me too," I said. If our lives got down to that one second and Gertie's shooting being our only defense, we were in deep trouble.

"Okay, then," I said. "Potty break, everyone, then we head out."

CHAPTER ELEVEN

Ten minutes later, we were on Saint Charles in the middle of something I couldn't even find the words to describe. People were crammed onto the street, shoulder to shoulder, and it was clear that many of them had been there all day and had consumed many drinks. They bumped and apologized and stepped on feet and waved beer in the air and shouted greetings to people they probably didn't know who were sitting up on balconies.

I gave the street a quick assessment and tried to decide on the best course of action. If we separated, we could locate Detective Bishop quicker. But then none of us would have backup and that wasn't the best idea. Of course, with the way the crowd was jostling around, we might get separated anyway. Finally, I decided it was safer to stick together and worst case, if we couldn't find Detective Bishop tonight, we'd hunt him up tomorrow. Since we had secured a place to sleep, that made it easier.

"Let's start left," I said, "and go to where the parade ends. Then we'll work our way back up the other side of the street. As we go, each of us can walk into a business and scan for cops, then we'll convene on the sidewalk again. If anyone finds Bishop inside one of the shops or bars, then send a text."

We started working our way through the crowd and when we got to the first bar, I sent Ida Belle in to scope it out. Gertie and I continued and she went into the next building, which housed a restaurant. I moved on to the next entrance and gave the tiny bar a quick walk-through before heading back out. Gertie and Ida Belle appeared a couple seconds later, both shaking their heads.

"This is going to take forever," Gertie said. "And what if he's one of those twenty-minute bathroom break kind of guys? We could check a business and not even know he's there."

"All we can do is give it our best shot," I said. "If you find any NOLA cop at all, ask them if they know what area Bishop is working. Maybe we'll get lucky."

"There's a cop," Gertie said, and pointed across the street at a cop, who took a big sip of coffee, then grimaced.

"He'll do," I said.

We pushed our way across the street and I spotted the cop headed inside a café.

"Can I get this reheated?" the cop was asking a man behind the bar.

"Nah, man," the bartender said. "I just made a new pot. Let me get you a hot one."

"Thanks," the cop said as he leaned against the bar, surveying the patrons. Then his gaze locked on the three of us and didn't shift. In all fairness, we probably looked like an odd trio. Three completely and normally dressed and sober women on Saint Charles Avenue was clearly not the norm. Not today.

"Excuse me, Officer?" I asked, making sure I checked his rank before I spoke.

"Yes. How can I help you ladies?" he asked.

"We're looking for a Detective Bishop," I said. "Dispatch

told me he was working the parade but didn't know what area he would be covering. I don't suppose you can help us out with that?"

He spent an extra couple seconds studying us, probably trying to assess the threat level. I found it both amusing and disappointing that he must have decided the threat level was low to zero when he pulled out a sheet and scanned it. If he only knew.

"Looks like Bishop is supposed to be between Poydras and Canal," he said. "Sorry I can't narrow it down any more than that."

"So you guys just walk the area you were assigned?" I asked.

He nodded. "And we keep walking until all these fools go home. Is there anything I can help you with? So you don't have to go looking for Detective Bishop in this madhouse."

"I don't think so," I said. "I might have some information about a homicide he worked about three years back. I'm not sure it will help, but I figure it doesn't hurt to give him the information."

"Yep, you're going to have to talk to Bishop directly if it's his case," he said. "If you don't run him down tonight, he'll probably be reachable tomorrow afternoon. Those of us who work the parade get a later start tomorrow."

"I imagine the whole city gets a later start," I said.

"Not the people you wish would," he said as the bartender handed him a huge cup of coffee. "You ladies enjoy the parade."

He headed out and we trailed behind him.

"Okay, which way?" I asked.

Ida Belle pointed. "A couple blocks that way and we hit Poydras. The distance between there and Canal isn't too bad. We lucked out on that part. If he'd been given streets closer to the start, we wouldn't have even made it over there by the time this thing gets rolling."

"It looks like it's already rolling," I said as a man bumped into me and dumped an entire cup of beer down my back.

"Sorry," he said, then gave me the once-over followed by a creepy smile. "Can I buy us both a drink?"

"Keep moving, buster," Gertie said. "Or I'll pull the gun out of my bra and show you how I use it."

I wasn't sure if it was the threat of the gun or the potential of seeing her bra or anything in it, but either way, it had the drunk moving on to find his next conquest.

"At least I smell the part now," I said.

"It's not Mardi Gras until you're wearing beer," Gertie said cheerfully.

"I'll be quite satisfied to return to the apartment dry," Ida Belle said.

"What if he's cute?" Gertie asked.

"I'm getting married," Ida Belle reminded her.

"Oh yeah!" Gertie said. "Sorry. That was never something I thought I'd have to take into account. But hey, now I can go with 'but you're not dead.'"

"When it comes to drunks dumping beer on me, there's the possibility that *someone* will be dead," Ida Belle said.

"Well, your argument got us to Poydras," I said. "You ready to start looking for Bishop?"

Gertie reached up with both hands and shook her chest.

"What in the name of all that is holy are you doing?" Ida Belle asked.

"My gun is digging into the right boob."

"Please tell me you don't have that Desert Eagle shoved in there," Ida Belle said.

"If I had the Eagle shoved in here, it would be digging into my kidney," Gertie said. "I went boring like the two of you. It's a nine-millimeter. And maybe some Mace. And a pocketknife."

"That's asking a lot of your bra," I said. "All I ask is that mine keep my boobs under my shirt when I'm in public."

"Well, if the rated-R portion of the evening is over, can we get this show on the road?" Ida Belle asked.

We proceeded up the street, repeating the process we'd used earlier, with each of us checking out a different shop. We were almost to Canal when I spotted a cop going into a café.

"There!" I pointed and picked up speed.

We hurried across the street and into the café. The cop was at the counter and we headed straight for him. I was a bit disappointed when I got a glimpse of his name tag but figured maybe he could guide us in the right direction.

"Excuse me, Officer," I said. "I'm looking for Detective Bishop. Dispatch told me I could find him around this area of Saint Charles. Do you have any idea where he might be?"

Okay, so Dispatch didn't tell me, but it was easier than explaining our process.

The officer looked momentarily taken aback and glanced across the café, then looked back at me. "Is there something I can help you with?"

I smiled. "You already have. I assume the gentleman in street clothes sitting at the table in the corner is Detective Bishop. You need to work on your poker face. Thank you for your help."

Detective Bishop had heard the entire exchange and watched the officer leave the shop. He was still shaking his head when we stepped up to the table.

Late thirties. Six foot two. A hundred eighty pounds. Excellent muscle tone. No weaknesses that I could see. Also extremely good-looking. Which didn't present a physical danger to me, but I could see where he might to a lot of women.

"If you're on break, we can wait until you finish," I said.

He shook his head. "If you do that, you'll be chasing me up and down the street in this crowd and hoping I can hear a word you're saying. I have another twenty minutes. If you don't mind my finishing my dinner while you tell me why you need to speak to me, I'm game."

"Of course we don't mind," I said.

"Heck, I was going to order," Gertie said. "That smells delicious."

"Pot roast," Bishop said. "This place has the best. And as it's the special today, no waiting required as long as you get it before they run out."

I waved at the server, and when she walked over, we ordered three pot roast dinners and three sweet teas.

"I take it you're not here for the drinking," Bishop said after we'd ordered. "Or are you pacing yourselves, unlike the thousands of fools outside the door?"

"I don't get drunk in public," I said. "It slows reaction time."

He raised one eyebrow and I passed him a business card.

"These are my assistants, Ida Belle and Gertie," I said.

He sighed. "You know I'm not going to talk to you."

I knew there was no love lost between cops and PIs. Cops saw us as interfering buttheads who likely couldn't get a job as a cop.

I held up a hand. "Look, I know the drill. But I'm not your usual PI. I'm a former CIA operative, for starters, and I'm doing this because retirement at my age is a huge stretch and I like puzzles. But after working for the government for a decade, I can't take any more of their red tape. That's why I went private."

"CIA? Really?" he said, clearly surprised. "And an operative.

That reaction time comment makes a lot more sense now. Have you killed anyone I'd know?"

"Probably, but I'm trying not to make a habit of it now that I'm a civilian."

He smiled and I could tell I'd won him over with my stellar wit and the possibility that I'd killed people he didn't like.

"So how can I help you, former CIA Operative Redding?" he asked. "Did I arrest a client of yours?"

"No," I said. "In fact, I don't have a client at all. I just have an interest in keeping people safe and there's a situation in my town that's gotten my attention. Things don't fit."

He nodded. The great thing about detectives was they got that statement because one usually didn't rise to the position of detective without having the ability to spot things that were out of balance.

"So where do I come in?" he asked.

I briefly explained the situation with Katia.

"You're sure it's homicide?" he asked. "Not a stray?"

I shook my head. "Trajectory was wrong."

"You could tell that by a look through a woman's clothes and a jacket, in dim light?" he asked.

"I'm sort of a specialist on trajectory," I said.

His eyes widened as he caught the reference. "Okay, then. How can I help? I've never heard of Katia Grekov and Lord knows, the sheriff's department wouldn't like me butting into their investigation. Not that I have any jurisdiction or grounds."

"Oh, trust me," Gertie said. "We know all about the displeasure of the sheriff's department when we 'butt in.' Doesn't matter that we've caught some of the worst criminals the town has seen in a while."

Bishop looked back and forth between Ida Belle and Gertie, and I knew he was trying to make sense of Gertie's statement, especially as it looked as though it was coming from an extra on *The Golden Girls*.

"It also doesn't help that Fortune is dating the lead deputy," Gertie continued. "Not that I'm saying she shouldn't date Carter. He's a great guy and perfect for her. He's just a bit too rigid about his job and following rules."

"Carter LeBlanc?" Bishop asked.

I nodded.

Bishop smiled. "I've heard about you. Carter has a couple buddies with the force. According to them, you've got some serious skills."

"Except for the ability to stay out of police business, that's true enough," I said. I didn't see any reason to hide what we were doing. I'd figured from the beginning that my talk with Bishop might get back to Carter. Not that I didn't plan on telling him. Just not right away. So hopefully, the usual law enforcement gossip train would be too busy with Mardi Gras to waste time carrying tales back to Sinful.

He laughed. "I'll bet Carter has his hands full. But you've got me curious. Why the interest in this murder? This woman was a visitor, right?"

I explained the similarity in appearance and dress between Katia and the woman she was visiting and that Katia had been standing there with the woman's daughter.

"So you think the wrong woman was killed?" he asked. "That seems a stretch. More likely, this Katia was into something she shouldn't have been and trouble followed her. Unless you think the husband did it. But even I can't see him pulling off that kind of stunt with his own kid standing right there. Even if he couldn't stand her anymore, he would have made sure his kid was out of the way."

"I think the wrong woman was killed because this is the second time Katia's friend has escaped death while someone else died. Three years ago, you responded to a homicide—a woman and her sister were attacked in a parking lot and the sister died."

He scrunched his brow for a couple seconds, then nodded. "Right. I remember. Russian girls. What's the connection?"

"Natalia Guillory was the woman who survived that attack. She's also the woman whom Katia was visiting."

He put his fork down. I'd finally gotten his attention.

"That *is* interesting," he said. "You got any theories?"

"Other than maybe Natalia is the real target and someone's bungled it twice? No. All I know is Natalia's husband is cheap and keeps to himself. It's a family policy. He works for the government and the word is he's intel. They moved to Sinful right after her attack into a house he inherited from his great-aunt. They attend church but no events at church. Their child is homeschooled. They are members of nothing and have no friends that they hang out with. It's hard to form a theory about people when you can't get any information on them."

He leaned back in his chair. "The plot thickens. So you're thinking that maybe this Natalia was into something before she met her husband that's got her targeted? Or is the husband the target and they're going for his wife to make an example?"

I shrugged. "Your guess is as good as mine at this point. But I don't like thinking that a killer could be lurking around Sinful, waiting for another opportunity. If Natalia was the intended target, then that makes two innocent people who've died because of whatever this is. I don't want anyone else caught in the cross fire."

He nodded. "Because the next time, it might be someone you know and care about. I get it. I'd be concerned as well. And I'll admit, the situation has definitely piqued my interest. But I still don't see how I can help. Even if I got you a copy of the police report, I don't think it's going to tell you anything."

"I already have it, and it didn't," I said. "Except for your name."

He narrowed his eyes at me. "You want to tell me how you got a copy of an open investigation report?"

I really didn't want to get into an argument over police documents and what was legal and not legal and the like, so I threw out my ace in the hole just to speed things along. After all, lunch hour was almost up.

I smiled. "Did I mention that we're staying right on Saint Charles Avenue? Big Hebert is lending us his place."

He stared. "Big Hebert? *That* Big Hebert?"

"Are there others?" I asked.

"I suppose not," he said. "So if you've read the report then you know as much as I do."

"Not really," I said. "We weren't there, and I know you don't put your hunches and basic observations into the official report. You can't without taking some flak for it. That's what I want. All the thoughts you had about the case that you would never have put into writing."

He blew out a breath. "That's going to be tough. It was years ago and with so little to go on, not much time was spent on it, either."

"Let's start with the obvious," I said. "Did you believe they'd been mugged?"

"No doubt about that," he said. "A camera about halfway down the street caught part of it before they fell outside of view. It was horribly grainy and black and white only, but you could see well enough how it started. Unfortunately, we were never able to track down another camera with a better view of the perps. Not that it would have mattered with those masks on, but we couldn't even track movement for more than a half a block."

"So both women were taken to the hospital," I said. "Were either conscious when you arrived?"

"Not really," he said. "I was only a block away when I got the call, but it was bad. One victim was barely breathing. The other was in and out of consciousness, mostly out. And when she was in, she wasn't coherent at all. Both of them got bashed in the head something awful. I've never seen so much blood. When we got to the hospital, they hauled them off for tests and surgery immediately. I didn't get to talk to Natalia again until the next morning. Her sister never regained consciousness."

"Where were their car keys?" I asked.

"In the purse we found," he said. "Natalia's wallet and cell phone were still in place as well. The young men who witnessed the perps running away claimed one dropped something as he ran. Since he didn't have time to strip the cash and credit cards out, I assume that wasn't intentional."

"Probably not," I said, "or they would have taken the car. Tell me about Natalia. How was she when you talked to her?"

"Bad off," he said. "I was there when she woke up screaming 'my sister, my sister' over and over. It was brutal."

"I can imagine," I said.

"Then she touches her head and the doctor tells her she was attacked, she's in the hospital, and has a head injury," he said. "I could tell she was terrified when she asked about her sister."

"Did the doctor tell her that her sister didn't make it or did you?"

"I told her," he said. "But she didn't believe us. She insisted on seeing her and she was so worked up that the doctor finally called for a wheelchair and we took her down to the morgue to show her the body."

"That must have been awful," Gertie said.

He nodded. "She fell apart, sobbing like I've never heard before. When she finally got a breath, I asked her what her name was. She was confused until I explained that we'd only found one purse belonging to Natalia Guillory but there was an old photo in her wallet of the two of them with 'Natalia and Annika' written on the back. We had assumed they were sisters since they looked so much alike."

"Sure," I said.

"She tells me she's Natalia," he said. "We'd already run her driver's license the night before but she no longer lived at that address. I had the computer guys trying to track down info on her—marriage license, employment records, social media, something—but they'd come up empty."

"What about her cell phone?" I asked. "I thought you said it was still in her purse."

"It was and it was completely clean," he said. "No address book. No call history. I was going to initiate a trace with the phone company that morning but then thought I didn't have to since she was awake."

He shook his head. "Thinking about that clean phone along with what you've told me has me wondering what really happened. Don't get me wrong, it had every marker of a typical mugging. But..."

"But what?" I asked.

"Well, who doesn't have contacts in their phone?" he asked. "And who deletes call history and texts right away? I mean, I guess it makes more sense now that I know her husband is intel, but it did seem odd at the time."

"I can see that," I said.

"Then things went really south," he said. "I asked her to tell me what happened, and she stared at me with this completely blank look then started to cry again, saying she couldn't remember. I figured she was just highly stressed and might feel better if she had a family member there, so I asked if she was married. She didn't have a ring on but that doesn't mean much these days. She starts to breathe really fast and then says she doesn't know."

"Amnesia?" Ida Belle asked.

He nodded. "The doctor took over then and started asking some questions and checking her out while he was doing it. I could tell he was trying not to freak her out even more. I went into the hall and called the computer guys and told them to keep looking for something because the victim wasn't going to be any help. It took them until that afternoon to get something, but they finally ran down a neighbor at the former address who gave us the husband's name. They found a new address for him in Virginia and sent the local PD to let him know what was going on."

"So how long was her memory gone?" I asked.

"It started to come back that evening, sometime after her husband showed up," he said. "I had my team working the video angle and figured I'd stay at the hospital in case she remembered something. I'll never forget it—he comes running through the door in a panic and rushes over to the side of the bed. She moves away from him, clearly afraid, and I ask him to step away from the bed as I don't know who he is either at that point."

We all gave him approving nods.

"So I grab the guy's arm and he starts yelling at me, asking what happened and where's the doctor. I drag him out of the room because it's clear he's scaring the hell out of her and I finally get it out of him that he's her husband. I explain that she's got some memory loss but the doctor thinks it will return and he finally calms down."

"I can't even imagine," Gertie said. "Your own spouse doesn't recognize you and in the midst of such a tragedy."

"It definitely took the wind out of his sails," Bishop said. "But he went back in and pulled out his wallet and showed her a picture of the two of them on a beach somewhere. He said it was their honeymoon and asked if she remembered. She didn't, so he tried a picture of their daughter. She stared at the picture for a long time, then shook her head. I don't think I've ever seen a man look so defeated."

"That's seriously harsh," I said.

Bishop nodded. "The doc said since her husband was there it might help her memory so I took off to give them some space. The doctor called me later that evening saying she'd begun to recall some things. Unfortunately, she still didn't recall the attack. She remembered walking to the parking lot with her sister, then seeing her sister fall, but then she remembered nothing until she woke up in the hospital. It took several more days before she remembered the entire attack up until the moment she was knocked unconscious, but I could tell she was straining for some of it. Like there were still gaps."

"She remembered Larry though, right?" Gertie asked. "And her daughter?"

"She said she did but her husband said things were still missing," he said. "For example, she still thought they lived at their former residence but they'd moved a month before. She didn't remember the new residence at all. She could remember her daughter's nickname but couldn't remember her middle name. The doctor said it could take weeks for it all to return and that given the severity of the blow and the extent of the swelling, it was possible she'd always be missing pieces. It was a really sad situation. I could tell the lapses were killing her husband."

"That has to be hard," Ida Belle agreed. "On everyone. I'd hate to lose my memory. That's the only place a lot of people I care about exist anymore."

Bishop nodded. "I got a few there myself. The weird thing, though, is she remembered her childhood in Russia, remembered her parents, her dog. The doctor said that's normal—that sometimes only one file gets damaged, so to speak."

"The mind is a strange place," Gertie said.

"That's a mouthful coming from you," Ida Belle said.

"Since you thought it was a random mugging, you didn't ask them if they had enemies and the rest of that line of questioning," I said.

He shook his head. "There wasn't any indication that we needed to, and since neither of them offered anything up in that direction, I figured we were all on the same page."

He looked out the window and frowned. "I always got the impression she was hiding something, though. Of course, that could mean anything from she spent too much money to she hooked up with a frat boy and didn't want her husband to find out, so that's not really saying anything. You know how it is."

I nodded. "Everyone lies about something. I worked for the government, so I'm used to it, but it does make it hard to solve cases when everyone's being less than forthcoming."

"Anyway," Bishop said as he rose, "we ran down the handful of leads we had but never came up with anything. I'm afraid that's usually the case with that type of crime. I have to get back on my route."

"Hey, what about your partner?" I asked. "Detective Thompson? Do you think he'd talk to us?"

"Probably, if you wanted to fly to Australia," he said. "He retired a year ago and moved down there to be near his daughter. She married an Aussie. But he couldn't tell you anything. Not the sort of thing you're looking for, anyway. Thompson ran the research and camera stuff. He never visited the hospital."

"So he never talked to Natalia?" I asked.

Bishop shook his head.

"Keep my card," I said. "If you think of anything else, no matter how small, give me a call."

He gave me a nod and as soon as he stepped out of the café, he was swallowed up in the crowd.

Gertie stabbed a piece of pot roast and looked at me. "Well? What do you think?"

"I'm not sure what to think," I said. "If Bishop thought she was hiding something, then maybe she was. But was it relevant to what happened or something completely different?"

Ida Belle nodded. "And then there's the memory loss. Bishop might have misread a legitimately confused state as intentionally holding back. I imagine it would look the same."

"Probably," I agreed.

"So what now?" Gertie asked. "Doesn't sound like pursuing Detective Thompson is worth the time, even by phone."

"Given that he never talked to Natalia, I don't think he's worth pursuing either," I said. "The facts, as slim as they are, are in the police report. I was looking more for the personal angle and general feel that detectives get. Thompson won't be able to help with that."

"We could try to find an emergency room employee," Ida Belle said. "Maybe a nurse who worked that night. I doubt we could convince the doctor to talk."

I nodded and scooped up a big bite of mashed potatoes. "That sounds like a plan."

"But in the meantime?" Gertie asked, looking hopeful.

"In the meantime, I imagine we'll get to see some of the parade as we have the walk back to the apartment," I said.

Gertie clapped her hands and bounced up and down in her seat. "I haven't been to a Mardi Gras parade in New Orleans in forever."

"There's a good reason for that," Ida Belle said.

Gertie waved a hand in dismissal. "You worry too much."

"Someone has to, since you don't worry at all," Ida Belle said.

"Look at it this way," I said. "If Gertie needs emergency medical attention, we might be able to run down the ER nurse who cared for Natalia while we're there. You know how I love efficiency."

"Just once, I'd like to visit an ER without needing to visit an ER," Ida Belle said.

"That *would* be different," I said.

"Well, hurry up and eat," Gertie said. "So we can get out there and work off some of this pot roast."

"I plan on taking all of my pot roast back to the apartment with me," I said.

"Please, you're young," Gertie said. "You've probably burned off those mashed potatoes just talking."

"If it worked that way, Celia would be the thinnest woman in the world," Ida Belle said.

I swallowed my last bite of pot roast and looked across the table. "Are we ready to do this?"

Ida Belle sighed. "One of us is."

CHAPTER TWELVE

The Mardi Gras parade was unlike anything I'd ever experienced. The floats were incredible with their artistry and they still didn't compare to the gowns and masks people on the floats wore. I finally understood why Gertie said some people planned for this for a year. A ton of items were clearly homemade, and the amount of time it took to get all those beads and sequins in place must have been staggering. The floats were a mixture of Louisiana themes, such as alligators, crawfish, and voodoo, and completely unrelated things, such as dragons, dinosaurs, superheroes, and one that had the main cast from *The Wizard of Oz*. It was absolutely spectacular.

But all of that paled in comparison to the crowd. Talk about an experience—and a lot of it on the sketchy side. We'd barely made it a block before I'd seen more boobs in that short span than I had in my entire lifetime, and I was including my own in that calculation. Men yelled and women yanked up their tops. Sometimes people cheered. Sometimes they groaned. But either way, they always tossed goodies. I found myself saying a prayer of thanks that Gertie had on a sports bra with a gun shoved in it. At least she wouldn't be tempted to join in the fray.

Of course, I was wrong.

We made it a whole block before Gertie saw people throwing LED beads, and everything she'd promised Ida Belle and me, everything she'd ever known about protecting herself, flew right out the window. She rushed into the middle of the crowd like she was saving a puppy from a speeding car.

Ida Belle and I tried to grab her but she got the jump on us. We scrambled after her, but Ida Belle got knocked into a street sign and I took an elbow to my ear that stunned me for a couple seconds and had me crouching as my vision blurred. By the time my vision cleared, I spotted Gertie through the sea of legs, rolling on the ground. She clutched a handful of beads with one hand and shoved a guy who looked like an extra from *Sons of Anarchy* with the other.

I sprang up, hoping I got her out of the fray before Anarchy guy got a good lock on her face, but Gertie had finally broken loose with the beads and jumped up, arms in the air and hooting like she'd just won the lottery. I yelled at her to get out of the street but no way could she hear me above the noise. I rushed forward but before I could get there, she was kidnapped.

By a parade float.

It was a giant crawfish, with claws up in the air but legs that hung over the side of the float. Gertie caught sight of me hurrying toward her and did one of those celebratory leaps just as the float approached. She jumped just high enough to get snagged in between the float and the first leg. And then there she was, dangling like a fish on a line.

I ran forward and tried to pull her out of the crawfish's grasp, but she was wedged tight and with the float moving, I couldn't get a good grip. Ida Belle dashed up and tried to assist but it was hard for two people to work in such a small space and get leverage while in motion. Finally, a couple of the men on the float noticed and leaned over the side to help. They each grabbed an arm and pulled her up onto the float.

Gertie cheered. The people on the float cheered. The crowd cheered.

Ida Belle and I watched her ride away, not even making an effort to move.

Ida Belle looked over at me. "Can I buy you a drink?"

"I thought you'd never ask."

We headed directly into the nearest bar and I sent Gertie a text with our location.

"This bar will be out of business before she gets off that float," Ida Belle said.

"I thought they might kick her off eventually."

"They're all drunk as Cooter Brown. They probably think she was with them."

"Or they got a peek of the gun in her bra and decided it was safer to keep her in beads and happy," I said, thinking about the view from the rescuers' perspective.

Ida Belle grimaced. "Things I hadn't considered and would have preferred not to."

She waved at the server, a harried-looking young man who trudged over and half-heartedly asked what we wanted. Normally, I would have been somewhat annoyed at the poor service, but given the circumstances, I just hoped he was off shift before he passed out from exhaustion.

"Two beers," Ida Belle said. "Whatever you have on tap is fine."

He looked a little less stressed when he realized our order was going to be easy and we weren't already drunk and belligerent.

She handed him a ten-dollar bill and gave him a sympathetic look. "That's to start. Hang in there. This day doesn't last forever. It just feels like it."

He smiled and perked up considerably. "Thanks, ma'am. Yeah, it's been a real bitch. Sorry, bear."

He headed off to get our drinks with a little more pep in his step. I looked over at Ida Belle and grinned.

"Look at you," I said, "being nice to people. It's a good thing no one else was here to witness it but me. They might get ideas."

Ida Belle waved a hand in dismissal, looking slightly embarrassed. "I've worked enough festivals, fairs, and church put-ons and the like to know that crowds of the general public can make you want to open fire. That's the reason I was never armed for events when we first got back from Vietnam. Too reactive. I even yelled at someone in the café one morning and insisted they give me twenty push-ups."

I laughed. "You were used to military discipline. The place where people actually follow orders."

She nodded. "Even if they didn't make sense. That was simply the way. Your commanding officer said so and that was as good as your mother saying so. You jumped and never asked why. It took me longer to reacclimate myself to normal people. Gertie never had much of an issue, but Gertie is a whole different story in most cases."

"Lord, isn't that a mouthful," I said.

The server returned and placed our beers on the table along with a plate of loaded nachos. "The guy who ordered them passed out and his friends just dragged him out of here. So they're on the house."

"Awesome!" I said, and grabbed a chip piled high with ground beef, queso, sour cream, beans, lettuce, tomatoes, and guacamole. "These look great. I can't believe I'm still hungry after that pot roast."

Ida Belle nodded and selected a less loaded chip. She took a bite and looked at me. "You know, I thought you were going to have a much harder time adjusting to normal life as a civilian. You've really surprised me there."

"I still get jumpy sometimes," I said. "I'm good with fireworks now because I force myself to assess before reacting. My ballistics training allows me to determine the difference, but I have to pause that half second to do it. I can see why so many vets have issues with them, though. If you can't stop your mind from heading straight into the past, then they would be hard to manage."

Ida Belle nodded. "We have some around town that make sure they're wearing noise-canceling headphones when fireworks are on the celebration menu. The problems come when the kids do things out of turn."

"Or when people go firing the real thing in the city," I said. "Like that idiot Ronald."

"Fortunately, that doesn't happen too often."

I raised one eyebrow.

"Sinful's not Chicago," Ida Belle said. "But yeah, we probably need some work."

"To be honest, I thought I'd have a harder time too. But it's almost like I had three lives—my childhood with my mother, my time with the CIA, and being here. I think moving to Sinful and becoming friends with you, Gertie, and Ally brought back so much of my good childhood memories that they tempered my CIA stuff so much I had no desire to go back."

"That's an interesting and perceptive observation," Ida Belle said. "I'm sure you're right. Perhaps if my mother hadn't kowtowed to my father, I would have had better feelings coming back here. But everything worked out in the end."

I knew Ida Belle's father had been a hard man and that

both he and her mother had passed when she was in Vietnam. They'd been a lot older when they had Ida Belle after a lot of years with no luck. Ida Belle's mother had been unable to have more children after her. Ida Belle contended that her father resented her mother for not giving him a son and Ida Belle for not being a boy. I didn't know much because Ida Belle rarely mentioned them. Most of what I did know came from Gertie, but I didn't go asking for details. I figured if Ida Belle wanted me to know, she'd tell me herself.

Besides, the past didn't matter unless you refused to let it go.

I looked out the window and frowned.

Or it came back to haunt you.

BY THE TIME Ida Belle and I got back to the apartment, updated Gertie on our location, showered, and changed into clothes that hadn't suffered the attack of Mardi Gras, Gertie was knocking on the door. She blew inside in a rush of stale beer and sweat, wearing so many beads, I wasn't sure how she was standing upright. I knew Gertie didn't sweat that much so I could only assume she'd picked up the extra scent from the float riders.

"That was the best time!" Gertie said.

"It smells like it," Ida Belle said.

Gertie refused to be deterred. "You two should have climbed up and joined us," she said as she started pulling off beads and putting them on the counter.

Ida Belle frowned, poured dishwashing soap into the sink, then plugged it and turned on the hot water. She grabbed the beads and tossed them into the soapy water as quickly as Gertie unloaded them.

"There was plenty of room and tons of cool beads," Gertie said. "I got all the extras, plus a bunch I swiped while I was pretending to throw them. And the guys invited us to a party later tonight in the French Quarter."

"Hard pass," Ida Belle said.

"Why not?" Gertie pouted. "They were cute."

Ida Belle stared. "We could start with I'm engaged, Fortune is dating Carter, and you don't know them. This is Mardi Gras, for Christ's sake. Might as well pick up men at a prison. At least then you could get a reliable background."

"You are so dramatic," Gertie said.

"Me?" Ida Belle sighed.

"If it was so much fun, how come you're not still there?" I asked. "The parade is still going strong."

"I got them to drop me off in front of the apartment," Gertie said. "The end of the parade is way down there. I'd never get a taxi and I didn't figure you'd be able to get close enough to pick me up."

"We wouldn't even have tried," Ida Belle said. "That SUV is not moving out of the garage until we are going home."

"Well, at least you two spoilsports can go out on the balcony and watch the rest of the parade," Gertie said as she pulled her pistol out of her bra and put it on the counter. Then she headed outside as Ida Belle swirled all the beads around in the sink.

I grabbed three beers out of the refrigerator. "Parade?"

Ida Belle took one of the beers. "We'll stand downwind on the balcony."

I clinked my beer with hers and headed outside to join Gertie, who didn't smell nearly as bad once she was mixed with the outside. Ida Belle and I grabbed chairs and sat to watch the fray from a safe distance. Gertie, who apparently had not collected enough beads, stood at the balcony, waving and yelling at the floats.

Ida Belle shook her head. "So help me God, if she took that gun out of her bra so that she could start flashing, I'm locking her out on this balcony for the night."

"She'd make so much noise you'd end up shooting her," I said.

"Probably true. How much beer did you buy when we stopped at the convenience store?"

"Two cases. I wasn't sure how long we'd be here."

"Good thinking. We're going to need it."

We made it through the first beer and went for a second round, watching the floats and the crowd. I had to admit that I enjoyed the float part. Some of the themes were really clever and the amount of work that went into them was incredible.

"I can see why people come from all over the country to see this," I said.

Ida Belle stared. "You're actually enjoying this melee?"

"Yeah. I mean, I don't want to be down there, and we owe Big Hebert something seriously cool for hooking us up with this place, but the floats are incredible and everyone seems to be having a great time."

"The floats are a sight to behold and we definitely got the hookup from Big," Ida Belle agreed. "I have to admit that I'm enjoying it myself. From up here. Not when we were down there. Sinful parades are enough excitement for me from the ground level."

"Well, we did have a murder, so that's kind of a high bar."

"True."

A huge cheer went up and something whizzed past my head. Immediately, I dived out of my chair and was reaching for my gun when Ida Belle yelled.

"It's just doubloons!"

I picked up a purple coin and stood up. Gertie grabbed it from my hand and started dancing around.

"This is one of the best ones!" she yelled.

I looked over at Ida Belle, who shrugged. The way Gertie was acting, you must be able to exchange the doubloon for a keg of beer or a box of puppies. The float was stalled in front of our balcony and Gertie stood at the railing, waving her hands and yelling for more goodies. An older lady on the float saw her and gave her a thumbs-up before digging in her bag for more doubloons. The lady tossed a handful of the doubloons at the balcony and Gertie leaned over the railing and stretched her arms out, trying to catch the goodies.

But she stretched just a little too far.

Her upper body flipped over the railing before I could stop her, but I made it there in time to grab on to one leg. Ida Belle rushed up and grabbed the other and we took a second to make sure we had a good grip before attempting to haul her up.

"We should let you drop!" Ida Belle yelled.

"We'll catch her!"

I looked down and saw a group of drunk frat boys standing beneath Gertie, hands extended. Half the hands held a beer and I didn't figure they could catch anything but a cold at that point, but the thought was there.

"Get me up!" Gertie yelled. "I'm showing off my new bra."

I looked down again and realized that Gertie's top had crumpled up at her neck and her new bright pink sports bra was clearly on display. Oh well, except for the frat boys, at least most people were only seeing the back. I nodded to Ida Belle and we both pulled at the same time, then grabbed her waist and dragged her back over the railing. Then I felt the hair rise on the back of my neck.

Immediately, I let go and Gertie fell to the ground with a

thump. I scanned the crowd, trying to find the source of my unrest, and saw him on the opposite side of the street. He was standing on the corner, leaning against the street sign, but he wasn't watching the parade. He wore blue jeans and a black hoodie, and his head was turned down. But I knew he was the one. He'd been watching me.

Six foot one. A hundred eighty-five pounds. No physical limitations to spot because he was too far away and wasn't moving.

Then he lifted his head in my direction.

My father!

CHAPTER THIRTEEN

I FLIPPED over the railing and dropped onto the sidewalk below, earning a round of applause from the frat boys. I heard Ida Belle and Gertie yelling behind me, but I didn't have time to stop and explain. I ran into the street, dived under a float, and rolled out the other side. He was no longer standing at the street sign so I shinnied up it to see if I could spot him. But it was no use. The crowd was too thick with too many people wearing the same type of clothes.

And my father knew how to disappear better than anyone I knew.

"Ma'am, I'm going to have to ask you to get down from that pole."

A voice behind me sounded and I whirled around and spotted a cop standing there frowning. Crap!

"How much have you had to drink?" he asked.

"Only a couple beers," I said.

"Uh-huh."

I figured he'd heard that one too many times tonight.

"I thought I saw someone I knew," I explained.

"And you thought diving underneath a float was the best option? Why don't you just send them a text?"

"Because they're supposed to be dead?" I offered, knowing exactly how it was going to sound.

The cop sighed. "Ma'am, I'm tired and it's getting close to the end of this nightmare, and I really don't want to fill out the paperwork on this. So will you do me a favor and stay on the sidewalk from here on out? Don't set foot in the street or on a street pole again. Understand?"

I held my hands up in surrender. "Completely. In fact, I'm just going to head back to my apartment."

"That sounds like a great idea."

"Uh, I have to cross the street to do it."

He sighed. "Then do it *in between* floats. Not underneath one."

He gave me one last shake of his head before heading off toward three guys trying to board one of the floats. Ida Belle and Gertie ran up as the cop walked away.

"What the heck was that?" Ida Belle asked.

"I'll tell you back at the apartment," I said, trying to slow my racing mind. "Let's get off the street."

I practically ran across the street, Ida Belle and Gertie scrambling to keep up, bolted up the stairs, then had to wait for Ida Belle to catch up with the key. Thank God someone was thinking. At least she'd locked the door before dashing after me. We hurried inside and I paced the kitchen, my hands hovering over my weapon. Ida Belle and Gertie slipped onto barstools and watched silently, probably trying to figure out if I was losing it.

I was trying to figure that out myself.

"I saw my father," I said finally.

Both of them jumped off the stools and hurried around the counter.

"Where?"

"Are you sure?"

I nodded. "Across the street. He was watching me. I felt it, and when I scanned the crowd, I spotted him there."

"You're absolutely sure it was your father?" Ida Belle asked.

"Yeah. He's older, of course. He's going gray and his hair is thinning. It looks like he had a nose job at some point and maybe even cheek implants, but it wasn't enough to get around the software and definitely wasn't enough to get around me. Besides, he can't change his eyes. It was him. I'd bet my life on it."

"Oh my God!" Gertie said. "What does this mean? What do we do? Good Lord, why did you run after him?"

"One thing at a time," Ida Belle said. "Fortune, you sit down and we'll decide on a course of action. Obviously, this is serious business and we need to make sure we do the right things and in the right order."

I nodded and headed for a barstool. Ida Belle pulled out the bottle of whiskey we'd bought and poured me a shot.

"I think a round is in order," Gertie said, looking more worried than I'd seen her in a long time.

Ida Belle poured the two of them a shot and me another, then looked at me.

"Okay, so we know your father is in New Orleans," she said. "What is the first action you need to take? Think like an operative now. Because that's how your father and anyone who's looking for him is thinking."

I whirled around and hurried over to the outside door to check the locks, then rushed from window to window along the patio wall, doing the same thing, pulling the shades as I went. Then I flipped up the panel for the security alarm at the front door and studied it.

"I need a code to set this," I said and pulled out my cell phone to call Mannie.

He answered on the first ring.

"I need to arm the security system at the apartment," I said.

"What happened?" he asked, immediately on alert.

"I just spotted my father across the street."

"I'll get right back with you," Mannie said and hung up.

I headed back to my stool but before I got halfway across the kitchen, there was a knock at the front door. I pulled out my gun and motioned to Ida Belle and Gertie, who had already grabbed their weapons. They took position several feet from each other and crouched behind the counter, guns aimed for the door and ready to fire. I unlocked the door and moved to the side, then turned the knob and flung it open, leveling my gun at what I hoped would be center mass of whoever was coming through.

I got the center mass part right. But it wasn't the enemy.

It was Mannie.

He stepped inside and glanced around, then gave us an approving nod. "I have to give it to you guys. You're suspicious and prepared."

I stuck my gun back in my waistband and felt some of the tension disappear from my shoulders and back.

"When you said you'd get right back with me, you really meant it," I said. "Did Big send you to make sure we didn't throw a party in his place?"

Mannie shook his head. "Mr. Hebert isn't concerned about his apartment. It represents something that is easily repaired or replaced. You, on the other hand, are not. After your discussion about the Katia murder, he was concerned, especially given Larry's intel ties. He thought my being close would be a good idea. Just in case you were kicking over a hornet's nest."

"That's sort of our status quo," I said.

Mannie smiled. "Exactly."

"So were you outside in the fray playing security guard all day?" I asked.

"Nothing so uncomfortable," Mannie said. "Mr. Hebert owns the building. He sent the tenant in the apartment next to yours on a nice vacation so that I could take occupancy."

"Told you he probably owned the building," Ida Belle said.

"That's a lot of expense for him," I said. "And seems like an overabundance of concern. You didn't tell him about my father, did you?"

"No," he said. "I would never break a confidence unless your life was in immediate danger. But it wouldn't surprise me if whisperings of potential trouble hadn't made it back to him. He has his fingers in many pots. I encourage you to tell him yourself, especially now that we know your father is in New Orleans. Mr. Hebert has resources in the state of Louisiana that few can match, including law enforcement and military."

"That's true," I agreed. "I was really hoping to keep people here out of it as much as possible, but it looks like that's not going to happen."

"First things first," Mannie said. "Let me provide you with the alarm code and show you how to work the system. Then you can fill me in."

He went through the buttons and gave us the code, which we all committed to memory. Operatives never wrote that kind of thing down. Then Ida Belle offered him a shot of whiskey and went to pour. I headed across the living room and turned on the stereo. Ida Belle and Gertie looked even more confused.

"Remember that long-range laser Mannie is trying to acquire for me?" I asked. "That's why we're staying in the kitchen."

"It's harder to get clear sound through the brick," Ida Belle said.

"Exactly," I said. "And the stereo distorts it even more."

"Tell me what happened," Mannie said.

I told him about spotting my father and my big leap to try to catch him. He stared at me the entire time I spoke, not saying a word. Just frowning. When I was done, he shook his head.

"You took a big risk," he said. "If your father found you here, so could others. They could have easily grabbed you in the crowd, chloroformed you, and dragged you off, pretending you were a drunk girlfriend."

"He's right," Ida Belle said. "This is the perfect environment for someone to disappear. You saw those people on the streets. How many of them are reliable?"

"I know," I conceded. "It wasn't rational, but I didn't think. I saw him and I just reacted."

"Understandable," Mannie said. "You haven't seen him since you were a teenager. Obviously, there's a lot of things you'd like to say to him."

"Or just get close enough to punch him in the face," Gertie said.

I nodded.

"Either is a bad idea," Mannie said. "Quite frankly, so is staying here. He knows where you are. Others might as well."

"If he knows I'm here then he followed us from somewhere," I said. "Since I seriously doubt he was lurking anywhere near the Heberts' office, I have to assume he's already located my home."

"And my SUV," Ida Belle said. "There's no way he followed us from Sinful to New Orleans without us noticing. Fortune and I are always looking."

I sighed. Why wasn't my mind keeping up with what was

going on? It was like my entire ability to think logically had been stripped away and replaced with something I wasn't used to at all. Confusion.

"He put a tracker on the SUV," I said.

Mannie nodded. "May I have the keys?"

Ida Belle would lend someone her boat or even her gun before she handed over keys to her beloved SUV, but she didn't even hesitate. She hurried back to her room and returned with the keys for Mannie.

"I'll take it somewhere and have it swept," he said.

"You need to assume you'll be followed," I said.

He smiled. "I hope so, but I'm guessing that he'll have eyes on this apartment. He'll know that you didn't leave."

"Will he?" I asked. "I've been known to escape a locked room before."

"I don't doubt that for a moment," he said. "But the way these buildings are constructed, there's only so many ways out and even one man can monitor them as long as he has some well-placed equipment."

I blew out a breath. "So what are we supposed to do? Because I'm sure you know that sitting in here with the shades drawn is not an option. Not for me."

"I think maybe we're getting ahead of ourselves," Ida Belle said. "You saw your father, but you didn't see anyone else and you haven't gotten a feeling of being watched until now, right?"

I nodded.

"Then maybe the people looking for your father don't know you're here any more than they know your father is here," she said. "They haven't located you in Sinful, so how would they know to look for you here?"

"I'm sure they know where I live by now," I said. "And it's highly likely that some have been through town for a peek.

They just haven't been lurking around long enough to draw suspicion from the locals."

"But there's nothing for them to see," Gertie said.

"Yet," Ida Belle said. "But you have to figure that if the people looking for Dwight Redding tracked him into this country then one of the assumptions they probably made is that he would make contact with his daughter. His *CIA operative* daughter."

"*Former* CIA operative," Gertie said.

"I'm not so sure they believe that," Ida Belle said.

"Ida Belle is right," Mannie said. "There are simply too many variables here and too many unknown players. I think we have to assume that people looking for Dwight will be here soon if they're not already, and they'll be watching Fortune, hoping to get a line on her father."

I threw my arms in the air, frustrated with the entire situation and angry with my father all over again for putting me and my friends in this situation.

"Well, that's just stupid," I said. "If I was still active, why on earth would I meet with my father? He's wanted by our government. For all we know, he's a traitor."

"Or he's not," Mannie said. "Regardless of his status with *this* nation, I can only imagine the amount of knowledge he might have about the nations he's traversed the past fourteen years."

Ida Belle and Gertie both gave me worried looks.

"With everything that's happening," Ida Belle said, "maybe we should head back home. At least you're better positioned to defend yourself there, and it's a lot harder for strangers to blend in Sinful. NOLA is full of strangers and they all look the same except to you."

I shook my head. "Not yet. I'd still like to try to find a hospital employee or two who looked after Natalia. Besides,

Mannie needs time to get the tracker off your SUV. I think we should stay put for now."

"I agree that going anywhere tonight isn't the smart move," Mannie said. "We can reconvene tomorrow and assess our options again. In the meantime, if you ladies need me, I will be right next door. Arm the system as soon as I leave."

He left and I locked the door behind him and armed the security system.

"I'm really sorry, guys," I said as I slumped onto a barstool.

"About what?" Gertie asked. "You didn't do this. Your father is the big stinker this time. God knows, you have more reason to want him in handcuffs than anyone else on earth. No one else suffered more loss at his hands than you did."

"I doubt the federal government sees it that way," I said. "In the big scheme of things, I don't matter. Not as his daughter, anyway. Even as an operative, I was only as good as the mission I was currently on. People are numbers to the government."

"Well, some of those *numbers* are more important than others," Gertie said.

"To us, of course," Ida Belle said. "But I'm afraid she's right when it comes to the big whirling machine that is our government."

"So what do we do?" Gertie asked. "We can't just sit here and wait for something to happen. That's not how we operate."

"No, it's not," I agreed. "But unfortunately, I don't have an answer."

"Are you going to tell Carter?" Ida Belle asked.

"I don't have a choice," I said.

"I meant tonight," Ida Belle said.

I nodded. "I think I need to. It's not fair for you guys and

Mannie to be in the loop and to leave him out. Plus, he needs to be on alert in case people come looking for me in Sinful."

In a rare loss-of-control moment, I picked up my shot glass and hurled it across the apartment, where it shattered against the fireplace. Ida Belle's and Gertie's eyes widened but they didn't say anything. I got off the stool and headed across the living room.

"I'm going to call Carter and then try to think of what to do," I said as I walked.

I had zero idea how I was supposed to accomplish either with any success.

CARTER DIDN'T ANSWER, so I left a message asking him to call when he had an opportunity to talk. I didn't tell him it was an emergency, because at that very moment, it wasn't. I was safe in Big's apartment, with a great alarm system, excellent dead bolts, two roommates armed to the hilt, and Mannie just next door. The governor probably didn't have security that good.

I flopped onto the bed and stared at the ceiling. What the hell was I going to do?

When I'd had my showdown with Ahmad, my biggest fear was that someone close to me would get caught in the cross fire. And when it was over, and my side suffered no casualties, I was thrilled and thankful.

I never thought I'd be facing the same thing all over again.

And it wasn't just Carter, Ida Belle, Gertie, and now Mannie who could get caught in the fray. Anyone in Sinful could be in the wrong place at the wrong time. And if the enemy got desperate, they might even take someone close to me to extort information. For the first time in a very long time, I thought about packing a bag and disappearing.

I kept a decent amount of cash on hand, as well as fake identifications, including Social Security cards, passports, and driver's licenses. I'd had some issued by the CIA, of course, but these I'd acquired on the side. The CIA could easily track what they'd issued, and as I'd learned the hard way, sometimes the enemy was in your own camp. So I'd created an out for myself and kept them handy and updated, just in case I needed to become a ghost.

I sighed. From spook to ghost. Was that going to be my life?

I couldn't remember the last time I was this angry. It might have been when my mom died. Then, I was angry at everyone —God for taking her, the doctors for not being able to save her, and her for leaving me. When my father was presumed dead, I was sad and scared, but not angry. Not even at him, even though he was the sole parent to a minor child and continued to put himself in jeopardy.

But boy was I mad at him now.

I thought I'd experienced the worst of my anger when Morrow called and told me he was still alive. I'd ranted most of the night to Carter, who was a sympathetic ear and not only in complete agreement, but angry on my behalf. But when I saw my father on that street corner, staring at me, every feeling of dismissal, apathy, and neglect from my childhood coursed through me, sending me over that railing and after him without a thought to anything else but making him answer for what he'd done.

Making him answer for ruining my life a second time.

I was an hour into thinking and still no closer to a solution when my phone rang.

Carter.

I took a deep breath. This was going to be bad.

"I assume since you called me from your cell that you managed to stay out of jail," he said.

I cursed my father again for rendering me unable to appreciate the joke and for having to spoil Carter's seemingly good mood.

"We're all handcuff-free and in for the night," I said.

"Did you find a place close to the Quarter?"

"Even better. We stopped to chat with Big Hebert on the way to New Orleans, and he lent us his apartment, which is right on the parade route. Huge balcony and all."

"You stopped just to chat with Big Hebert?"

"Yes. We chat sometimes. He likes me. Why else would he lend us his apartment? He could probably be getting a million dollars for this place right now. The master bathroom shower is bigger than my living room. But I also wanted to check in with Mannie and fill him in on my father."

"I think that's a good call."

"Yeah, well, something's happened."

"What?" His voice was immediately tense.

"I saw my father."

He must have moved the phone away from his mouth but I still heard the cussing.

"When and where?" he asked. "Give me all the details."

I told him the entire story, down to a somewhat modified version of Mannie's arrival. I did tell Carter that Mannie was staying in the apartment next door. I just didn't reveal that his arrival had been somewhat before I'd ever caught sight of my father. When I was done, he was silent for so long that I checked my phone to make sure we were still connected.

Finally, I heard him exhale.

"Are you all right?" he asked.

I blinked. It was the absolute last thing I expected. Where was the yelling, the admonishments, the outright what-the-heck-were-you-thinkings? Just when I thought I knew Carter LeBlanc, he surprised me. I blinked again, this time because I was getting a little teary.

"I'm all right," I said finally. "I mean...I don't even know."

"I can't even imagine. How do you settle for one thing? Surprised. Angry. Sad. Confused."

"All of the above and a few more. I've got a pretty good case of whiplash."

"Yeah. Well, at least you guys are safe. I have no doubt Big Hebert installed the best security system available and despite my misgivings about your odd and sketchy friendship, I'm glad you're in his place. And even more glad that Mannie is watching out."

And there he went and surprised me again.

"So am I," I said. "More eyes are never a bad thing, especially when they have Mannie's résumé. I told you he's going to have Ida Belle's SUV checked out and remove the tracker we figure is on it, but that's almost symbolic. You know what this means."

"Your father knows where you live."

"Exactly. So what do we do about that?"

"Honestly? I have no idea. I have to admit that even though I figured a man with your father's connection and skill set could easily locate you, I never really thought he'd come looking for you."

"Neither did I," I said. "I was sorta expecting the other side, you know?"

"Me too."

There was silence again and I knew Carter was trying to process everything. Given that I'd just spent over an hour lying here and still hadn't made sense of any of it, I doubted he was going to come to a revelation during our conversation.

"What could he possibly want?" I asked. "No way will I

ever buy a father-daughter reunion. Dwight Redding has never been sorry for anything a day in his life. I don't care what he's been doing for the last fourteen years. Nothing changes a person's character."

"Maybe he wants to warn you that people will come looking. There's a huge gap between ducking out on being a father and letting your child get hurt on your account."

"I was in danger from Ahmad. You think he wasn't aware of that? I never heard a peep out of him then."

"Since we don't know what he's been up to, we can't be sure he was in a position to get information to you. And besides, the threat from Ahmad was well known. It wasn't like you needed to hear it from him."

I sighed. "Look. I appreciate what you're trying to do but it's not going to work. And you don't have to try to cushion the blow for me. There's nothing to cushion. I figured out who my father was a long time ago. All these latest events do is up the ante."

"I'm sorry, Fortune." His voice was low and broke just a little when he said my name.

I felt my heart clench because I could feel how much he meant it. This man loved me and would lay down his life for me. Of that, I had no doubt. It was a little overwhelming and yet at the same time, I couldn't imagine how I lived before this.

"I'm sorry too," I said. "Morrow can deal with my father. He's the CIA's problem as far as I'm concerned. But I won't be able to live with myself if this falls out on the people I care about. How can I protect them? That's my priority."

"*Our* priority. For starters, when you get back home, I'm moving in for a while. When I'm not at work, I'll be with you."

"What about Tiny?"

"He and Merlin can hang out."

"That might be worse than the terrorists gaining entry."

"Fine," Carter said. "He can stay with my mom for a while. But you know we're going to have to introduce them sooner or later. Unless you plan on living in separate houses forever."

"I, uh...I guess I hadn't thought about it."

Good Lord, I'd only just gotten used to being in a serious relationship. And yeah, we spent some nights at each other's houses. But officially cohabitating was a place my mind hadn't gone yet.

"You plan on breaking up with me?" he asked.

"We're not sixteen, Carter. Adults don't 'break up.'"

"They do on those reality shows."

For the first time in hours, I felt a smile tug at my lips and I knew I was on my way back from the dark side.

"You watch reality shows?" I asked. "I wasn't planning on breaking up before, but I might have to consider it now."

He chuckled just a tiny bit, probably more for my benefit than because what I'd said was actually funny.

"Nothing is going to happen to you or the people you care about," he said. "You can trust me on that."

"I know."

And the best part was, I wasn't even lying when I said it. Not even a little bit.

CHAPTER FOURTEEN

IT WAS close to midnight when I walked into the living room. Ida Belle and Gertie had moved from the barstools to the couch and were drinking hot chocolate.

"I can make you one," Gertie said.

"That would be great," I said.

"We stayed on the barstools for a while," Gertie said as she stood, "but then our heinies went to sleep so we had to opt for the couch."

"I think it's fine," I said, and sat in a recliner. "I was just reacting like my training told me to. And Ida Belle is right. If the guys looking for my father were watching us, I'd know. I'm sure they're not far behind, though."

"There's a cheerful thought," Gertie said and popped a cup in the microwave.

"What did Carter have to say?" Ida Belle asked.

"He was shocked," I said. "But what can he say—'sucks your father's a butthole and came back from the dead to ruin your life'?"

"That's a little more polite than I would have put it," Gertie said.

Ida Belle nodded. "Did you tell him about the tracker on my SUV and Mannie being here?"

"I told him everything he needed to know but not necessarily in the order they happened," I said.

"Meaning you didn't tell him Mannie was already here before we called," Ida Belle said. "Or that you gave him the lowdown on your father in your kitchen last night."

"No. I told him I filled Mannie in when we stopped to chat with Big."

"Smart," Ida Belle said. "We need Carter at 100 percent. We can't have even one ounce of him focusing on his aggravation over your relationship with the Heberts and Mannie."

"I don't think he's focused on it at all for a change," I said. "In fact, he said he was glad Mannie was here and that we were staying in Big's place as the security would be top-notch."

"Did he have any thoughts?" Ida Belle asked.

"Nothing that we haven't already considered," I said. "How could he? We don't really know anything. Not where my father has been for the last fourteen years, what he's been doing, or more importantly, who he's been doing it for. It's all a black hole. And without more information, I don't see how we could do anything but speculate."

"And unfortunately, most of the speculation is bad," Ida Belle said.

Gertie returned with my hot chocolate. "And the only person who can give us information is the one man we can't just pick up the phone and call."

Ida Belle shook her head. "I just don't understand what he could possibly want from you. If he needs to tell you something that badly and refuses to do it by phone, mail, carrier pigeon, or whatever, then why did he hide when you went after him? That was the golden opportunity for a face-to-face with no one around to back you up."

"I wish I knew," I said. "I've thought about it until my head hurts, but I can't think of a single reason that he has any use for me. And no way do I believe it's personal."

My cell phone signaled an incoming text and I pulled it out, figuring it was Carter.

It was Mannie.

Are you still awake? I have some information for you.

I sent a reply.

Yep. Still up. Come over and fill us all in at the same time.

I didn't get a response so I took that to mean he was on his way. I jumped up from the couch and headed to the door, then realized I'd left Ida Belle and Gertie sitting there, slightly startled and wondering what the heck was going on.

"Mannie's on his way," I said.

His knock sounded by the time I reached the door. I looked through the peephole to verify it was him before turning off the alarm and letting him in.

"We should establish a code word," I said.

"Agreed," Mannie said.

"Why would you do that?" Gertie asked.

"Because people can be easily summoned, then shot through a peephole," I said. "Please don't ask me how I know."

Gertie's eyes widened and she nodded.

Mannie sat with us in the living room and looked at Ida Belle.

"I found the tracker on your vehicle," he said.

"That was fast," Ida Belle said.

"You're good!" Gertie said, and I added a nod of agreement.

"I appreciate the compliments, but it wasn't that difficult," he said. "For a device to be well hidden, you need time, and since Ida Belle keeps her SUV in the garage at night, that only leaves opportunity when she's parked somewhere else."

"Can we shoot it?" Gertie asked.

Mannie smiled. "Despite everything that's going on in the city right now, I think a round of gunfire in this neighborhood would still stand out."

Gertie looked a bit disappointed. "The police are always in the way of good fun."

"In cases like this, you don't want to destroy it," Mannie said. "It's better to misdirect. So this is what we'll do. Since we have to assume you're under visual observation, Redding will know when you leave but he won't follow because he doesn't think he has to. When you ladies leave New Orleans to return to Sinful, I'll remove the device from your vehicle and place it on one of my people's cars. They will leave the city when you do but once they reach the interstate, will head in the opposite direction."

"Can we reverse that?" Gertie said. "Your guy can go to Sinful and we'll just continue on down the interstate to Florida."

"Either can be arranged," Mannie said. "But I'm going to hazard a guess that Fortune isn't up for a vacation at the moment."

"Gertie doesn't even need to show her face in that state after our last vacation," Ida Belle said. "They've seen enough of the rest of her as well."

"So I'll play down my sexy and buy a one-piece this time," Gertie said.

"As much as I am tempted to go flop down on a beach for a while, we're not taking a vacation," I said. "My father aside, in case you've forgotten, we have a murder in Sinful and we can't be sure another isn't forthcoming. We need to get as much information as we can on that."

Mannie frowned. "Yeah, that's the second thing. Since we had surnames, I made some calls about Natalia, Annika, and

Katia. All three were recruited out of college to work for the same corporation—Natalia in marketing, Annika in the internal training department, and Katia in sales. It's based in Russia but has offices internationally."

"What's the line of business?" I asked.

"I found several—commercial and residential properties, hedge fund investing, some film and television interests, a marketing branch that handles advertising for their own lines as well as for other corporations, and a sales department for unloading the real estate when they were ready to turn it."

"Big money," Gertie said.

"Huge," Mannie agreed. "Natalia only worked there three years before she quit and took a job at a small art museum. Larry met her in Russia eight years ago and he married her there and brought her to the US. They lived in DC initially. Katia Grekov took a promotion about a year later and relocated to New York. Annika never left Russia except for the one trip she made to New Orleans to visit her sister, where she ultimately met her demise."

"That all sounds fairly innocuous," Ida Belle said. "The background part, I mean."

"And that's exactly how it's supposed to look," Mannie said. "But my sources tell me that the corporation is under investigation by the FBI."

"For what?" Gertie asked. "Money laundering?"

"Among other things," Mannie said. "But the most interesting reason is that it's suspected to harbor spies."

"Wow," I said and slumped back on the couch. "Well, that explains why Larry was mad when Katia showed up at his house unannounced."

"And it makes Katia the most likely target, especially if she was a spy," Ida Belle said.

I nodded. "Remember what Larry said—that Katia was

close to Annika, but not really to Natalia. That's why she'd never met Lina before."

Gertie's eyes widened. "You think Annika was a spy as well?"

"As crazy as it sounds, all of this would make more sense if she was," I said.

"Or at least if both of them were up to their neck in illegal activity for the corporation," Mannie said.

"If Natalia didn't want any part of it," Ida Belle said, "that would explain why she quit working there and then married the first steady older American she could find."

"Who just happens to be US government intel," I said. "Does that sound suspicious to anyone else?"

"It did to me," Mannie said. "But as far as I could find, Natalia never left the country after moving here with Larry and there was nothing to indicate that she wasn't exactly what she appears to be—a housewife and mother with the same hermit tendencies as her husband."

"I wonder if the FBI questioned Larry about his wife's involvement with Katia," I said.

"If they didn't before she was killed, they will now," Mannie said.

"Either way, Larry's temper will be in volcano territory," Ida Belle said. "If Katia was really working for the Russian government, then her connection with Natalia could cost him plenty."

"Or even land him in jail if anyone thought he had knowledge of it," I said. "So given all this new information, the big question is, why did Annika visit Natalia three years ago, and why did Katia visit Natalia now?"

"I think if you figure that out, you'll know who killed them both," Mannie said, and stood. "This murder just kicked up in danger factor by about a hundred notches. If the Russian government ordered the hit on Katia, then anyone taking an interest will be viewed as a threat. If you're going to continue pursuing this, you'll have to be very careful."

"What about Carter?" Gertie asked.

"He's an exception," Mannie said. "They will expect him to do his job and come up with nothing. Then the issue can slowly fade away. But Fortune is not Carter."

"If a former CIA operative is caught asking questions about a murdered Russian spy, that changes the game," I said. "I get it."

"Jeez Louise," Gertie said. "We're going to have to walk around with rearview mirrors with all the back-watching we need to do."

Mannie smiled. "A little obvious but not the worst idea you've had. I'm going to head back to my apartment. I don't want to get in the way of your plans, but I'd appreciate a heads-up when you plan on hitting the streets tomorrow and your intended destination. That way, if I can't make contact with you, I know where to start looking."

"You're not going to follow us too?" Gertie asked.

"No," Mannie said. "Redding will have already seen me entering this apartment and will be looking out for me. I'd say your best bet to ditch him in the city is to pull a switch on him."

"What kind of switch?" Gertie asked.

"Misdirection," I said. "I'll figure something out."

When we were somewhere else. Somewhere that would be harder to overhear.

Mannie said good-night and headed out. I got us locked and secured once again and suggested we all head to bed. They both nodded and we trailed silently down the hall. I knew they wanted to talk more, but I was tapped out and it was better to have any discussion that entailed our movement happen someplace where no one could listen.

Of course, Big might have the whole place wired, for all I knew.

I rolled over and closed my eyes.

If the CIA had taught me anything, it was that someone was always listening.

THE NEXT MORNING, we were all dragging a bit as we trudged into the kitchen. I knew none of us had slept well. I could hear Ida Belle tossing and turning most of the night and since I couldn't hear Gertie snoring, I knew she wasn't out for the count, either. We'd had a whole lot to process in one day. Especially me.

I had barely finished putting coffee on to brew when I got a text from Carter.

Just doing a morning check-in.

I texted back.

We're all up but not alert. About to have coffee.

He sent me a heart back and then another text that said he'd check in later that morning. I sat on a barstool silently willing the coffeepot to brew faster. Ida Belle was even more impatient. She stood next to it, clutching a cup as if she could will it into being. Gertie was the last to arrive and eased onto the stool next to me. She put her arms on the countertop, then grimaced and dropped them down again.

"My armpits are killing me," she declared. "They haven't been this sore since I accidentally ate two pot brownies at a party and thought I could fly. Spent half the night standing on the couch and flapping."

"Why did you eat two?" I asked.

"No one told me they had extra ingredients," Gertie said. "It was brownies. How many would you have eaten?"

"Good point." I would probably still be on the couch flapping.

"I've avoided other people's brownies ever since," Gertie said.

"Where were you that you ran across pot brownies anyway?" I asked.

"A birthday party," Gertie said.

"Really?" I said. "I'm surprised anyone has gotten away with it given that you can't even sell alcohol in Sinful. Seems like pot brownies would be a first-class ticket to a jail cell."

"It was Sheriff Lee's party," Gertie said.

I shook my head. I hadn't had enough sleep and hadn't had *any* coffee. It was far too early to contemplate that situation. The coffee finally finished brewing and Ida Belle actually gave a half-hearted cheer, then poured everyone a cup. We all sat and drank in silence for a couple minutes.

"So what is the plan for today?" Gertie finally asked.

"I was thinking we'd go to the casino," I said.

They both looked at me as if I'd lost my mind and I pointed to my ear. Their expressions shifted from confusion to understanding.

"That sounds fun," Gertie said. "Maybe I'll hit one of those big jackpots. I think they're giving away a Harley-Davidson."

"The world does not need you on a motorcycle," Ida Belle said. "We have enough to worry about."

"Oh, I wouldn't keep it," Gertie said. "I'd give it to you."

"Then I totally approve of this winning-a-motorcycle plan," Ida Belle said. "What time do we leave?"

"Maybe an hour," I suggested. "That gives us long enough to shower and dress or whatever."

"Whatever meaning finishing another pot of coffee, I

hope," Gertie said. "I'm exhausted. All last night I dreamed of parades. And in almost every one of them, I ended up running as a float with a giant Mickey Mouse trying to eat me."

"Sounds scary," I said.

"And weird," Ida Belle said.

"Oh, you don't even want to know about the one with Winnie-the-Pooh," Gertie said.

"You're right," Ida Belle said. "We don't."

Gertie managed to lift her middle finger on the coffee mug. I laughed and got up to serve up the rest of the pot and brew another.

"Anyone want breakfast?" I asked.

"Not me," Ida Belle said. "I need to wake up more first. What about you?"

"I'm not really that hungry," I said.

"Well, heck," Gertie said. "I guess I'll have a granola bar until the two of you find your appetites again. Here we are in a city full of fantastic restaurants and you guys aren't hungry. It's like I'm still asleep. Another nightmare."

I smiled. "I'm sure we'll be ready soon and then we'll find something excellent."

We polished off another pot of coffee and Gertie had two granola bars. Then we headed down the hallway to get ready. But as we approached our bedrooms, I motioned them to the master bedroom suite and waved them into Big's shower.

Gertie looked at me as if I'd lost my mind. "I love you like a daughter," she said. "But I don't want to shower with you."

Ida Belle sighed. "She brought us in here because nothing can hear through the walls and the shower tile. This thing is solid stone."

"Oh!" Gertie said. "That's a great idea. We should have gotten in here last night when Mannie came."

"I didn't think about it then," I said. "Anyway, this is my

plan. We take a cab to the casino and have them drop us off out front. We go straight through the casino and out the back, then walk a couple blocks and pick up another cab and head to the hospital where Natalia was treated."

"That's a solid plan," Gertie said. "You're very good at this sneaky stuff."

"She was CIA," Ida Belle said. "What's she supposed to be good at? Knitting?"

Gertie frowned. "I knit and I'm sneaky and dangerous."

"You got part of it right," Ida Belle said. "Although the definition of dangerous is up for interpretation."

I had to smile. It was hard not to around those two. "That's it as far as the sneaky planning goes," I said.

"Then let's get this show on the road," Gertie said. "Or in the cab."

We all changed into our "for public viewing" clothes and headed out. I was strapped with a nine at my waist, another nine in my ankle holster, and a switchblade in my pocket. I had no doubt that Ida Belle was well armed and there was no way I was asking Gertie what she had in her purse. It was one of her largest ones—basically the size of a beach bag. I figured if worst came to worst and we had to kill someone, at least we had a way to transport the body.

We left the apartment and stood at the corner until we flagged a cab. Once there, we went straight inside the main entrance and made our way to the other side of the casino. When we got to the exit, I headed for the door, then stopped. I had that feeling again. I whirled around, almost knocking Ida Belle and Gertie over, and shoved them back behind a potted plant.

"What's wrong?" Ida Belle asked.

"Maybe she has to pee," Gertie said. "I do."

"You should have gone again before we left the apartment," Ida Belle said.

"He's out there," I said.

"You saw him?" Gertie asked, her voice rising in volume and pitch.

"No," I said. "But I know he's there. I can feel him."

"Then let's go out another way," Ida Belle said.

"Wait here," I said, and grabbed a cardboard sign advertising one of the restaurants and walked to the exit door with it in front of me. I peered around it, trying to see if I could spot him, but the feeling had passed. Cars drove by. People walked by. But no one was standing in place. Still. I knew he'd been there.

I headed back in and Gertie gave me an anxious look.

"Did you see him?" she asked.

"No," I said. "But he was there. I'm sure of it."

"If you're sure, we're sure," Ida Belle said. "Maybe we can try another exit."

I shook my head. "If he's circling the block in a car, we'll never get out of here and far enough away that he doesn't see us."

"Even in the crowd?" Gertie asked.

"He could pick us out in a second from a block away," I said. "We have to be able to do that. Sometimes a crowded street is the only opportunity we get."

"Then what do we do?" Ida Belle asked. "Go back to the apartment? Go home?"

"Why don't we just go stand out on the sidewalk and see what the heck he wants?" Gertie asked.

"So all the people looking for him could get a two-for-one?" Ida Belle asked.

"Yeah, I guess that's a bad idea," Gertie said. "But we don't know that the bad guys are out there too."

"We don't know that they're not," Ida Belle said.

"We also don't know that my father isn't one of the bad guys," I said.

"Well, I'm choosing to believe he isn't until proven otherwise," Gertie said. "At least when it comes to national security. As a father, no discussion is necessary."

"So?" Ida Belle said. "What now?"

The truth was, I had no idea. I had really been hoping we could lose him with the casino move but I should have known better. Dwight Redding had been at the game twice as long as I had. There was probably no way I was going to ditch him. But I couldn't afford to go about life normally, either. I gazed across the casino and blew out and breath. And that's when I saw him.

CHAPTER FIFTEEN

"THIS WAY," I said, and headed for one of the big signs that indicated restrooms. I managed to walk normally so I wouldn't give anything away, and Ida Belle and Gertie—God bless them—trusted me enough to follow without question. When I made a hard turn into the women's restroom, curiosity won out.

"I knew someone else besides me would have to pee," Gertie said.

"I don't need to use the restroom," I said. "I saw someone in the casino."

"Your father?" Ida Belle asked.

"No. A guy I saw on the street yesterday at the parade. He was walking the same direction as us but on the other side of the street. Then I saw him later when we were on the balcony. I didn't think anything of it then because it looked like he was with a group of guys near a bar."

"Which would be easy enough to do," Ida Belle said. "Just stand with them and chat, cheer, offer up beer, and it will look like you came together."

I nodded. "And when he was walking down the sidewalk, I figured he was on his way to meet them once I spotted him with that group. But he's in the casino now and there's no sign of his buddies. Three times is way too many to run into the same person in a city this crowded."

"Agreed," Ida Belle said. "So how do we lose him?"

I stared at the wall for a moment, considering.

"We don't," I said finally.

"We don't?" Gertie asked.

"No," I said. "We go back out and gamble."

"Oh," Gertie said. "Then he might think we're really here vacationing."

"Even if he does, it won't change his directive," I cautioned. "Especially since I'm sure he saw me jump off a balcony yesterday and run across the street. The irony is, the man he was looking for was probably forty feet from him and he never even noticed."

"Your father is really good," Gertie said.

"Yeah, I know," I said. "That's part of the problem."

"What does this guy look like?" Ida Belle asked.

"Midthirties," I said. "Six foot one. One hundred ninety-five pounds. Slight limp on the left side stemming from old knee injury. Short, spiky brown hair with cowlick on the right side. Nose has been broken before. Tan that didn't come from vacationing. Weapon at his waist. Wearing blue jeans and navy polo shirt. Tennis shoes are white Nikes with blue stripe. Not one of our guys. Moves differently."

"Good Lord, that's impressive," Gertie said. "You saw all of that in a matter of seconds and from a distance?"

I shrugged. "It's what I do."

"Still impressed," Gertie said.

"Me too," Ida Belle agreed.

"Okay, so we go out and play," I said. "If anyone catches sight of this guy then let me know. If we're too far apart to speak, then text. Does everyone understand the directive?"

"Heck yeah," Gertie said. "I get to play some slots. Hey, is this considered a business expense?"

"Since we're not on a case, then no," I said.

"What if you're the client and the detective?" Gertie asked. "You know, solving the mystery of your father for the sake of your ongoing business. And potential health."

"Then I'd have to pay myself and it would all be a wash," I said. "Is that it?"

"One more question," Gertie said. "Can I pee now?"

TEN MINUTES LATER, we'd exchanged cash for casino cards and found some available seats. It wasn't going to be easy to stay in view of one another because the casino was packed. But no way was I risking letting either of them out of my sight. Too many people had already seen us together and were already calculating if and how they could be used as leverage. A little old lady was an easy target—at least, that's what they'd be thinking. I knew different, but I also knew that even the best could be gotten to.

I sat at a stool at the end of a row and Gertie snagged the one next to me when a woman who looked like she'd been there for a day or two got up and declared the machine a "good waste of a month's salary." I cringed but Gertie seemed thrilled with the opening. Ida Belle located a stool on a row across from us and facing the other direction. She gave me a nod as she sat.

Excellent.

Between Ida Belle and me, we had a view of several different directions. No one could get close to us without us seeing him coming. And since neither of us was lacking in the aiming department, if they approached with a firearm, I had no doubt we could take them out. The last thing I wanted was Gertie opening fire, especially inside a casino. I didn't have enough money or years left on my life to handle that scenario.

I stuck my card into the slot machine and pushed the button, trying to look as if I were having fun. Gertie didn't have to pretend. With every poke of the buttons, she bounced up and down, yelling directives at the machine as though her voice was going to make the magical combination of unicorns and rainbows appear. I found the whirling, dinging, singing, and other odd noises of the machines to be incredibly annoying but then, I was in operative mode.

I figured it was best to let Mannie know what was going on just in case anything went down, so I pulled out my phone to send a text.

Spotted an unknown at the casino. Pretending to gamble until we can evade.

His reply came back almost instantly.

Will walk the perimeter. Describe.

I sent the description I'd given Ida Belle and Gertie earlier.

Excellent.

That was it. I slipped my phone back into my pocket and went back to attempting interest in the frolicking dolphins on the screen in front of me. If only I had a little bit of Gertie's lack of attention span, I'd probably *have* more fun and *be* more fun. But I feared I was destined to be logical and practical before anything else the rest of my life. Of course, that's the way Ida Belle was, and she seemed perfectly happy. She definitely had a lot fewer injuries.

I got an incoming text and pulled out my phone. Ida Belle.

Moving toward us. Your six o'clock. Hands in pockets. Advise.

Hold position but be ready.

Gertie looked over at me, waiting for instruction.

"Just keep playing," I said and hit the button to spin the reels again. There was no way he could drag one of us out of here without causing a scene. And none of us was going down for the count.

Approaching you quickly. Hands still in pockets.

I put one hand up on the machine and pulled out my gun with the other. Several seconds later, I heard the shuffling of feet on the carpet and felt the presence of someone behind me.

"Fortune Redding," a man's voice said, low and just above my neck. "If you come with me, no one has to get hurt."

"You mean you?" I asked. "Because that pressure you just felt on your crotch isn't because I'm interested in a good time. I'll unload this into you and you'll bleed out before you ever get off a shot."

"You wouldn't dare," he said.

"I think we both know better," I said. "So back away slowly and I might let you leave here on two legs."

I heard a loud crack and swung around just in time to see him stagger back a couple of steps. Ida Belle stood there with a serving tray that she'd apparently delivered into the side of his head. He blinked a couple times and that's when I saw the desperation. This was not going to end well. I dived into him as he reached for his waist and tackled him onto the carpet. People started yelling and I could hear the loud calls for security.

I had surprised him but he was too strong for me to keep down. He flipped over and was scrambling to get away when

Gertie clocked him in the face with her handbag. He yelled and clutched his nose for a moment, but that didn't stop him from still attempting to run. My firm grip on his leg was preventing it.

"Clock him again!" I yelled.

Gertie swung the purse back to Mexico, then came around as though she were Babe Ruth. It hit him right in the side of the head and he wobbled for a moment, then dropped. Unfortunately, the momentum she'd created sent the purse bouncing off his head and continuing on its circular trajectory. It hit the slot machine Gertie had been playing, flinging Gertie over the stool and headfirst into the row of buttons. The machine whirled, then stopped and set off an incredibly loud display of music and flashing lights.

"She won the motorcycle!" someone said.

Ida Belle pulled zip ties from her pocket as I rushed over to check on Gertie. She didn't respond when I called her name and my heart jumped into my throat. Then I saw her chest move and relief coursed through me. But we still weren't out of the woods. Unconscious meant potential head injury.

"Someone call 911!"

"I already did it." A woman's voice sounded nearby. "I asked for an ambulance and the cops."

I looked up and saw her walk over and kick our assailant in the crotch. "Men like you are why women have to watch their backs every second. Pervert!"

A casino manager had run up just in time to see the kicking portion of the morning and took a step away from the woman and looked down at Gertie. "Is she all right?"

"She's breathing but unconscious," I said.

He nodded. "What happened?"

"That man made a suggestion I didn't care for," I said. "Things devolved from there."

"I'm really sorry," he said. "The hospital isn't far away. They should be here soon."

He'd barely gotten the words out of his mouth when a pair of paramedics rushed up. I pointed to Gertie, who they began to check out. She groaned and opened her eyes and a cheer went up through the crowd. The paramedics helped her sit up and then one retrieved the gurney they'd brought in.

"You have a nasty lump on your head," one of the paramedics said. "We need to take you to the hospital to be checked out."

Gertie looked up at the slot machine, which was still heralding her win, and her eyes widened. "No way I'm leaving here without my motorcycle! The hospital can kiss my—"

"Please don't worry about that." The manager rushed forward. "I'll take your information down and when you are cleared you can come back and fill out all the paperwork. But please go get checked out. I insist."

Of course he insisted. He was probably thinking the motorcycle was the least of his losses. An old woman attacked and injured while playing in his casino was a far bigger worry. Even if she'd sort of attacked herself.

Gertie motioned to her handbag. "Get him my driver's license."

I picked up the bag and cracked it open, afraid to let anyone huddled around us get a peek. Good Lord Almighty! If the police asked to search the "weapon," Gertie was going under the jail as soon as she was released from the hospital. There were far too many sticks of dynamite. One was too many for law enforcement, but I could tolerate a stick or two. Gertie, however, looked like she was about to start a commercial construction project. There were two pistols in there, duct tape, two switchblades, Mace, and a crowbar. And that's just what I saw before I found her wallet.

I pulled the wallet out and hastily zipped the purse, then handed her ID over to the casino manager, who took a picture of the license and of Gertie, who by then was on the gurney and grinning, giving him two thumbs up. The police chose that moment to arrive and rushed up, trying to determine what was going on.

I pointed to our assailant. "That man tried to force me to leave the facility with him by threatening to harm me. I'm pretty sure he has a gun."

The cops looked down at the man, then at Gertie and her thumbs up on the gurney, and frowned. Clearly, they needed more to go on.

"I resisted," I said. "My friend clocked him with a serving tray and my other friend hit him with her handbag after I got him on the ground."

"And you carry zip ties around with you?" one of the cops asked.

"Doesn't everybody?" Ida Belle asked, giving him a derisive look.

"Okay," the cop said. "We're going to need you three to come down to the station and give a statement. And we'll need to get the name and contact information for everyone who saw what happened."

"This lady is not going anywhere but the hospital," one of the paramedics said.

"And we're going with her," I said. "You've got the guy. The statement can wait."

"What about him?" one of the cops asked. "He's unconscious too."

"Only room for one," the paramedic said. "The next crew can deal with him but I highly suggest you go along and make sure he's handcuffed and monitored. We don't need people attacking senior citizens in casinos or harassing women, especially during Mardi Gras. It's really bad publicity."

The cops looked both frustrated and aggrieved and I felt a little sorry for them. I'll bet they all wished Mardi Gras didn't exist. Their days must be filled with all sorts of this type of nonsense because the one thing they didn't look was surprised.

"Can we at least get your names?" the cops asked as they followed us as we were following the paramedics.

I gave them our information as we walked and promised to go in and give our statements as soon as we were sure Gertie was all right. They were still staring down at our assailant, shaking their heads when we left.

"Can we ride along?" Ida Belle asked. "We don't have a car."

"No problem," one of the paramedics replied. They loaded Gertie up, then we all climbed in and we were off.

I knew we were all dying to talk on the way to the hospital but we couldn't risk doing it in front of the paramedics. It seemed to take forever to drive there, then get Gertie admitted. The staff put her in a room and told us it would be a while before they could get to her as they had a bunch of frat guys come in earlier who'd managed to collapse a balcony.

They allowed Ida Belle and me to stay in her room, which was unusual, but the staff appeared so exhausted I couldn't blame them for not wanting another argument. I could hear the frat boys yelling down the hall and figured they were probably relieved to see three women, two of them seniors, whose only request was to sit in the same room.

As soon as the nurse closed the door, Gertie grinned.

"Well, I got us to the hospital and no one will be the wiser about why we're here," she said.

"Good God, woman," Ida Belle said. "We're here because you got knocked out by that purse of yours. You should have to register it as a weapon."

"The purse and the contents," I said. "But she does have a point. I'm sure we're still being watched, and at least this way we have a medical reason for being here. And since we're in the ER, it wouldn't hurt to ask some questions."

"Oh! Speaking of weapons," Gertie said and pulled a pistol out of her bra. "Better stick that one in my purse with the rest in case they want to do an MRI."

"Because that's our biggest worry," Ida Belle said.

I heard more shouting down the hall and Ida Belle shook her head.

"On the upside," she said, "once the staff is done with that group, they'll probably be too tired to care about questions. We just have to hope someone who took care of Natalia still works here and is on duty today."

"Speaking of questions, let's get up to speed before anyone comes," I said. "We need to have our stories straight for the cops."

Ida Belle nodded. "I was planning on saying that I saw the guy walking up and staring at you, then he leaned over and told you to leave with him or he'd hurt the old lady."

"Old lady!" Gertie protested. "Why do I always have to be the old lady?"

"Because you're the one in the hospital bed," Ida Belle said.

"That's good," I said. "I will back that up and say I refused and that's when you clocked him with the tray, so I jumped on him. I'll say he was getting the better of me so Gertie leaped in and hit him with her purse, then fell into the slot machine, knocking herself out. How does that sound?"

"You're going to tell the cops he was getting the better of you?" Gertie asked. "That's almost funny."

"Well, I couldn't exactly pull my usual moves right there in the casino," I said. "Besides, we don't want to raise suspicion. It's already somewhat out of character for three women, two of them more advanced in years, to take out a youngish, fit dude."

"More women should follow our lead," Gertie said.

"I agree," I said. "But for our purposes, it's better if the cops see us as potential victims."

"Works for me," Ida Belle said.

"I still don't like being the old lady," Gertie said. "But I suppose it's the easiest way to explain it. So what will happen to the stalker?"

"I don't know," I said. "Hopefully an assault charge, but we can't count on it."

"Maybe he won't recover," Gertie said.

"I know I'm going to regret this," Ida Belle said, "but what do you have in that purse? I hit him with that tray like I was auditioning as cleanup for the Yankees and he still had the energy to wrestle Fortune."

"I got a peek when I was looking for her wallet," I said. "It was part gun shop and a little bit Home Depot." I looked at Gertie. "Why do you have a crowbar in there?"

"In case we need to break in somewhere," Gertie said.

"Woman, you've got to have the strongest shoulder in the state," Ida Belle said.

My cell phone signaled an incoming text. Mannie.

Saw an ambulance leaving the casino. Was afraid it might be you.

Good guess. But we're all fine. Just a knock on Gertie's head.

Can you talk?

Sure. One minute.

Because I didn't want to get kicked out of the room, I stepped into the lobby to make the call. There were no cell phones allowed in the ER and I was hoping to stay on the good side of the nurses.

Mannie answered on the first ring and immediately asked what happened.

I explained and by the time I was done, he was chuckling.

"I guess that's one way to get to the hospital without anyone knowing what you're doing," he said.

"That's what Gertie said. Don't encourage her."

"So where is the guy now?"

"He was still hog-tied on the floor of the casino when we left. A second set of paramedics were supposed to be on their way for him, so I assume he's at or on his way to a hospital."

"If it's yours, make sure he's handcuffed and even then, be ready."

"No one has arrived here since us, so either he's not here yet or they decided he needed to go directly to jail. He was starting to come around when we left."

Mannie was silent for a bit, then he said, "I think it's time to bring the Heberts in on the entire story. They have connections with the New Orleans Police Department that could be useful."

"You're right. Bring them in. I should have when I was there yesterday, but I was trying to minimize exposure of civilians."

"Of course. That's your training. But the Heberts aren't your typical civilians, although I expect they'll be both touched and amused at your attempt to protect them. I didn't catch sight of your father anywhere around the casino, but if he was there watching, he might have followed the ambulance."

"Yeah, I was thinking about that—we need a way to get out of here without needing to check back in, if you get my drift."

"When they release Gertie, call me. I'll pick you up and transport you to the apartment."

"Thanks. I really appreciate everything you're doing for us."

"I'm happy to help. This is my forte, although I prefer that those on the line be people I'm unfamiliar with rather than people I like."

"Ditto."

"I'll be standing by."

He disconnected and I headed back to Gertie's room and brought them up to date.

"So do you think it was your father outside the casino?" Ida Belle asked. "Or do you think your stalker has a friend?"

"I think it was my father," I said. "Just a feeling, of course, but that's all I've got."

"Why do you think that guy tried to abduct you?" Gertie asked. "That flies way past risky and right into just plain stupid."

"He's desperate," I said. "I could see it in his expression and knew he was going to make a bad move. And when he looked at the two of you, he saw what most people see—two nice little old ladies—so he completely underestimated you."

"There's that 'old' thing again," Gertie said. "But I get what you're saying. I suppose that's an advantage we have, really."

"Definitely," I said. "And it's an advantage to me. If that had been Ally sitting next to me, I might have reacted differently."

"Meaning you would have just shot him on the spot," Ida Belle said.

"I would have waited for him to go for his weapon," I said. "But it would have been a legal nightmare. It's better if we don't have to kill people."

"I think it's better when some of them die," Gertie said.

"No argument there," I said.

A nurse pushed the door open and came inside to check Gertie's vitals. "We're going to get you back for a CT scan in a couple minutes," she said. "Do you have any metal plates in your head?"

"She's so hardheaded, you'd think so," Ida Belle said.

The nurse was clearly tired but smiled. "My mom says the same thing about my aunt Maggie. My name is Lois. Let me know if you need anything."

"Lois, if you wouldn't mind, could I ask you something?"

"I suppose," she said, looking a tiny bit apprehensive.

"Were you working here in the ER three years ago?"

"I started about three years ago," she said. "Why do you ask?"

"There's a woman we know, a friend, who might be in trouble. She and her sister were attacked in the French Quarter and brought to this hospital three years ago. Her sister died. Two Russian women, blond hair. Thirtyish."

"I remember that," Lois said. "I was training on the ward at the time."

"A friend of the woman that survived was recently killed," I said and showed her my PI credentials. "I'm trying to figure out if this woman is in danger. Anything you could tell me about that incident would help."

She frowned. "I hate to hear that, and I wish I could help, but I wasn't assigned to either of them. The woman you need to talk to is Gilda Jackson. She was the charge nurse at the time and handled the most critical cases."

"Does she still work here?" I asked.

"She does but she's on vacation," Lois said. "Since she's senior, she gets her pick of time off. I used to wonder why she left the city for Mardi Gras because it's such a good time. Then I worked a couple of Mardi Gras in the ER and had my answer."

"I don't suppose you know how to reach her, do you?" I asked. "I wouldn't ask but it's rather urgent."

She looked at me, then at Ida Belle and Gertie, bit her lower lip, then finally nodded. "I have her number in my cell phone but we're not allowed to have them on shift. I can get it for you, though."

I gave her my card with my phone number on it. "Just text it to that number. And thank you."

"Of course," she said. "The tech will be back for Ms. Hebert soon."

"Well, that's that," Gertie said, looking disappointed.

"It's not the end of the road," I said. "As soon as we get out of here, I'll leave a message for her and maybe she'll get back with us."

"Would you get back with total strangers asking you to violate HIPAA laws, especially while you were on vacation?" Gertie asked.

"You lost me at total strangers," I said, "so I'm really not the person to ask."

"All we can do is try," Ida Belle said. "Maybe she'll get back with us. Maybe she won't. Either way, we just keep moving."

Gertie sighed. "What a waste of a good concussion."

IT TOOK another hour before the tech came to the room to retrieve Gertie and by that time, it was all Ida Belle and I could do to keep her from walking out. She swore she was fine, and I figured she probably was, given the things I'd seen her survive, but you never played Russian roulette with a head injury. I finally managed to get her settled by reminding her that a medical report would be a solid addition to our police reports.

Ida Belle and I exited the room behind the tech and she said she was going in search of coffee. I told her I was going to try to call Carter and bring him up to speed and to grab me the largest cup she could find. I needed something in my stomach because I was going to starve to death before we got food. I should have joined Gertie eating granola bars earlier. I started walking in the direction of the lobby when a man in a janitorial uniform and hat opened a door and grabbed my arm.

My father!

CHAPTER SIXTEEN

HE MOTIONED me inside the supply room, and everything I thought I would do if I came face-to-face with him fled my mind and I found myself unable to do anything at all. Then the moment passed and I yanked my arm back and pulled out my pistol. He put his hands up and nodded, then motioned to the room again.

"I have to speak to you," he said. "It's a matter of national security."

Crap! There were only two things that could get me to step into the lion's den—my friends and national security.

I waved my gun at him and he stepped backward, keeping his hands up. He was fast but no way could he pull a gun on me before I got off several shots. And only one would do.

"Speak," I said as the door closed behind us. "And keep your hands up while you do it."

"I need you to get information to Director Morrow," he said.

"Why don't you do it yourself? You could probably accost him somewhere in a hallway."

He shook his head. "The CIA and intelligence agencies for

most countries have him under surveillance and have for months. Just like you. I've been trying for days to find a way to get to you that didn't cause you more problems, and with all the people milling around this city, this was the best opportunity."

I stared. "Are you serious? *More* problems? You abandoned me as a child after I'd already lost my mother. Pretended to be dead for fourteen years, then pop up alive and suspected of being a traitor, and I'm still not convinced you're not. You've done nothing but cause me problems. My entire life before Sinful consisted of nothing but trying to get out of your shadow, and when I finally did, you show up to ruin everything again. I should shoot you right here and save all of us a lot of trouble."

At least he had the decency to look somewhat contrite. "Look, I know what I did to you was wrong but at the time, I thought it was the best choice. I was a crap father and husband, for that matter. There was only one thing that I did well, and when the military made me an offer to go under deep, I thought it would be better for you and the country if I disappeared and did what I do best."

"You've been working for the military for all these years?" I still wasn't convinced.

He nodded. "You won't find my name on a payroll check, of course, but yes. I infiltrated a major terrorist cell over a decade ago and have been handling communications between cells for several years."

"How did you convince them you'd sold out?"

"I took a lot of money and withstood years of scrutiny. The military never planned on getting regular updates from me. I was in place only to alert if things were about to go bad on a global scale. But my military channels are compromised. The one person I know I can trust is Morrow. But I can't get to him."

"So you decided to get to me instead. Now that I'm old enough to do something for you. Not that you ever did much of anything for me."

"I know you don't believe it, but my leaving *was* for you. I knew Morrow would look after you. I just didn't ever consider that you would follow in my footsteps. If I had known how things would turn out, I would have done everything differently."

"No. You wouldn't have." I studied him for several seconds. "You know that some think I was an even better agent than you. Do you really think you can lie to me and I can't tell? In so many ways, I am my father's daughter."

His expression went totally blank, and for a moment, he looked just like he did when I was a child, which said a whole lot about the first sixteen years of my life.

"Fine," he said. "Neither of us is looking for some big Oprah father-daughter reunion, so I'll get right to the facts. In ten days, there is a meeting in London between the top security personnel of several countries. The president will be there. The prime minister of Great Britain will be there and several other leaders."

I frowned. "And what's going to happen?"

"There's a massive hit planned. The hotel that the visiting leaders stay in has been rigged to attack them with sonar. Even if they make it through the attack alive, they probably won't ever be the same again. Simultaneously, assassins have targeted the prime minister during his dinner. His entire family will be poisoned."

"Sonar? But won't that cause widespread problems?"

He nodded. "It's likely that everyone in the hotel will be affected—guests and staff. It will kill or cripple several hundred people at once, mostly people whose only mistake was being in the wrong place at the wrong time."

"Who's behind this?"

"It's a joint effort among several terrorist groups but I haven't been able to determine who is leading the charge."

"And what's the purpose?"

"The same as it always is—to injure the strong."

"I don't get it. Why are you telling me this? You've managed to become invisible for over a decade and you really think you couldn't have gotten this information to Morrow another way?"

"You were an excellent operative. I don't have to explain to you the difficulties one experiences when there's corruption within the ranks. There's a sheet of paper on the table behind you that contains twelve names. Those people are traitors working within the intelligence community of each government that will be represented at this meeting. Three of them are CIA. One is the man currently sitting in federal prison for leaking information on you."

I felt my pulse tick up a notch. "And the man in the casino?"

"One of your old friend Ahmad's captains. But there's been no hit ordered on you. The guy in charge now has been looking for a way to take over Ahmad's group for years. You did him a favor. His only interest in you now is the same as the others—leading them to me."

"Before you can get information to the right parties."

He nodded. "You are the only person I can trust to deliver this for me. Most don't believe that you've been deactivated, but they've been unable to prove differently."

"Maybe because it's true."

"Is it really?"

He stared at me and I knew he was doing the same thing I

do—watching every inch of my face for that telltale sign that I was lying.

"My reasons for becoming an agent are no longer important to me," I said. "I have a new life. A life that I vastly prefer to the one before."

He watched me silently for several more seconds, then nodded. "I'm sorry to hear that. You're a real asset to this country."

"Yeah, well, I've found some people who appreciate me even more, and now they're in danger."

"Yes. I can only assume the man you dispatched at the casino broke surveillance and approached you. The clock is ticking and the closer to the meeting they get, the harder they'll work to ensure their plan goes off without a hitch."

I cursed loudly and he glanced nervously at the door.

"My life will never be normal," I said. "All because of you. You should never have married. You should never have had kids. You knew who you were. It wasn't fair to shove other people into your trajectory."

He was silent for a few seconds, then lowered his head and sighed.

"You're right," he said. "I shouldn't have pursued your mother but she was unlike anyone I'd ever met before. Just being near her made light brighter. I'd never felt like that. I would have given her whatever she asked for, and what she wanted more than anything was a child. I was selfish. It wasn't fair to her or to you. I hoped by leaving that I could avoid making you as miserable as I made her."

"You're 0 and 2."

"I know. And the last thing I wanted to do was drop this in your lap, but I don't know any other way. You needed to know what was happening, so you could get the information to Morrow and so you could protect yourself. I never would have risked coming out of hiding and exposing you further, if it wasn't critical."

"So that's it? You just dump this on me and disappear again?"

"No. I'll make a 'slip' somewhere so that they can gain temporary position on me, then leave the area in an attempt to draw them off. Good luck, Fortune."

He dropped his hands and inched for the door. I stepped back and let him go. There was no point in holding him there any longer. Nothing he could say would change the current situation or make up for the damage he'd done. He opened the door and slipped out.

I heard a faint "I'm sorry" before the door closed.

And then I started to cry.

I GRABBED the paper with the names and scanned them, my blood running cold, then I sprinted out of the room. But my father had already disappeared. A nurse coming down the hall gave me a funny look but I just turned and took off for the lobby. I stuffed the paper in my pocket and pulled out my cell phone. Then I stopped. Who was I calling first? I needed Ida Belle back in my sight. I needed to warn Mannie that the situation had just gone from fifty to one thousand. But mostly, I wanted to talk to Carter. Just because.

As I was trying to decide, Ida Belle came through a side door clutching two huge coffee cups, and some of my tension eased. She took one look at my face, set the cups on a table and rushed over.

"What's wrong?" she asked. "Is it Gertie?"

"No," I said.

I headed for the restroom, motioning for Ida Belle to

follow. I didn't like the big glass front that the lobby had. Too much exposure. When we got inside, I checked to make sure it was empty, paced a couple times, then stopped, took in a deep breath, and slowly blew it out.

"My father was here," I said.

Ida Belle plopped the coffees on the counter.

"Are you okay?" she asked.

I shook my head. "We need to get out of here. Everything has changed."

"What did he tell you?"

I shook my head. I couldn't involve Ida Belle and Gertie in this. Or Mannie for that matter. It was too big. Too frightening. It went so high up on the food chain that it was an apex predator. Several were high-ranking military officials in three different countries. One was the CIA operative who had effectively replaced me in the Middle East. The other was the deputy director of the CIA—Morrow's right-hand man.

No wonder my father had come out of hiding. No wonder half the world's bad guys were gunning for him and shadowing me. But now it was my problem. And I had to think like an operative in order to complete the mission, but this time was different. This time I had to consider the survival of people other than myself. It was a lot.

"We need to get back to Sinful," I said.

On the surface, it sounded counterintuitive—as if I were just leading the bad guys right to my front door and exposing the entire town to my burden. But the reality was, the bad guys were already there. If I disappeared, it left everyone there at risk of being kidnapped to draw me out. The only way I could keep them safe was to put myself on display, and the best place to do that was where strangers stood out and neighbors were nosy and called the police about everything.

I could try to convince the people closest to me to go into

hiding, but without time to prepare documents and without a system in place to move several individuals at once, it would have been hard to do successfully. And even if a foolproof plan could be established, I knew they wouldn't leave. So it wasn't an option.

"What about the police statements?" Ida Belle asked

Crap! If we didn't give our statements, one of the bad guys would be back on the job. I figured there were more where he came from, but taking him out of commission for a day or two was an every-little-bit-helps sort of situation.

My phone rang and I saw it was Mannie. I knew he wouldn't call unless it was important so I answered.

"Your casino friend escaped police custody at another hospital," he said when I answered.

"How did that happen?" I asked.

"No idea," he said. "All I know is that Big called a contact with the NOLA PD and found out. He's got them running scared as he's claimed you are a close personal friend, but you know how hard it will be for officers trained to work civilians to try to locate one guy, especially with Mardi Gras in full swing."

"I get it," I said. "I think we need to get back to Sinful immediately."

"I agree. What do you need from me?"

"Move Ida Belle's SUV somewhere we can pick it up without being seen. That might give us enough lead time to make it back to Sinful without incident."

"No problem. I'll need about thirty minutes."

"That will work. Gertie isn't released yet but should be soon."

"I'll pick you up when you're done," he said.

"Are you being followed?"

"I was earlier, but they couldn't hang. They don't know the city, and I can use that to my advantage."

"Text me when everything is in place."

"Will do. Watch your back."

"Always."

I slipped my phone in my pocket. "Our friend got away, so the statements aren't going to be an issue. We need to get Gertie and get out of here."

We located the charge nurse, and she told us Gertie was back in her room and the doctor would be there soon. We headed back and found Gertie sitting up and raring to go. I brought Gertie up to speed as much as I had Ida Belle at least, making sure she knew to hold in her thoughts—which were likely to be stringent and loud. I could tell she was straining not to let out her anger and squeezed her arm, indicating that I knew exactly how she felt.

The doctor walked in about twenty minutes later.

"Your tests look good," he said as he checked Gertie's head and shone a light in her eyes. "How do you feel?"

"Bored and restless," Gertie said. "I'm ready to leave."

The doctor frowned. "I'd prefer to hold you overnight for observation."

"The only way you're holding me overnight is if we're dating and it has to include dinner first," Gertie said. "If I'm not dying, I'm getting out of here."

"I'll get you a release form to sign," the doctor said. I could tell he wasn't happy when he left the room, but he also knew better than to try to argue.

"You know," Ida Belle said, "this is the first and I hope the only time I see you check yourself out of the hospital against doctor's orders."

My cell phone signaled an incoming text. Mannie.

SUV in place but enemy is positioned outside hospital. Spotted three on foot and two vehicles so far. Probably more. Building is surrounded.

Crap! I figured after our friend at the casino got away, he'd alert his people and they'd set up shop outside the hospital, hoping for a chance to grab one of us as we left, but I hadn't expected that many. Of course, that was before I knew that several terrorist groups had decided to make friends and get together for one big hurrah. But that didn't mean they'd trust one another, which meant all of them had sent operatives to come after me.

Ultimately, they'd show up in Sinful, but we needed to get a jump on them. The lone highway between New Orleans and Sinful was filled with long stretches of nothing, which gave ample opportunity to force us off the road. Or worse. If the enemy even suspected for a second that my father had gotten information to me, they'd kill me just to be sure. How many people were surrounding me at the time wouldn't matter. In fact, they'd just assume it was safer to get us all.

I repeated the text to Ida Belle and Gertie, and they gave each other worried looks, then looked back at me, clearly expecting me to come up with a solution. In my past life, I would have shot my way out and gotten a lift from a helicopter, but that didn't seem like the best idea at the moment, even if I had a helicopter at my disposal.

Then a thought occurred to me. I sent a text to Mannie.

Is ambulance still parked outside ER entrance?

Yes.

Send coordinates for SUV, then stand by.

10-4.

I looked at Ida Belle and Gertie.

"I have an idea."

CHAPTER SEVENTEEN

A couple minutes later, Gertie had signed the papers officially relieving the hospital of any and all responsibility related to her release and had absolutely refused to get into a wheelchair unless they sedated her. The exhausted hospital nurse just told her to go and advised Ida Belle and me to assist her. I grabbed her elbow to steady her as we walked down the hall. She was reasonably good except for the occasional sway that came with a bout of dizziness.

I glanced back every so often to see if the hallway was clear of personnel. As we inched closer to the supply room, the nurse who'd brought Gertie the discharge papers slipped into a room and left the hall empty. I opened the door to the supply room and we all hurried inside.

"When I was in here earlier, I saw two hazmat suits," I said. "The ambulance is still parked outside and I noticed the paramedic left the keys in it."

"You want to steal an ambulance?" Gertie asked.

"There are at least five terrorists outside," I said. "Do you have a better idea?"

"No," Gertie said. "I think it's a great idea. It's just that it sounded more like something I'd suggest than you."

"Desperate times," I said.

"Let's do it," Ida Belle said.

"But you said there were two hazmat suits," Gertie said. "How is that going to work?"

I pointed to a body bag.

Gertie shook her head. "No way! I'm not getting in that thing. I'll suffocate."

"I'll cut a hole in it," I said. "In order for the hazmat suits to pass muster, we have to be transporting someone contagious. And it's the only way to get all three of us into the ambulance without arousing suspicion."

"Then let Ida Belle do it," she said.

"You were swaying when we walked down the hall," I said. "If we end up having to run, you'll be a hindrance. Is that what you want?"

Gertie frowned. "Fine. But I want to lodge an official complaint about always having to be the dead person."

"I always have to be the slut," I said. "We all have roles to fill."

"Stop your complaining," Ida Belle said. "It's a much bigger stretch for Fortune to play a slut than for you to play a dead person."

Gertie stared. "As soon as I'm not dizzy—"

"Yeah, yeah." Ida Belle waved a hand in dismissal. "Let's get this show on the road before a call comes in and that ambulance is no longer there for the taking."

Ida Belle and I suited up, and then I cut a hole in the body bag and we got it onto a gurney and Gertie inside.

"What about my purse?" Gertie asked as I started to zip the bag up. "We might need that stuff."

"As much as I hate to admit it," Ida Belle said, "she's right."

I unzipped the body bag and sat her purse on her stomach. "There, now you're pregnant."

Gertie gave me a look of dismay. "I prefer dead."

Ida Belle grinned. "See. Things can always get worse."

Gertie moved her arm, probably to give Ida Belle the finger, but before she could manage to do it, I zipped her in place.

"No noise," I said. "Corpses don't speak."

"They fart," Gertie said.

"Go right ahead," Ida Belle said. "You're the one zipped up like a sandwich."

I peeked out of the storeroom to make sure the coast was clear, then pushed the gurney into the hallway.

"Just go straight through the lobby without stopping," I said to Ida Belle. "Even if the front desk clerk tries to stop us."

I picked up speed as we went, hoping that going fast would further indicate the urgency of the task. As we burst into the lobby, the front desk clerk jumped a bit, then her eyes widened.

"Oh my God!" she said. "Is everything all right? Wait! You need to sign out."

"No time," I said, forcing my voice low. "The suits are only good for two hours. We'll sign when we get back."

The clerk stood there staring as we hurried out but didn't make a move for her phone. She must have been new and didn't know protocol very well. Either that or she'd seen everything under the sun and this didn't rank high on the oddity list. We hurried out the doors and the gurney started rocking from side to side when we hit the parking lot.

"Stop moving," Ida Belle said.

"I have a wedgie," Gertie complained.

"Dead people don't get wedgies," Ida Belle said.

I breathed a sigh of relief when I saw the ambulance still

sitting in its reserved parking spot, but as we started to turn the gurney in its direction, Gertie must have gotten in a good tug. The gurney tipped to the right and before we could stabilize it, it fell over, sending Gertie to the ground with a crash.

She let out a strangled cry, and an older lady being helped to the hospital by a younger man took one look at the body bag and made the sign of the cross.

"Sometimes they come back," Ida Belle said.

The woman's eyes widened and she swayed a bit as the younger man practically pulled her toward the entrance. Ida Belle and I bent over to lift Gertie back onto the gurney.

"Good God, woman," Ida Belle said. "You have to stop eating like crap."

"It's not me," Gertie said. "It's my purse. I'm about to puke with this thing sitting on my stomach."

We plopped her on the gurney, then hauled it for the ambulance before someone reported us to the hospital staff. Or the CDC. Ida Belle opened the back of the ambulance and we got the gurney folded and into the back. Then she hopped in with Gertie and I went around to take the driver's seat. The keys were in the ignition, just as I'd seen before, and I said a quick thanks for the employee who hadn't followed protocol while also asking him silently for forgiveness when Human Resources came down on him.

I started up the ambulance and backed out, scanning the parking lot as I went. I spotted a man standing next to a car and watching the ER entrance. He had his cell phone to his ear but he'd forgotten to move his lips, so his acting needed work. Another man walked down the sidewalk, but instead of glancing at the sea of hot women who were passing just to the right of him, his gaze was locked on the ER entrance as well.

No wonder Mannie had spotted them. They were practically waving flags. A flash of something caught my eye as I pulled onto the street, and I looked up and saw a man with a sniper rifle on the roof of a neighboring building. I felt my pulse spike as anger coursed through me. The sniper wasn't there for me. He was there for my father. But any one of us could have caught a bullet meant for him. If the operatives were willing to attempt an assassination in broad daylight and right in front of a hospital, then I needed to get back to my house and get secured as soon as possible.

My father had said he'd attempt to draw them off and for whatever crazy reason, I believed him. But they'd still be watching and the more time that passed, the bolder they would become. I had to secure my home and my family first and figure out a way to get that information to Morrow without leaving Sinful and without it being intercepted. I had a few ideas on the first and only one on the second.

"Get me out of this thing!" Gertie complained.

"I forgot you were in there," Ida Belle said as she pulled off her headgear and grinned at me. "There better not be a fart waiting for me when I unzip this thing."

"Would serve you right if there was," Gertie said as Ida Belle unzipped the bag. "But unfortunately, I couldn't work anything up. Probably because I haven't eaten since Moses was a baby."

"I'm surprised you don't have a buffet in that handbag of yours," Ida Belle said.

"I swapped it for a dart gun," Gertie said.

I cast a nervous glance in the rearview mirror but Ida Belle didn't seem concerned. I supposed in the big scheme of things, Gertie and a dart gun were small potatoes. I stopped at the corner and paused long enough to check my text messages for coordinates to the SUV.

"So what's the plan?" Gertie asked. "I hope it includes lunch."

"It does if you have a casserole ready to go," I said. "But no stops until we get back to Sinful."

"We're taking this thing all the way to Sinful?" Gertie asked.

"Okay, one stop," I said. "We'll retrieve Ida Belle's SUV on the other side of town where Mannie has it ready to go. Then we head straight home."

"Do you think this will buy us enough time to get home without incident?" Ida Belle asked.

"I hope so. Because I don't think sending his guy to Florida with the tracker is going to help. My guess is my father put that tracker on your SUV, and he won't be looking for us again. The question is whether the rest are all clustered in New Orleans watching me."

"Or waiting in Sinful," Ida Belle said.

"When they can't find us in New Orleans, they're going to figure we went home anyway," Gertie said.

"Yeah, but I'd prefer to get there before they do," I said. "Gives us time to prepare."

"Just how many people do you think are involved?" Ida Belle asked, looking worried.

In my haste to get out of New Orleans, I'd completely forgotten that Ida Belle and Gertie only knew part of the story. My heart tugged as I realized that these women had followed my directive to steal an ambulance and flee the city based on nothing more than my saying it was necessary. Words couldn't begin to describe how much I loved them for the trust and respect they had for me.

The problem was, how much did I tell them—none of it, all of it? At that point, it probably didn't matter. The enemy would assume knowledge if they decided my father had made contact with me and that would be that. But I couldn't go down that road. For my own sanity, I had to assume that they didn't know my father had made contact.

Because that was the only way we had a chance to come out of this unscathed.

But it wasn't fair to leave them in the dark. They needed to know what we were risking our lives for. That was only fair. So I told them what my father had conveyed, minus the personal stuff and the names on the list. When I was done, they both sat in stunned silence. Finally, Gertie spoke.

"Do you believe he's telling you the truth?" she asked.

"I do," I said. About the coup. Not about being sorry.

"I think we have to believe him," Ida Belle said. "Why else would he be here? It's a huge risk to him. Even his own government is looking for him. If some catch sight of him, they'll lock him up. The rest will just kill him. And besides that, I can't imagine contacting Fortune was something he ever wanted to do."

"Coward," Gertie said. "I'm sorry. I know he's all 'I'm trying to save the world' but to me, he'll always be a douchebag."

I felt my heart clench at Gertie's tone.

"I don't think anyone is going to disagree with you," I said. "Least of all me. But the coup planned would produce global unrest, which then produces chinks in the armor. We can't have that kind of lapse in our national security. Not even for a second. And the list of people scares me. It goes far up the food chain."

"Do you know any of them?" Ida Belle asked.

"I know all of them," I said.

Ida Belle blew out a breath. "Wow. That's beyond words. I feel like I keep saying this, but what's the plan?"

I spotted Ida Belle's SUV parked at the curb of the side street where Mannie had left it and pulled up behind it.

"First, we get out of these suits and into your SUV," I said. "Then I'll let Mannie know we're mobile and he'll send his guy off toward Florida with the tracker, then head for the highway, hoping to intercept us on the way home. You're going to take over driving from here, and I'm counting on you to know a back way to the highway, just in case they're watching the main exits from the city."

"I'm on it," Ida Belle said as she shrugged off her suit.

Gertie looked disappointed. "I was hoping we could keep those. Halloween isn't that far off."

"They're too expensive," I said. "I don't want the poor guy who left the keys in the ambulance to never work again."

"I suppose he did give me a ride to the hospital," Gertie said.

I stepped to the back and pulled my suit off as well and we hauled Gertie out of the body bag. Then I opened the back door of the ambulance and stepped out. I didn't pause because stationary targets were easier to hit. I didn't think things had progressed to that level, but if my situation with Ahmad had taught me anything, it was that when dealing with terrorists, you couldn't always rely on common sense.

Ida Belle and Gertie hurried after me as I located the keys under the back wheel where Mannie had indicated they'd be. I tossed them to Ida Belle and jumped into the passenger's seat and we were off. I pulled out my phone and sent Mannie a text.

Clear. Send your guy out.

On it. Avoid the area around the hospital.

Already have a plan.

10-4.

I slipped my phone back into my pocket and hoped my plan was good enough.

"Aren't you going to call Carter and fill him in?" Gertie asked.

I shook my head. I'd already gotten several texts from him and my responses had been short but normal. If he had any idea what was going on, he'd rush to New Orleans and that was the last thing I needed him to do. The fewer people outside of Sinful, the better. It was time for everyone to get in the castle and pull up the drawbridge.

"This is the sort of conversation that needs to happen in person," I said.

"What if the bad guys are already in Sinful?" Gertie asked.

"Then they picked the wrong place," I said. "Carter is already on alert. No one can take him by surprise."

I clenched my hands until my nails dug into my palms.

At least, that's what I was telling myself.

IDA BELLE MANEUVERED around the streets of New Orleans until the buildings turned into neighborhoods, which then turned into more rural areas with acreage instead of lots. I'd been watching the mirrors carefully but so far, there was no sign of unwanted company. Mannie had texted that he was performing evasion procedures and would try to fall in with us on the highway. He was in a black Cadillac sedan with limo-tinted windows.

It seemed like hours had gone by when we finally passed our last cow and pulled onto the service road for the highway. I pulled Ida Belle's binoculars from the glove box and scanned both sides of the road but didn't see anything of merit. There were only a few cars and they looked to be common for the area—older-model sedans with a bit of rust, huge pickup trucks, and minivans with those stick figures on the back. It occurred to me that one of those vans would make an excellent cover and make it easy to haul firepower, but I didn't credit the enemy with that much creativity.

We were ten miles or so down the road when a black Cadillac sedan pulled onto the highway behind us. I lifted my binoculars to see if I could ascertain that Mannie was the driver when the headlights began to flash in an odd rhythm. It took me a second to realize it was Morse code.

G-O-O-D-J-O-B

I grinned. Yep, that was Mannie. I filled Ida Belle and Gertie in and they both relaxed some. Despite things being easy so far, I could tell that they were both as on edge as I was. Not that I blamed them. This was serious business. And with multiple factions at play—all unreliable—it just made things harder to predict.

We were twenty minutes from Sinful when trouble hit.

CHAPTER EIGHTEEN

A CAR HAD BEEN PARKED behind the embankment for an overpass. As we went by, it dashed onto the highway right behind us, intercepting Mannie in the process. There were metal guards low over the tires and I had no doubt the hood was reinforced as well. The windows were tinted so dark I couldn't see inside, but I had zero doubt as to who was in that car.

"Floor it," I told Ida Belle, and hopped into the back seat with Gertie.

The SUV leaped forward, pressing Gertie and me into the back of the seat as we peered over. Unfortunately, the car had something special under the hood because it lost only a little ground before covering the gap again. Mannie had dropped back, his sedan unable to keep up. Ida Belle's time machine was fast but the weight difference between it and the enemy's car evened them out.

Gertie and I aimed our pistols over the back seat and waited as Ida Belle lowered the glass.

"Aim for the driver's-side windshield," I said as I squeezed off a round.

The bullet hit the glass and bounced right off. The fact that the driver kept coming rather than slamming on his brakes told me everything I needed to know.

I cussed. "Bulletproof glass." I looked at Gertie. "Do you have the Eagle with you?"

"No," she said. "You guys kept complaining about me carrying it."

"She picks now to care what we think," Ida Belle said and handed me her .45. "Try this."

I didn't figure I was going to have any more luck with the .45 and I was right. I tried two rounds—one in the windshield and one in the hood—but both ricocheted off. Even worse, the car kept inching closer and I saw a pistol come out of the passenger window. Ida Belle didn't have guards around her wheels. If they took out one of her tires, then we were in trouble. The three of us and Mannie could probably handle one car, assuming we were all operational after the crash, but there was always the chance that this unit had already called for backup.

We had to dispatch them now or we weren't going to make it home.

Ida Belle must have seen the arm extending out the window in the other car because she began to do evasive maneuvers, swerving back and forth, making it harder for the shooter to hit his target. Gertie and I clutched the back of the seat as the SUV swayed, trying to keep our balance. Two shots rang out from their car, but both were misses. The arm ducked back into the car and I was afraid that was a sign that they were about to try something with more oomph.

"In the back of the SUV, pull up the carpet," Ida Belle said. "There's a rocket launcher under there."

I blinked. "A rocket launcher?"

"Gertie's not the only one who can shop illegally," Ida Belle said. "Hurry up before they take out a tire."

Ida Belle closed the back window so that the shooter couldn't see inside. I scrambled over the seat and pulled back the carpet, then wriggled around so that I could remove the cover. Sure enough, there was an RPG and a single rocket. I said a quick prayer of thanks and another that these women never stopped surprising me. I grabbed the launcher, got it loaded, and scrambled back over the seat where I'd have access to the sunroof.

Then I remembered Mannie.

I pulled out my cell phone and sent a text.

Hang far back. Now!

I saw Mannie's car drop away as if he'd slammed on the brakes, then I crouched on the back seat, ready to pop up, take aim, and fire. I told Ida Belle to open the sunroof and maintain a straight line. My pulse was racing as the sunroof opened, one thought flashing over and over in my mind—*you only have one shot*. As soon as I had clearance, I stood up and placed the launcher onto the roof of the SUV, then leaned in to take aim, said a quick prayer, and fired.

The rocket took off, sending me and the launcher tumbling down into the SUV and on top of Gertie. Ida Belle gave the SUV the last acceleration it had remaining and it leaped forward. Gertie and I scrambled up and peered out the back as the driver of the sedan slammed on his brakes and yanked the wheel to the side.

But it was too late.

The rocket hit the hood of the car and it exploded into a million pieces.

Gertie and Ida Belle both cheered and I managed a thumbs-up before collapsing into the bottom of the SUV. I hoped to God no one remembered that car and Ida Belle's

SUV because I had no idea how I would explain things to the police. I was pretty sure even Morrow couldn't make that one go away.

Mannie's car burst through the flames and smoke and Ida Belle slowed to a more manageable speed of a hundred miles per hour. We were only minutes from Sinful and unless there was a roadblock ahead, we were going to make it.

"Good Lord!" Gertie said. "I've never seen anything like that. It was fantastic! Can we do it again?"

"No!"

Ida Belle and I both responded at once.

"I'm hoping we don't have to," I said. "That's not the sort of attention I want to draw. Besides, using something of this caliber on a mostly empty stretch of road is one thing but using it inside the town limits would be very bad."

"You could point it at Celia's house," Gertie said.

I smiled. "Okay. Maybe one more."

IDA BELLE DROVE straight to my house and we hurried inside. Mannie arrived a few minutes later, explaining that he'd cased the block to make sure nothing looked out of place and all was clear. I grabbed us all a beer and Ida Belle, Gertie, and I sat at the table. I motioned to Mannie to take a seat but he shook his head.

"I have some things to do," he said. "Your package arrived, and I need to pick it up, assuming you still want it."

"Heck yeah," I said. Any diversion right now would be more welcome than a lottery win.

"And I need to call in some reinforcements in case that rocket of yours doesn't scare others off," he said and smiled. "Nice job, by the way."

"I can only take the credit for good aim," I said. "Ida Belle is the one who acquired the goods."

He raised one eyebrow at her. "We're going to make you into an outlaw. Just wait."

Ida Belle waved a hand in dismissal. "I've been an outlaw since the crib. I just don't flash my goods around all the time like some other people."

"There's no point in having goods if you're not going to flash them," Gertie said.

Mannie's smile wavered and I laughed.

Gertie looked back and forth from Mannie to me and frowned. "You know, if it weren't for Carter, I'd be thinking you two were a great fit."

Mannie continued to smile but shook his head. "I don't think so. Fortune is an exceptional operative and an even better human, and I'm willing to admit that my interest in her does exceed a professional capacity. But being in a relationship with someone like her requires a kind of strength I don't have."

Gertie nodded. "Translation—Fortune is going to give Carter a heart attack one day and Mannie doesn't want to go out that way."

"Something like that," he said.

He pulled out his phone and started a video. We all leaned in and saw Ida Belle and me pushing Gertie out of the hospital and into the ambulance.

"How did you know it was us?" Gertie asked.

Mannie raised one eyebrow.

"Never mind." Gertie waved a hand in dismissal.

"But that was you just getting started," Mannie said as he queued up another video. This time it was his view of the car chase after he'd slammed on his brakes. About two seconds into the video, the enemy's car blew sky-high. Gertie cheered at the video and Ida Belle grinned.

"That was even better the second time," I said.

"And therein lies my earlier point," Mannie said. "You ladies stay safe. I'll text you when I have the product in hand and you can let me know when I'm clear to deliver it."

"Thanks for everything," I said. "And please give our thanks to Big for letting us use his place and our apologies for not cleaning up before we left."

"We didn't even get our bags," Gertie said. "And I had my new sexy bra in it."

Mannie looked slightly dismayed. "My associate has collected all of your things and put the apartment back into its previous condition. I will bring your items when I deliver the laser."

"You need some of those associate people," Gertie said to me. "They get everything done."

"*You* are supposed to be my associate people," I said.

"Oh, right."

We all laughed and Mannie headed out.

"Good God, woman, break out the food before we all waste away," Gertie said.

"I have to agree with her," Ida Belle said. "Between the fear and the excitement, I've probably burned ten thousand calories today."

I got up and assessed the refrigerator. "Already cooked, I have leftover pot roast, four hamburgers and some franks, baked beans, and potato salad. What do you guys want?"

"Yes," Gertie said.

I laughed and started shoveling containers out of the refrigerator. Gertie and Ida Belle took over with the stove, oven, and microwave and before long, we sat down to our extremely late breakfast and lunch.

"This is better than the casino buffet," Gertie said.

"The school cafeteria is better than the casino buffet," Ida Belle said. "They plan for everyone to be half drunk and short on sleep. That way, they don't care about the food."

"Well, I'm not drunk but sleep is on the questionable side," I said. "Still, this all tastes better now than it did when I first had it."

"I hope you have dessert," Gertie said. "I'm going to need to wash all this protein and carbs down with some sugar."

"I have chocolate chip cookies and key lime pie," I said.

"Key lime pie?" Gertie said. "That's not your standard fare."

"Ally's trying out recipes," I said. "I am her helpful and thankful guinea pig."

"How do I get that job?" Gertie asked.

"If you started eating for Ally as well as yourself, I'd have to get stronger shocks on my SUV," Ida Belle said. "Just stick to your own fattening creations and leave testing Ally's stuff for when we're at Fortune's."

Gertie shrugged. "Works for me. We're over here all the time anyway."

"And that's about to become a more permanent thing," I said. "I can't risk you two staying alone. That stunt today shows just how desperate they're getting."

Gertie frowned. "Yeah, that was weird. Why were they trying to kill us? Dead people don't talk."

"I don't think that was their goal," I said. "I think they wanted to stop us somewhere on the highway and take me or all of us hostage. If someone died that would have been unfortunate but probably not the end of the world."

I heard a boat engine outside that seemed to cut off when it got near my house. I put my finger over my lips and got up to grab my laptop off the kitchen counter. I opened a blank document and typed.

No talking about my father except to misdirect.

I pointed to the kitchen window and they both nodded. If I could purchase a laser, so could the enemy.

"Well, I don't know what they think they're going to accomplish," Ida Belle said. "You are the last person your father would want to see."

"That's true enough," Gertie said. "Fortune would probably shoot him on sight."

"I don't know that I'd shoot him, but a hard right hook to the jaw is definitely in order," I said. "But you're right—even if he needs help, there's no reason for him to contact me, especially now that I'm no longer active. There's nothing I can do for him."

"Do you think he's a traitor?" Gertie asked.

"I don't know," I said. "And I don't care anymore. He made his choices. He can live with the consequences. I'm just angry that the rest of us have to live with them as well, especially you guys."

"It's not your fault," Gertie said. "None of it. You left that life."

"Yeah, unfortunately, it didn't leave me," I said. "But let's talk about something more cheerful. Gertie, tell me about that new television series you started watching. Is it any good?"

Gertie gave me a confused look and I pointed to the door and signaled for them to keep talking. Then I hurried out the front door and around the side of the house. I could use the hedges between my house and Ronald's to get close to the water. Maybe it was just a fisherman who'd stopped nearby to try his luck. Maybe it was someone who'd run out of gas. Maybe it was kids stopping to sunbathe or drink beer out of their parents' sight. But with everything going on, I had to be sure. There was only one highway into Sinful, but the hundreds of waterways that led to the town made securing it more difficult than it originally seemed.

When I got to the end of the hedges, I peered around and caught a glimpse of a boat just past my house and partially hidden by my giant oak tree. The engine wasn't running, but the boat wasn't anchored. It appeared to be moving with the flow of the bayou. A second later, the engine fired up and the boat took off away from my house. I ran to the edge of the water but barely caught a glimpse of the back of it before it rounded a corner in the bayou.

I headed back inside and waved Ida Belle and Gertie into the downstairs bathroom as it was in the center of the house and contained no windows.

"It was a white ski boat with blue and red stripes," I said. "That's all I could see before they took off."

"But they were stopped behind your house?" Ida Belle asked.

"I don't think so," I said. "I think they cut their engine right before they got here, then drifted back down the bayou."

"So your security camera wouldn't have caught them," Ida Belle said.

"No," I said. "Which I'm sure was intentional. I couldn't get a good look from the hedges, either. I ran to the edge of the water when they took off but only saw the tail end when they rounded the corner. I saw four figures in the boat but couldn't make out anything more."

"Could be kids out for a joyride," Gertie said. "They tend to do that in boats around here rather than cars, especially if it's sunny."

Ida Belle frowned. "A ski boat does sound more like kids but I can't think of anyone in Sinful who has one that looks like that. Gertie?"

She shook her head. "Doesn't ring a bell. We should ask

Walter. Scooter does a ton of boat repairs down at the shop. He might know."

Ida Belle pulled out her phone but Walter didn't answer. She left him a message to give her a call when he had a chance and then looked back at me.

"So I guess Gertie and I need to pack bags again?" she asked.

"I think that's the best idea," I said. "We're stronger standing together than each of us alone."

"Won't Carter mind us crashing your sexy house party?" Gertie asked.

"Carter minds all of this," I said. "But he wants you safe, just like me."

"Then we best get going," Gertie said. "I need to give Ally a call and ask if she can handle Francis a bit longer. Plus, it's going to take me a while to pack up my goodies, and I don't mean the eating kind although I'll be bringing some of those as well."

Ida Belle nodded. "I have a couple of nonedibles that I'd like to get in here as well."

"Do you have another rocket launcher?" Gertie asked.

"No. That was a onetime purchase," Ida Belle said. "And not a cheap one, either. Honestly, I don't even know why I bought it. I was on one of those deep web sites for gamers and military and someone had it for sale. Might have been an adrenaline high. I'd just beaten the crap out of most of them in our game."

"Well, I for one am thrilled you spent the money," I said. "Still a bit surprised, but thrilled."

"Oh, is that a tax deduction?" Gertie asked.

"We weren't on a case," I said. "And even if we had been, I'm not sure how 'rocket launcher' would look on a depreciation schedule."

"I just call everything office supplies," Gertie said.

"One day, you're going to get audited and they're going to put you in Martha Stewart prison," Ida Belle said.

Gertie shrugged. "I'll just smile and play dumb. Tax evasion is illegal. Not knowing how to interpret their stupid tax law isn't."

Ida Belle shook her head. "Let's finish up lunch and get going. Fortune needs to call Carter and try to explain all of this and she doesn't need us hanging around listening."

"You always make us leave when things are going to get good," Gertie groused.

I followed them back to the kitchen, frowning. There was nothing good about my upcoming conversation with Carter.

Nothing at all.

CHAPTER NINETEEN

I'd barely gotten Ida Belle and Gertie out of my house when I got an incoming text. Carter.

Explosion on the highway. Are you guys home?

I sighed.

Yes. You better get over here.

If Carter was alone, I could about imagine the string of expletives that were coming out of his mouth. He wasn't going to be any happier once he had the whole story. At least this time, he couldn't pin the blame on us. Not exactly. I mean we did sort of lie about why we really went to New Orleans but none of our trouble stemmed from that. We would have had fallout even if we'd stayed in Sinful. And it probably would have involved dead men on my lawn rather than pieces of men scattered on the highway. The second was easier to get away with.

I heard Carter unlock the front door and call out as he entered. I already had a shot of whiskey poured for him before he even got to the kitchen. He took one look at me standing there with the shot glass and sighed.

"How bad?" he asked.

I gave him the shot and waited until he got it down, then motioned for him to follow me. When I went into the bathroom, his eyes widened.

"Are you under audio surveillance?" he asked as I closed the door behind us.

"I'm not sure. There was a boat earlier that stopped right behind my house. With that kitchen window..."

He nodded. "You're right. Better to be safe. So what the hell is going on? Why are the state police scraping up bodies on the highway?"

I told him everything that had happened, only leaving out the stuff that had to do with Natalia. When I was done, he looked as if I should have brought the rest of the whiskey bottle into the bathroom with us. He stared at me silently for so long, I was about to check his pulse. Finally, he moved toward me and gathered me in his arms, squeezing me tightly.

"I'm so glad you're all right," he said when he finally loosened his grip.

"Me too," I said. "I have to admit, it was touch and go for a minute on the highway. If Ida Belle hadn't bought that rocket launcher..."

He flinched and shook his head. "I'm going to pretend I didn't hear anything about that and hope to God that the team working that explosion don't find any parts of the rocket they can identify."

"It was an explosion that killed people. They're going to keep looking until they find at least part of the device."

"Yeah, but if those guys are part of a terrorist cell, the experts will assume something went wrong with their own equipment. Or that a rival faction took them out. Assuming they can't locate a serial number."

"That would have been the first thing Ida Belle took care of. But you're assuming they'll be able to identify the men as part of a terrorist cell. My guess is the men and the car aren't accounted for anywhere in this country. So what happens then?"

"Assuming no one comes forward with a missing persons complaint that might fit, then it will probably go down as unsolved and ridiculously weird and get shoved in a box."

"Good enough for me."

"Okay, so this list your father gave you. Can I see it?"

I shook my head. "I stashed it behind a set of lockers at the hospital."

"Why would you do that? How can you get the information to Morrow if you don't have it?"

"I have it." I tapped the side of my head.

"I forgot about your recall. But are you certain you have the names right?"

I looked down. "They're hard to forget when you know them."

Carter rubbed his head and cursed. "You need to tell me those names."

"I can't. We both know everyone is safer if you don't know. Right now, no one but me, you, Ida Belle, Gertie, and my father know I have the information. If anyone else thought that, they would have popped me right on the balcony during the parade or in the casino."

"Then what was that stunt on the highway?"

"A kidnapping attempt is my best guess. A plot to draw my father out."

"They really don't know the guy, do they?"

"Understatement of the year."

"They're going to keep getting bolder," Carter said. "If your father doesn't manage to draw them off..."

I nodded. "I'm not worried about myself. But I *am* worried about Ida Belle and Gertie. The terrorists will take one look at them and think they're an easy target to get to me."

"That would be a mistake on the terrorists' part."

"It would be, but we don't know how many they'll send. I'm having them move in with me until this is over."

"That's a good idea. I suppose if worst comes to worst, it's all over in ten days."

"We can't let that happen. If their plan goes off, it could seriously cripple the US and our allies. I have to get the information to Morrow."

"But how are you going to do it? You can't go to DC. They'll shoot you as soon as you set foot off the plane or before you board. I suppose the military could land a helicopter in your backyard and take you to DC by military transport, but I'm guessing Morrow is being watched by more people than the Superbowl."

"Trying to deliver in person or by electronic methods aren't options, but there is a way. I just need some magazines."

"Magazines?"

"Yeah. Stuff a guy would read. Three would work. Current month editions."

"I can handle that. Are you going to write the names in the magazines then mail them to Morrow?"

"Sort of. Just get me the magazines and I'll explain."

"Is there anything else you need to tell me?" he asked. "I probably have a couple hairs left that didn't go gray while you were talking."

"Gertie won a motorcycle at the casino," I said.

He stared at me in dismay. "Way to bury the lead."

His cell phone rang and he checked the display and frowned. "I have to get to work but I will be back here as soon as I can be. Lock your doors. Turn on your alarm. And watch those cameras. If you see anything moving out there besides your idiot neighbor or that danged alligator that Gertie treats like a stray dog, arm up and call me. In that order."

"Can I fire first, if necessary?"

"I wouldn't expect any less. But maybe no rocket launchers in the neighborhood."

I shrugged. "She only had one rocket."

IDA BELLE and Gertie returned two hours later and it took us about forty-five minutes to unload Ida Belle's SUV. If the whole detective thing didn't pan out, we had enough inventory to open a gun shop. And maybe a bakery. There was a thought. Because who didn't love guns and pie? When we'd finally gotten everything sorted and positioned in the best location for each weapon, we flopped down in the living room with bottled water.

"I feel like I've lived ten lives in one day," Gertie said.

"If you're talking about some normal person's life, then maybe," Ida Belle said. "If you're talking about yours then this is maybe a week or two of it."

Gertie grinned. "We do have some fun, don't we?"

Ida Belle shook her head and looked over at me. "She's the only person I know who went to Vietnam and had fun."

"It's all in how you view life," Gertie said. "And how you want to feel about it."

"I view life from the breathing standpoint," Ida Belle said. "And so far, so good."

"How did your talk with Carter go?" Gertie asked.

"Better than I thought it would, actually," I said. "I think he was so happy we were all alive that he didn't want to say much about the why part of it all."

"Make sure he never sees that video Mannie took," Gertie

said. "He'll have you handcuffed to him day and night...oh, on second thought, maybe show him the video."

"How does he feel about our slumber party?" Ida Belle said.

"It's the same call he would have made," I said. "I know everyone around here looks at Carter and sees the genuinely nice guy with sometimes unlimited patience and a huge heart, and all of that is true. But he was still Force Recon. And no matter how you try to distance yourself, the training is there first, before anything else."

Gertie cast a nervous glance at the window and I knew what she was thinking.

I got up and walked over to the window. "While you guys were gone, I rigged up a little something to help with our audio concerns."

I lifted the blind and pointed to the window seal. "Didn't you notice that annoying rattle when you sat down?"

"As a matter of fact, I did," Gertie said. "I thought maybe a storm was coming up and you needed to check into replacing your windows up here."

"You're partly right," I said. "See here in the corner? I have the windowpane tethered to that fan. I removed some of the caulking so the movement of the fan causes the window to vibrate. That distorts the sound that a laser can gather."

Ida Belle gave me a nod of approval. "We're going to make a solid redneck out of you yet."

Gertie got up and walked over to the window for a closer look.

"The boat!" Ida Belle said, almost jumping in her seat.

"Did you hear back from Walter?" I asked.

"Yes. But he didn't know the boat," Ida Belle said. "But then I had an interesting conversation with Myrtle, and she said one of the petroleum engineers who is new to the area came into the sheriff's department this afternoon to report his boat stolen."

"Let me guess," I said. "He owned a white ski boat with blue and red stripes."

"You got it," Ida Belle said.

"Well, there's our answer," I said as I texted a message to Carter to let him know that it was better if law enforcement didn't try to stop that boat. No telling what kind of firepower it held.

"So I was right," I said. "Someone was checking up on us. Let's hope none of them are as bold as our friend in the casino."

"I'm hoping that guy is bird food on the highway," Gertie said.

Ida Belle nodded in agreement.

"So it's safe to talk in here now, right?" Gertie asked, and tapped the window. "This is so cool. Did you do the kitchen?"

"Yep," I said. "I'm glad Marge was hot-natured. She had fans everywhere."

"She wasn't hot-natured," Gertie said. "She had horrible gas. Eating all those greens has side effects besides good health."

I grimaced. "I'll file that under things I never wanted to know."

"Gertie's full of things you never wanted to know," Ida Belle said. "Most of them about herself."

"Did Mannie bring your special order yet?" Gertie asked.

"No. He should be here any minute though," I said.

"What about Carter?" Ida Belle asked.

"He got held up by the state police," I said. "They wanted his take on a mysterious car explosion on the highway."

"He probably has a cold sore from biting his lip," Gertie said.

I nodded. "By the time he got back to Sinful, he still had paperwork to do for a case going to trial next week that he had to finish today. He'd barely sat down in his office when he was summoned to the Swamp Bar. Apparently, there was a problem involving a boat, a keg of beer, two goats, and a naked woman."

"That sounds interesting," Gertie said.

"That sounds like some more things I don't want to know about," Ida Belle said. "Well, if history is any indication, Carter will be sorting that mess out for a while."

"That's what I figured," I said. "So I thought after Mannie leaves, maybe we could do a little surveillance ourselves. You know, get back to being the spies, not the ones spied upon."

Gertie looked excited for a moment, then sobered. "Do you think it's safe?"

"I don't see why not," I said. "We're going to enlist Phyllis's help, so all it will look like is three people going to visit a friend."

"Carrying a large case," Ida Belle said.

"Right," I said. "Which is why we'll also be carrying food and a bottle of wine and we'll be putting something extra on the case."

I went to my office and returned with a colorful sticker for an essential oil company.

"Genius," Ida Belle said. "They'll think we're having a hen party."

"That's pretty smart," Gertie said. "But you should have made it something cooler, like one of those sexy toy companies."

"That would be the biggest mistake ever," Ida Belle said. "This town likes to pretend it disdains such things, but you know as well as I do that if anyone saw Fortune with a case with that sort of label, the race would be on to get a peek inside of it. Everyone runs when someone mentions essential oils. Now, there's an idea. Maybe I should become a salesperson. Would cut down on all that social stuff people keep inviting me to."

"So we're really going to do this?" Gertie asked.

"Of course," I said. "Why wouldn't we?"

She shrugged. "I don't know. I guess I just figured with everything else you've got going on, you might just leave this thing with Katia to Carter."

"Carter has so many law enforcement irons in the fire right now that he doesn't have the time he needs to devote to that case. If it turns out something shady is going on with Larry or with this questionable coworker of Katia's, we're in a better position to find out than Carter."

"And since we aren't hindered by things like the law, we can do it quicker and more efficiently," Gertie said.

I cringed a little at her comment about the law, but she wasn't too far from the truth. I certainly didn't mind skirting it or outright jumping over it if it got the job done.

"We do have an advantage," I said. "All we need to operate on is speculation and we've got plenty of that. Carter needs hard evidence to make certain moves."

Ida Belle nodded. "Besides, Carter's attention is split right now with trying to do his job and worrying about you."

"Worrying about someone else is far worse than being the one worried about," Gertie said.

"So we're agreed," I said. "We visit Phyllis and see if we can get anything from Larry and Natalia. If we get something that Carter can use to make a move on, then we'll fill him in on the what and the how."

"Maybe you can handle that one," Gertie said. "And then I can avoid him for a while afterward."

"That's going to be hard to do when you're sharing the same coffeepot," Ida Belle said.

There was a knock on my front door and I got up to let Mannie in. "I'll handle Carter. Let's just concentrate on getting him enough information to put the person who killed Katia behind bars."

Mannie came in and we gathered in the kitchen as he placed the case on the table.

"It has instructions," he said. "They're all basically the same but I'd scan them for the few differences that equipment sometimes has."

"I will. What do I owe you and how do you want me to get you the money?"

"35k but I'll get with you later on the money."

He glanced at the window, and I knew he was thinking that someone could be outside with the same equipment, listening to everything we were saying. I walked over to the window and lifted the curtain to show him my additional makeshift window dressing.

"Clever," he said. "Have you seen or heard anything since you've been back?"

I told him about the boat and he frowned.

"I figured they would move in soon," Mannie said. "But I still don't like it. I think I'm going to stick around Sinful tonight. Keep watch on things."

Gertie shook her head. "I don't think there's any room left at the inn."

Mannie smiled. "I doubt the good deputy would approve of my taking up residence here. But I'll be fine. I've managed in far worse."

"Nonsense," Ida Belle said, and pulled her keys out of her pocket. "Here's the keys to my house. It's sitting empty and at least you'll have a place to eat, shower, and sleep if you want to."

"Thanks," Mannie said, and took the keys. "That gives me a

base for operations. I'll probably patrol tonight and perhaps I can get a few hours of sleep tomorrow. I'm going to head out now. You might want to let your neighbors know that your third cousin is visiting."

"Good idea," Ida Belle said, and pulled out her cell phone. "God knows, I don't want anyone accosting you with a gun, trying to play hero."

"I promise not to kill any of them," Mannie said as he opened the front door. "It's bad manners unless your name is on the deed."

After he left, we took my new toy and scanned the instructions, then ran a few tests with it in the house as well as the backyard, checking first for unwanted visitors. The clarity was really amazing. Somewhat unfortunately so, we found when we turned it on the back window of Ronald's house and got a blast of him singing opera.

"Where do you think they are?" Gertie asked as we stepped back into the kitchen.

"I don't know," I said. "Watching the highway for sure. The only other way in is by boat, so all they'd have to do to cover the bayou behind my house is keep both ends in view."

"That's not going to be as easy in stolen property," Gertie said.

"I let Carter know not to approach them," I said. "He sent me a thumbs-up, so he understood the message."

"Hopefully, they'll stay on land, and no one sent for your father will draw the attention of Deputy Breaux or Sheriff Lee," Ida Belle said.

"Carter instructed them to report any strangers directly to him and said I had been notified of a potential problem due to my previous line of work," I said.

"That probably scared Deputy Breaux into staying inside

the sheriff's department unless absolutely necessary," Gertie said.

"He's better off there," I said. "Everyone is better off staying out of this. So, the sun's down. If you guys are ready to get this show on the road, I'll pop on that sticker and we can get to work."

"Do you want me to give Phyllis a call and let her know we're coming?" Gertie asked.

"No," I said. "It's harder to say no when people are standing in your doorway."

Ida Belle grinned. "You're getting good at this small-town thing."

CHAPTER TWENTY

The lack of notice turned out to be unnecessary. Phyllis was thrilled to see us. Her forty-six cats were not. At least it seemed like forty-six. She claimed it was her baker's dozen, which Gertie explained to me meant thirteen, but I wasn't convinced. Every item that could hold a cat on top of it or under it had eyes glaring at us. I only had one cat and barely made it out of the bedroom every morning without physical damage. I was surprised Phyllis was still alive.

"Come in, come in," Phyllis said, dithering all the way back to the kitchen. "I just made a batch of sweet tea, or if you're dieting, I have some unsweet tea or water, or if you'd like, I can make coffee. While you're thinking on that, let me put out some goodies."

Phyllis began shoveling food from her refrigerator and her kitchen counter onto the table at an alarming rate. "Let me just grab a few more things out of the utility-room pantry," she said, and hurried off.

"She has more food here than a hotel buffet," I said. "All that can't be just for her. Does anyone else live here?"

Ida Belle shook her head. "Her second husband died about ten years ago."

"Diabetes?" I asked.

"Because he wanted to," Gertie said.

Ida Belle elbowed her as Phyllis came hurrying back into the room with boxes of crackers.

"I have plain and wheat and some kind of three-grain thing," she said. "I haven't tried them but I saw on Facebook that they are great with cheese. Anyway, sit, please, while I pour the drinks and we can catch up. It's been a while since you came for a visit."

"Wasn't planning on coming again until her wake," Gertie said under her breath, and Ida Belle elbowed her again.

"Actually," Ida Belle said, "we didn't come for a chat."

Phyllis froze and her face fell. "No?"

"No," Ida Belle said. "We came about your neighbor, Larry."

Phyllis flushed. "What's he done now? The man is a menace. He yelled at me the other day for standing in my own backyard."

"You were just standing there?" I asked.

"I might have been on top of the picnic table," Phyllis said. "But that's just because I was checking my roof. You never know when you might be missing a shingle."

"Uh-huh," Ida Belle said. "Anyway, I'm not sure if you've ever met one of our new residents, Fortune Redding." She pointed at me.

"Not officially," Phyllis said. "But, of course, I've heard all about you—CIA. So exciting! Next time one of my cats is missing, I know who to call."

I just nodded and Gertie coughed, holding in a laugh.

"Well, Fortune is now a private investigator and opened her own firm recently," Ida Belle continued. "She has a client who needs information on Larry and we were hoping to enlist your help."

Phyllis's eyes widened. "You want *my* help?"

"Yes," Ida Belle said. "Your help could make this case. *But...* everything has to be confidential. You'll need to sign a form stating that you'll never repeat anything you saw or heard here."

"Not even to the police?" Phyllis asked.

"Not unless they ask specifically," Ida Belle said. "Client confidentiality is very important in our line of work."

"So you two work with Fortune?" Phyllis asked. "Are you detectives as well?"

Ida Belle shook her head. "We're analysts, which means we assist on investigations but we're not licensed."

"But you still get to go along and do things, right?" Phyllis asked. "I could do that. Hey, I want to be an analyst. I probably have a résumé somewhere. Let me go look."

"I'm not hiring right now," I said. "The business is just getting started and I don't have enough clients to hire more personnel. But if it grows enough that I need to add people, you'll be the first person I think of."

As the person I would never, ever hire.

Phyllis bounced up and down, causing her bun to come loose and trail down her back. She grabbed the offending wad of hair, twisted it around on top of her head, and stuck a bread knife through it. I made a mental note to never eat bread at her house.

"So what can I do?" Phyllis asked. "What do I need to sign?"

I pulled out the fake confidentiality document that we'd put together and handed it to Phyllis. "You can have your attorney go over that, if you'd like. But if you do, we won't be able to enlist your help. Unfortunately, my window of opportunity is closing for my client, so I have to get information tonight, or I'll have to let the client know I can't help them."

Phyllis ran for the counter, yanked a pen out of the drawer, and signed the document without even reading a single word. Then she thrust it back at me.

"His other wife is your client, isn't she?" Phyllis asked. "I knew I was right about him. It's all going to come back to roost. 'Don't gossip, Phyllis.' 'You're crazy, Phyllis.' Well, we'll see who's crazy once you're done exposing Larry Guillory for the bigamist that he is."

"I can't divulge my client's name or their interest," I said.

Phyllis winked. "Of course not."

I held in a sigh. If we didn't get out of this woman's company soon, I was going to need a drink. Maybe even a horse tranquilizer.

"So what do I need to do?" Phyllis asked.

"Nothing at the moment," I said. "What I really need is access to your backyard."

"Oh." Phyllis looked somewhat disappointed. "That's it?"

"For now," I said. "But in a few days, I might need you to tell me about Larry's comings and goings."

Phyllis pointed to a notebook on the counter. "I've been keeping a log. I can tell you every time that man has left or entered the house for the last three months."

"You don't sleep?" I asked.

"Yes, of course," Phyllis said, "but I set up one of those nanny cams in my bedroom window. It overlooks the front of their house."

"That's very interesting," Ida Belle said.

"That's scary as hell," Gertie mumbled.

"Well, the back door is right there," Phyllis said and pointed. "Do you want a tour?"

"No. I'm pretty sure I can figure it out," I said.

Since there wasn't an inch of space left on the kitchen table, I pulled out a chair and sat the laser case on it. Phyllis leaned over to look at the logo and blushed.

"Essential oils..." she stuttered. "I don't think...I mean..."

I held in a smile. Even crazy Phyllis had an aversion to the essential oil movement.

"Don't worry," I said. "That's just to throw people off. People don't ask questions if they see the logo."

"I would imagine they don't speak at all," Phyllis said.

I flipped the lid back and Phyllis looked in the case, her expression like a five-year-old on Christmas day.

"Oh," she said, now frowning. "What's that?"

"A laser," I said.

Her eyes widened and she gasped. "You're not going to kill him, are you?"

"Of course not," I said. "I'm just going to direct this over your fence and try to listen to any conversation occurring inside the house."

"This thing can do that?" she asked.

"I hope so," I said.

She ran her finger down one of the legs on the stand. "Can I get one of these at Walmart?"

"They're more of a special-order sort of thing," Ida Belle said. "If you have the right military connections."

Phyllis looked disappointed and I said a silent prayer of thanks that the Phyllises of the world couldn't afford military hardware.

I set up the laser and recording device and prepared to head out the back door.

"I need Ida Belle and Gertie with me," I said. "Phyllis, if you could watch the front to make sure no one is lurking around, that would be great. If you spot a vehicle you don't recognize, let Ida Belle know."

"You mean there's other people checking up on Larry, too?" Phyllis asked.

"We think so, and we don't want to cross paths with them," I said. "They might try to steal our ideas."

"And they're all Yankees," Gertie said.

Phyllis drew herself up straight, her jaw set. "We'll just see about that," she said as she stomped off to the front door.

"Nice," I said to Gertie as we headed outside.

I scanned the backyard, trying to determine the best place to attempt to use the laser, and finally settled on the far back corner that contained a huge oak tree. The porch lights from the houses didn't reach that far and the tree would provide me some cover without getting in the way of the signal. I was pleased to see that cheap Larry's security concerns only extended to a camera at the front of the house. The back was clear.

"Let's drag that picnic table under the tree," I said.

The table was surprisingly solid and fairly heavy, but we managed to get it under the tree and next to the fence.

"This should give me enough height to get the laser directed at the kitchen or bedroom window, depending on where we see movement," I said.

I pulled the laser and tripod out and set them up, then did the same for the receiver. I adjusted the height and aimed for the kitchen window, since that was the one with a light on, and then hooked up the recording equipment. Lastly, I put on my headphones and handed Ida Belle a pair.

"Handle the receiver," I said.

"Why can't I handle the receiver?" Gertie asked.

"Because you couldn't read the display even if we gave you the Hubble telescope to look at it with," Ida Belle said.

"Fine, I'll get new glasses," Gertie said. "Then you two will have no excuses for leaving me out of the fun stuff."

"I need you on field ops," I said. "First, go make sure that Phyllis is watching the front, and then check yourself since I don't exactly trust Phyllis's idea of questionable activity."

"Phyllis is a nutbag," Gertie said. "But at least she's impressionable. She took to your story in a heartbeat. What do I do after checking on Phyllis?"

"Take position at the fence gate," I said. "Open it a crack and watch for any passing cars that you don't recognize or suspicious people walking by."

Gertie set off across the lawn to the house and I looked at Ida Belle, who pulled her headphones in place and gave me a thumbs-up. I powered up the laser and checked the aim again, then prayed someone was in the kitchen talking about something besides the weather or what to eat for dinner.

"Look," Larry said. "I'm sorry about Katia but she never should have come here. After what happened with Annika, why would she put you at risk?"

"She was scared," Natalia said. "I think something was wrong."

"Of course something was wrong," he said. "I told you years ago that the two of them were up to their neck with people that you don't play around with—Mafia, drug traffickers, and God only knows what else. You left the company yourself because you had too many questions about their practices. They chose to stay, and if that's what they wanted to do with their lives, then it's none of my business. Until they bring it to my home. Have you forgotten that you almost died when you ran off to New Orleans against my wishes to meet Annika?"

"Of course I haven't forgotten. I sent my sister home to my parents in an urn!"

"And she almost took you with her. Your daughter would have grown up without a mother. I thought that would prove to you just how dangerous it was to be involved with them. You should have sent Katia packing. She's shown no interest in you since we married. Why come here now?"

"Maybe she needed to regroup."

"Well, you see how that worked out. Your daughter witnessed a homicide. The woman's chest practically exploded right next to her."

"Stop! Just stop! Do you think I wanted any of this? But I couldn't turn her away. She was like family. I never thought—"

"And that's your problem. You've never thought. I always suspected that if the situation arose, you'd put Katia ahead of Lina and me, and now I know for sure. I'm not going to pretend that we have any big romance. I know you married me to get out of Russia. But I thought we were reasonably happy, and once you had Lina, that changed everything. It's not about you or your sister or her childhood friend anymore. It's about our daughter."

"If I didn't know any better, I'd think you were happy Katia is dead."

"I don't like how it happened, but I'm not about to mourn the loss of someone who brought serious trouble to my family's doorstep. The sooner she's in the ground and that nosy coworker of hers is out of this town, the sooner we can get back to our lives. And they'll be much safer now that no one is left to bring their bad choices here."

"I hate you!" Natalia screamed.

A door slammed.

"You reap what you sow," Larry said quietly, even though the room must have been empty.

Ida Belle looked up at me and mouthed, "Wow."

I nodded and pointed to the light that went on in the bedroom. I shifted the laser to the bedroom just in case Larry followed Natalia to continue the fight but instead, I heard what appeared to be Natalia on a phone call.

"I can't hold any longer," she said. "As soon as the police are done with this investigation, I'm leaving."

There was a pause as she listened, then she spoke again.

"You think I don't know that?" she said. "But what am I supposed to do? No judge is going to give me custody of Lina. Not with Larry's connections. Besides, for all his faults, Larry loves Lina. She'll be safe with him."

Another pause.

"Can you get everything in place in time?"

Then everything went silent for a while. The light was still on in the kitchen and I could see Larry's lone shadow, which meant Natalia had left the room or something was interfering with the signal.

Then I saw two shadows in the kitchen again and moved the laser back to the kitchen window.

"I'm going out for a while," Natalia said.

"At this time of night?" Larry said. "Where are you going?"

"Nowhere," Natalia said. "I just need some air."

"Now is not the time to be gallivanting about," Larry said.

"Why not? The enemy is dead, as you just reminded me."

The door slammed and I assumed that was Natalia leaving. Then I heard Larry again, apparently on a phone call.

"We've got a problem with Natalia," he said.

There was a pause, then Larry spoke again.

"You know she hasn't been right since her sister was killed. But it's getting worse. I can't continue to take these risks with Lina."

Then his shadow disappeared from the room and everything went silent.

No! I couldn't miss what was happening now. It might answer everything.

"Stay here and keep recording," I said to Ida Belle, and hopped over the fence just as Gertie was returning from inside.

"Where's she going?" I heard Gertie ask.

I didn't hear the answer because I was creeping down the dark side of the yard toward the house. I hadn't seen a shadow in the bedroom so I assumed Larry had moved to the front of the house, maybe the living room. If I could get over the fence and down the side of the house, I might be able to hear through one of the living room windows on the side.

But as I approached, I heard a car slam on its brakes and then Natalia started to yell.

"What are you doing out here spying on me, you crazy old bat!" Natalia screamed.

Crap! I had no doubt Phyllis was the culprit. She'd breached the front window and must be out in her yard taking notes as Natalia was trying to make her getaway.

"I...you..." Phyllis stuttered, then I heard the front door of her house slam and assumed she'd retreated inside.

The car screeched off and I heard stomping inside the house, moving to the back again. I crouched down behind a trash can and next to the fence, waiting to see where Larry landed. Unfortunately, he landed in the backyard. The back door banged open and I saw a spotlight start sweeping the yard. The laser equipment was mostly camouflaged by the tree, but Ida Belle was on the ball and I saw the equipment disappear from the fence line. Unfortunately, Larry appeared in the middle of the backyard and then turned my way.

"Are you out here, you psycho?" Larry called out. "I've had it with your meddling."

I yanked out my cell phone and sent a text to Ida Belle and Gertie.

Trapped on far side of yard. Need a diversion now!

CHAPTER TWENTY-ONE

I PEERED around the trash can and saw Larry swing his light toward the fence then start walking my way. What worried me wasn't the spotlight in his left hand but the nine-millimeter in his right. He had every right to shoot me, and after what had happened to Katia, no one would blame him. But I had no reason to shoot Larry, nor did I want to. And that's where things got sticky.

I heard movement in the middle of Phyllis's yard and saw a cat fly over the fence and drop onto the ground. It froze for a moment, probably still trying to figure out what the heck had happened, then the fence panel where the cat had appeared from broke off of its posts and fell over into Larry's yard, Gertie clinging to the top of it.

As the cat shot off toward the back of the property, Larry swung around in Gertie's direction with the spotlight. I used that moment to scale the side fence to the front yard, then ran around to Phyllis's house. I barreled through her gate, then hurried to the fence disaster, praying I got there before Larry decided he'd had enough conflict for the night.

When I got to the broken fence panel, Gertie was kneeling

with her hands up in the air. Ida Belle was standing close by, trying to talk sense into Larry, who appeared to be completely out of sorts.

"I couldn't find him up front," I said as I stopped, then turned to the side and pretended to see Larry for the first time. "What the heck?"

"Answer me," Larry said, looking down at Gertie. "What are you doing spying on me?"

"She's not spying, you nut!" Ida Belle yelled. "She's looking for Phyllis's stupid cat."

"You're lying," Larry said.

"Good God Almighty, man," Ida Belle said. "What has gotten into you? Gertie climbed the fence to see if the cat was in your backyard. That's it."

"And if you weren't so cheap, the thing wouldn't have collapsed," Gertie said.

"Not helping," I said, and kicked her foot.

"I'm sick of that woman poking her nose into my business," Larry said. "She's always there at the window with her notebook, spying, making notes. She's nuts."

"Of course she's nuts," I said. "Why do you think we're out here trying to find her cat? If we don't, she'll be knocking on the door of every house in Sinful. I'm sorry the fence broke. I'm sure we can find someone to fix it, but you need to put that gun away."

"Where's my baby?" Phyllis ran out the back door of her house, wailing.

I cringed. The last thing we needed was Phyllis and her crazy out here in the middle of this. I saw something move across a patch of dirt at the back fence line and pointed. "There!"

Phyllis practically ran across the yard and scooped up the cat, then ran past us, shooting daggers at us as she went.

"I accidentally let him out," Gertie said. "I think she's mad."

Larry stared at all of us for several seconds longer, then threw his hands in the air. "You're all mad! Just get off my property. I have enough to deal with right now without all this tomfoolery going on."

We headed back into Phyllis's yard and waited until Larry went back into the house before attempting to retrieve the laser. I sent Gertie to turn off Phyllis's back porch light but Phyllis was so mad about her cat that she wouldn't open the door. That didn't deter Gertie for a minute. She picked up a garden gnome and smashed the light bulb. I could hear Phyllis wailing inside but that didn't matter. Ida Belle and I gathered up the equipment and headed for the back door.

"She's done lost her mind," Gertie said.

"She never had it," Ida Belle said.

"Well, I need the case for this laser, so opening that door isn't an option," I said.

"We've got bigger problems than the case," Gertie said. "My purse is in there."

The thought of an angry and emotional Phyllis alone all night with Gertie's purse had me pulling out a knife and jimmying her back door. It's a good thing that Phyllis was as cheap as Larry about some things. A five-year-old could have managed it.

I pushed the door open and walked inside. Phyllis stood in the middle of the kitchen, clutching the cat in one arm and an iron skillet in her other hand.

"Are you going to cook us to death?" Gertie asked.

"You tried to kill my baby!" Phyllis wailed. "Now you've broken into my house. Get out or I'm calling the police."

"You mean you're going to call Fortune's boyfriend?" Gertie asked.

Phyllis stared at us in dismay as she remembered the connection.

"We're only here to retrieve our property," I said. "Just calm down. We're leaving as soon as we get everything we came with."

I packed the laser and we headed for the front door. I looked back at Phyllis, who was lurking in the kitchen doorway, and said, "Remember the agreement you signed. You say nothing about what happened here tonight. Are we clear?"

I didn't especially like scaring her, even though she was an idiot and probably deserved just a little payback for all the aggravation she must heap on her neighbors every day. Her eyes widened and she swayed a bit. I figured it was best to get out of there before she passed out so I closed the door and we hurried to Ida Belle's SUV. I wondered if Larry was watching us leave or if he was back on the phone with whomever he'd called, trying to figure out what to do about Natalia.

"Well?" Gertie asked as we drove away. "Did you get anything or did I risk poor Mr. Pickles and that shred of sanity that Phyllis is holding on to for nothing?"

I looked back at her. "Mr. Pickles?"

"Shred?" Ida Belle asked.

She waved a hand in dismissal. "Come on. Stop holding out. Anything?"

"Plenty," Ida Belle said. "And if we only knew what it meant we might be in good shape."

"I'll play everything for you as soon as we get back to my place," I said to Gertie. "I need to hear it all again to try to get a handle on it and I want your input."

When we arrived at my house, Gertie practically jumped out of the SUV and sprinted for the porch.

"What's taking you guys so long?" she complained.

I hurried up the porch with the laser, unlocked the door,

then turned off the alarm. As soon as everyone was back inside, I locked the door, pulled the dead bolt, and turned the alarm back on. We headed to the kitchen and I grabbed my laptop.

"Let me do a quick sweep of the cameras before we get started," I said, and queued up the security camera footage for the time frame we were gone.

"It's going to take forever to watch all that video," Gertie said.

"I don't have to watch it all," I said. "Just when they detect movement."

I scanned the couple of places where the recording was flagged for movement but two were stray cats and one was a bass boat cruising past. I recognized the guy as a regular at the café, so nothing concerning.

"Maybe they decided to step back," Ida Belle said when I closed the laptop.

"Wouldn't you when you heard about the exploding car?" Gertie asked. "Maybe they had misgivings about just how far Fortune would go. I seriously doubt they have them now."

I nodded. "It's possible the rocket sent a message to hold position. And since I came home instead of boarding a plane, they have no reason to assume that my father ever made contact."

"And I guess they're not worried about email or phone because they can intercept it on one end or the other," Gertie said. "So maybe you're in the clear?"

"We won't know that until the big day passes," I said. "Until then, we have to stay alert. Now, who wants to hear the argument between Larry and Natalia?"

Gertie's eyes widened. "An argument? Woo-hoo! Fire it up!"

Ida Belle had already grabbed us some sodas and put a

container of cookies and a bag of chips on the table. Gertie and I looked at her and she shrugged.

"I felt like something salty," she said. "You need peanuts or something."

"I'll add them to the grocery list," I said as I pulled out the recording device and set it to play.

Larry and Natalia's voices sounded out, clear as day, and we all sat stock-still, listening to the entire exchange, then their individual phone calls. Ida Belle hadn't captured anything after I left, so that was it. When it was done, I looked at them.

"What are your thoughts?" I asked.

"Sounds like Mannie was right about Katia and Annika being into shady business," Ida Belle said.

"No wonder Larry was mad," Gertie said. "First his wife goes against his wishes to meet her sister and almost dies, then this childhood friend shows up and there's another murder."

I nodded. "I don't think I'd want anyone from Natalia's past showing up either, given those odds, especially since she worked for that same company for a while."

"Do you think she quit because she caught on to the shadiness?" Gertie asked. "Maybe that's the real reason Annika and Katia didn't visit her. She married Larry to get away. And if they moved around a lot, which is kinda what it sounds like, maybe she didn't tell anyone where she was. Remember her driver's license when she was attacked had her old address but they were getting ready to move again. No telling how old it was."

"Entirely possible," I said. "And given that Larry's line of work is intel, he might know things about the company and even about Katia that Natalia doesn't. For all we know, he could have been aware of problems with the company back when Annika was killed, which would explain his anger over Natalia meeting her sister in New Orleans against his wishes."

"So given potential inside knowledge of the corporation's sketchy dealings and Annika's death, if he thought Katia's presence posed a threat, how far would he go?" Gertie asked.

"I think if a man knew that a person posed a threat to his family then he might do a lot of things he wouldn't otherwise," Ida Belle said. "The real question for me is not *would* he do it but *could* he? Meaning could Larry make that shot? Was he confident enough to risk that kind of shot with his daughter right there?"

"Without knowing the full nature of Larry's job, it's hard to say what his training might have entailed," I said. "A lot of tech intel still have to go into the field because they're the only ones who can reprogram equipment on the fly. If Larry was trained for fieldwork, then he would have spent some time on the firing range. And despite his geeky appearance, Gertie saw what kind of shape he's in. What if the computer geek story is a complete fabrication to cover his real job? It wouldn't be the first time."

Ida Belle nodded. "He also claims he's retired and clearly that's not true either. Not completely."

"Maybe when he leaves and goes to DC he's not necessarily going to DC," Gertie said. "He could be roving all over, doing the kind of work Fortune used to do. For all we know, he could be the geeky James Bond and whoever he works for gave him the order to kill Katia."

I shrugged. "Anything is possible."

"Well, he had motive and opportunity," Ida Belle said. "We do know that. Natalia was looking for Lina's jacket but why wasn't Larry there with his family? I don't think anyone has ever said."

"I bet Carter knows but he's not going to tell us the answer," Gertie said.

"It wouldn't matter anyway," I said. "If Larry is the one who shot Katia, he's hardly going to say that's what he was off doing. He'll claim he was in the porta-john."

"True," Ida Belle said.

Gertie frowned. "Why not just tell Katia to leave? I mean, unless it was a job-related hit. He didn't have to let her in the front door if he didn't want to."

"That's a good point," I said. "But it's clear from their conversation that their marriage is on the rocks. Maybe Larry was afraid to turn her away because he thought it would send Natalia packing."

"It sounds like Natalia is out the door anyway," Ida Belle said.

"And leaving her child behind," Gertie said. "That's desperation. But if she already had someone arranging things, why didn't they plan for Lina as well?"

"Natalia said to whoever she called in the bedroom that Lina would be safe with Larry because he loved her," I said. "Which indirectly implies Natalia *isn't* safe with Larry because the feelings aren't the same. Do you think a domestic abuse situation is possible?"

"I hate to think it, but I guess so," Gertie said. "Maybe that's the real reason they move a lot and don't socialize with locals or send Lina to public schools. It's easier to keep things hidden if people can't see them."

"But if Larry is abusing Natalia, then what was his phone call about?" Ida Belle asked. "Based on his comment, it had to be someone familiar with Natalia and her medical issues after her sister's death."

I nodded. "And there's something strange about that conversation. Here, listen."

I played back the piece of recording where Larry made the phone call. "Did you catch that? Larry said 'we've' got a problem with Natalia. Not 'I've.'"

"You're right," Ida Belle said. "That is strange."

"It can't be anyone from Natalia's family," Gertie said. "They cut her off when she came to the US, and even Natalia said how she'd lost everyone after Katia was shot. So who the heck was Larry talking to?"

"That's a darned good question," Ida Belle said.

"An even better one is who was Natalia talking to," I said. "If she supposedly had no one left, then who did she trust with an escape plan?"

"A secret friend?" Ida Belle suggested. "Women's organization?"

"Both possible but difficult to keep a secret from someone with Larry's skill set," I said. "And here's another thing to consider—how stable is Natalia's mind? Larry said on that call that she'd never been the same since her sister's death, and if that's the case, this shooting could have sent her right back over the ledge. Remember, Detective Bishop said she was practically hysterical in the hospital, so her desire to run could be a factor of an unstable mind and not necessarily a long-term plan."

"PTSD?" Gertie suggested.

"Given the situation, I imagine that would be high on the possibility list," I said.

"Considering what Mannie told us about Katia and Annika possibly being spies, maybe Larry was talking to his superiors," Ida Belle said. "They could be coming down on him because of Natalia's prior connection with the company, especially with Katia killed on his watch."

"I hate to think it was Larry who killed Katia," Gertie said. "But it does make more sense than someone tracking Katia to Sinful and taking a shot at her during a local parade."

"Except someone *did* track Katia to Sinful," I said. "Vitali Fedorov was here when she was shot."

"That's right!" Gertie said. "Good Lord, how does he fit into this?"

"I wish I knew, because it presents a whole different set of options," I said. "Natalia said she thought Katia was in trouble, and if that was trouble on the professional side of things, then maybe the company sent him to do cleanup. But there's another option."

"Which is?" Gertie asked.

"What if Katia and Fedorov were involved?" I asked.

"But you said Fedorov denied having a relationship with Katia," Ida Belle said. "Wouldn't you have been able to tell if he was lying?"

"I thought Fedorov was lying about everything," I said. "I got the impression he was playing a role and it's something he's used to doing. Assuming he's been trained on how to evade questioning, I might not be able to pinpoint which statements are lies. In his case, the entire exchange came across as ungenuine."

"So if Fedorov and Katia were involved, maybe she was looking for a place to hide because she was afraid of him," Gertie said. "Given what the company is suspected of, Katia would have known what Fedorov was capable of, right? Maybe it's that simple—that she was running from him."

"Entirely possible," I said.

Ida Belle sighed. "We have a whole lot of suspicion but no actual proof."

"That seems to be our status quo," I said.

"I thought this detective thing would get easier when we had more experience," Gertie said.

"I think the problem is that people are the ultimate variable," Ida Belle said.

"Maybe you can coerce something out of Carter tonight,"

Gertie said. "Use your weapons...and I don't mean the metal ones."

"I don't think I have anything on my person that's going to make Carter give me information on an open investigation," I said.

"Then you're not using them right," Gertie said.

"You're underestimating Carter's stubbornness and honor," Ida Belle said.

"You're underestimating his being a man," Gertie said.

CHAPTER TWENTY-TWO

CARTER DIDN'T GET to the house until close to midnight and I could tell he was exhausted. Ida Belle and Gertie had retired to their rooms thirty minutes before, and I'd showered but couldn't wind down enough to attempt sleep. He was hungry when he got there, as he usually was when he'd been slammed all day and had barely managed to fit in a bag of chips or a protein bar. I fixed him up a plate of leftovers and set it and a beer in front of him at the kitchen table. Then I grabbed a bottled water for myself and sat across from him.

He stared at the table for a couple seconds, then turned around and looked at the window. "What is going on with that window?"

I showed him the fan and explained about the caulk removal.

"Smart." He picked up his fork and sighed before taking a bite.

"I don't want to be that person and ask if it was a rough day," I said. "So I'll just skip the pleasantries and get right to asking what happened with the car explosion."

He shook his head. "Aside from the frame of the car and a

couple of larger metal pieces, there is nothing left that you couldn't fit into a shoebox, including the occupants. You've succeeded in making three state troopers and one forensics guy sick. They were still looking for pieces of people when I left."

"And do the state police have any thoughts on what happened?"

"None. The VIN on the car is gone, as is the license plate, so no way to track things down by the owner. No one thinks this was a manufacturer's error, though."

"How could they? No manufacturer gets it that wrong."

"So I'm sure they're thinking explosive and targeted, but they can't figure out what kind of explosive."

"How hard do you think they're going to look?"

"Hard to say. The problem is not being able to identify the driver or any passengers. They don't know how to prioritize something when they don't know who the victim is."

"Is that supposed to matter?"

"It does in Louisiana, especially if the victim has any political connections."

"So other than waiting to see if someone comes up on a missing persons report, what else can they do?"

"Nothing much. My guess is a team will work the wreckage and if no one raises the alarm over someone important disappearing into the fine Louisiana sunset, they'll eventually shove it all in boxes and label it unsolved."

I nodded. "Best possible outcome for us."

"You know, normally I would be all angry and ranting about Ida Belle having a rocket launcher in her SUV, but I have to say, in this case, I'm kinda happy with her and Gertie's absolute disdain for the rules."

"Me too. What about the Katia situation? Anyone on the potential arrest list yet?"

"You know I can't discuss the case, but I will tell you that it's not going anywhere fast."

"The general gossip is that Katia was running with a dangerous crowd and she showed up here to evade them."

"Well, if that's the case, she didn't do a very good job."

He motioned to the magazines on the table. "Did you work your magic there yet?"

"Yes. And I'm going to need another favor tomorrow."

"What kind of favor?"

"You're always so suspicious. This is an easy one. I just need you to mail these magazines. No postage needed. Just send them the way they are. But you have to make sure no one is watching you because it's imperative that they're not intercepted."

He picked up the magazines, then flipped them over and looked at the stickers with Morrow's home address and postage on the back.

"Is the information taped in the magazines?" he asked.

"No. Before I resigned my position, Morrow and I established a covert method of communication in the event that either or both of us was under surveillance and couldn't use normal channels, even those that were previously assumed to be safe."

"So you have some sort of code?"

I nodded. "We went old school. Invisible ink indicates the lines he needs to take the letters from. The code we established will give him the order."

"How will he know the magazines are from you?"

"I'll use another established tip in a phone conversation I'll have with him tomorrow. He'll know to be on the lookout for something out of the ordinary."

"In this case, the magazines."

I nodded. "But to the enemy, it just looks like a regular subscription delivery."

Some of the tension went out of his shoulders and he shook his head. "That's genius. It was so smart of you and Morrow to establish a method of communication before you resigned."

"Well, we couldn't be certain that the Ahmad issue wouldn't resurface in another form. I don't think either of us imagined we'd be using the plans for this reason, though."

"How could you? Last time I checked only one man came back from the dead."

"Yeah, well, leave it to my father to try to one-up Jesus."

Carter gave me a sympathetic look. "I'm so sorry about all of this. I hoped after last year that things could settle into some sort of normal."

"Me? Sinful? Normal? Isn't that asking a lot?"

"Probably. So let's change the subject to something more pleasant. What did you guys do tonight?"

Made a crazy lady sign a fake contract. Illegally listened in on Larry and Natalia. Almost got shot. Scared at least five lives out of Mr. Pickles.

"Nothing much," I said.

"That sounds lovely."

I nodded. It would have been.

CARTER and I turned off all the lights downstairs and prepared to head up to bed when I heard a noise outside. I signaled to the backyard and pulled out my gun. Carter grabbed my laptop and thrust it at me so I could access the cameras. I accessed up the two covering the backyard but didn't see any movement. Then over in the corner of the backyard, near the bayou, I saw a figure standing in the shadows. It was cloudy, so the moonlight barely trickled through, but there was no doubt in my mind that it was a person standing there.

I pointed to the hedge with the shadow and motioned to the front door. We separated in the front yard, each heading around the house in a different direction. We didn't know if the man was alone or working with someone and couldn't afford for either of us to be flanked. I was on the side where I'd identified the threat. Carter had taken the unknown. I skirted silently down the hedges toward the bayou, thankful that moonlight was at a premium and that I'd been required to do this so many times that I knew the way by heart.

I stopped about twenty feet from the place where I'd seen the shadow and waited for any sign of movement. Finally, I heard the rustling of footsteps on leaves just ahead of me. Then another set off to my right, coming from Ronald's yard. Even farther out to my left near the bayou, I heard movement as well but couldn't see anyone.

I inched closer to the movement ahead of me, figuring that was the shadow I'd seen. Whoever was on my right in Ronald's yard was still on the move but not very quiet. I could easily discern every step and gauged the distance from me at about twenty feet. As I eased toward the end of the hedge, the steps to the right picked up speed and a man burst through the bushes right in front of me, crashing into the shadow person.

I froze. That couldn't have been Carter. He was on the other side of the house and darn well knew how to be quiet when he walked. So was it another terrorist? Was there infighting among the foot soldiers? Suddenly, the moon peered out from behind the clouds and I got a good look at what was happening on my lawn.

Two men were locked in a battle on the ground. The one who'd gotten knocked down had the guy on top of him by the throat. I didn't recognize the guy doing the throttling but the guy on top was wearing camouflage gear and a motorcycle helmet. The pink ballet slippers gave him away.

Ronald.

What my insane neighbor was doing tackling strangers in my yard I had no idea, but what I did know is that he'd picked the absolute wrong time to be nosy. The guy strangling him wouldn't loosen his grip until Ronald had taken in his last breath. I stepped out of the hedge and leveled my pistol at the enemy.

"Let him go or I blow your head off," I said. "And you know I can."

He rolled over, taking Ronald with him, then rose up, dragging Ronald in front of him as a human shield. Ronald was limp and I worried that it was too late, but then he coughed. The enemy immediately shoved a gun to Ronald's head and started walking backward, dragging Ronald with him.

The helmet made it impossible to get a clear shot of the enemy's head, and his gaunt body was blocked by Ronald's larger frame and overabundance of gear attached to his camo. I followed him, gun leveled at Ronald's head, waiting for an opening. Because I had no doubt that when he got near the bank, where he must have a boat stashed, he'd ditch Ronald and take a shot at me.

It would be the last shot he ever tried to take.

We were a couple feet from the bank when trouble arrived in the form of a partner in a boat with a rifle trained on me.

"What are you waiting for?" the guy who had Ronald yelled. "Shoot her!"

Before he could even finish the sentence, a shot rang out and I immediately dropped and rolled behind the grill. I popped up to look and saw the guy in the boat fall over the side and into the bayou. The guy who had Ronald flung him to the side and ran for the boat. I sprang up and took aim but my bullets weren't necessary.

As soon as his foot hit the water, Godzilla launched up and grabbed his arm. He screamed and dropped his pistol, trying to wrench his arm from the gator's powerful jaws. I steadied my aim, just in case he was able to work himself loose, but Godzilla didn't disappoint. The gator yanked the man backward, then whirled around in the water and dived, dragging him under the murky water.

Carter ran up as the bubbles rose and I hurried over to Ronald, who was struggling to stand. I grabbed his shoulder and helped steady him. He pulled off his helmet, threw both arms in the air and gave a loud woot.

"Did you see that?" he said. "That gator saved my life. I love him! I love Godzilla."

He turned around and took off for his house.

"Wait!" Carter yelled. "Where are you going?"

"I have to bake a casserole," Ronald said. "That's what he likes, right?"

He didn't even wait for a response. In fact, he shifted from a fast walk to skipping and singing. I looked over at Carter, who was staring, mouth open.

"Can I please shoot him for trespassing?" I asked.

"I have a feeling it would save both of us a lot of trouble in the future, but I'm pretty sure we're not supposed to do it," he said.

"What about for wearing ballet slippers to accost terrorists?"

"That one might actually be on the books."

The back door banged open and Ida Belle and Gertie ran out with pajamas on, curlers in place, and guns drawn. Carter took one look at them and smiled.

"The cavalry is here," he said.

Gertie scanned the yard, looking for something to shoot. "We always miss all the fun. Why didn't you call us when the targets showed up?"

"There were only two of them," Carter said. "I got one and Godzilla handled the other."

"We saw from the upstairs window," Ida Belle said. "Might be the highlight of my year, but the year's still young."

Gertie stared at the bayou and shook her head. "That man is going to be really bad for Godzilla's digestion. He's used to eating cooked food."

"Don't worry," I said. "Ronald is off to bake a casserole. He's a big fan now."

Gertie looked dismayed. "I hope he doesn't think that means we're friends or something. I can't be seen talking to Ronald. I have a reputation to protect."

"Are you wearing Deadpool pajamas?" Carter asked.

Gertie grinned. "Sexy, aren't they? Comes with the mask, but I thought it would get in the way of my aim."

Carter looked slightly pained.

"So how do we handle this..." I waved my hand at the bayou. "Whatever this is?"

Carter blew out a breath. "There's a good question."

"Are you going to sweep for the bodies?" I asked.

"No point," he said.

Ida Belle nodded. "Tide's going out. They'll be in the lake by now, except for what Godzilla consumed."

It was probably wrong of me, but the last part of her statement made me smile.

"So two unknown suspects attempted to break into Ms. Redding's home and were accosted by her neighbor and a rogue alligator," Ida Belle said.

"Godzilla's not a rogue," Gertie said. "Clearly, he's a trained watch-alligator."

"He *is* more efficient than a dog," Ida Belle said. "That I'll give him."

I nodded. "And no cleanup required."

Carter sighed. "I just shot a man. I have to go in and write this up. I'll figure out something."

"If Ronald hadn't witnessed the whole thing, we could have just pretended it didn't happen," Ida Belle said.

"That situation could be rectified," Gertie said.

"No rectifying Ronald," Carter said. "I need you three to get inside, secure the house, and don't come out for any reason."

"No need to," Gertie said. "Obviously Godzilla has things under control."

We went back into the house and Carter grabbed his keys, gave me a kiss, and left. I locked everything up, turned on the alarm, and then headed for the kitchen to fill Ida Belle and Gertie in on what they hadn't seen. Finally, all three of us were yawning so bad we couldn't finish a sentence.

"Let's go to bed," Ida Belle said. "Surely no one else is going to attempt anything tonight."

"We don't even know what they were attempting," Gertie said.

"And we never will, but I'll bet it was nothing good," I said.

"I can't believe Ronald is cooking for Godzilla," Gertie said as we headed upstairs. "My, how things can change."

"He was still lurking around my yard," I said. "In ballet slippers."

"Some things will never change," Ida Belle said.

We headed into our rooms and I closed the door and hopped into bed. The sheets were nice and cool and I was definitely exhausted, but as I lay there, I couldn't get my mind to stop whirling. I'd had entirely too much input in a short amount of time. And although I would never admit it, seeing my father face-to-face had affected me more than I'd expected it to. It was one thing to think the only parent you had left had chosen a dangerous mission and died rather than stick to a desk job and raise you, and it was a whole other thing to realize he'd faked his death and abandoned you. But seeing him had brought out so many emotions I didn't realize were still lurking within me. Mostly anger. But with a large dose of hurt.

Finally, I gave up, threw the covers back, and headed downstairs. As soon as all of this was over, I was getting a television in my room. I don't know why I hadn't already. There were too many nights I needed a distraction, and Carter couldn't be there for all of them. Plus, sometimes he wasn't the kind of distraction I needed. Like now. He'd know something was bothering me and would ask. And I wasn't ready to talk about the things that were bothering me the most.

I slumped onto the couch and turned on the television to the Hallmark mystery channel. It was innocuous enough to put me to sleep but not nearly as annoying as those Christmas movies Gertie loved so much. I stared at the screen, not really listening, and eventually drifted off to sleep.

When you're nearing the end, always go back to the beginning.

The words from one of those mysteries were echoing in my mind as I drifted into consciousness...with a horrible crick in my neck. It took me a minute to realize that I wasn't in my bed but half sitting, half lying on my couch. And the angle I'd finally arrived at was the reason for my neck protesting. I sat up and moved my head from side to side and finally felt that big pop that let me know everything was back in the right place.

I looked at my watch and saw it was barely even 6:00 a.m. Carter had never shown up and I figured that meant he'd spent a long night at the sheriff's department. I checked my cell phone and saw a text from him at around 4:00 a.m. saying that something had come up and he probably wouldn't see me until early morning. That probably meant soon, so I headed into the kitchen to put on coffee. It wasn't as though I was going back to sleep. I had important business this morning.

I heard Carter's truck pull into the drive, disarmed the alarm, and opened the door to let him in. He gave me a hug and quick kiss before sniffing the air.

"Is that coffee I smell?" he asked.

"I just put it on. Are you hungry?" I asked as we headed for the kitchen.

"Not really. More sleepy than anything. Hopefully I can grab a couple hours at lunch."

I poured us both a cup of coffee and we sat at the kitchen table. "You have to go back to work right away?"

He nodded. "Something came up with the case."

"Katia's case?"

"Yeah. The company she worked for is under investigation by the FBI."

"For what?"

"Channeling money for the wrong people."

"You think she was going to blow the whistle?"

He hesitated, then nodded. "I shouldn't be telling you this and I expect you to keep it confidential—and that includes Ida Belle and Deadpool."

"My lips are sealed until the case is closed."

"Larry's government work is intel and he's not exactly retired, even though that's the story he puts out there."

"So the theory is that Katia was going to give Larry information and someone capped her?"

"It fits the narrative for that set of facts but I'm afraid that's all I've got—a nice story." He frowned. "Then there's something else."

"What?"

"In checking with previous neighbors, a few of the women have speculated that things were odd in the Guillory household."

"Odd how?"

"They weren't sure but one of them said that Natalia had a certain look that reminded her of herself before she left her abusive husband."

"You think Larry is a wife beater?"

"It would put an entirely different spin on things, if you assume that shot was intended for Natalia and not Katia." He watched me for a moment, then narrowed his eyes. "You don't seem remotely surprised by any of this."

"I was a CIA operative, my father just returned from the grave, and I've been living in Sinful for months. Very little surprises me anymore. But I hadn't failed to notice that Katia and Natalia were dressed alike, with similar builds, and both had long blond hair in ponytails. From a distance, in the dark, and with Katia standing there with Lina, it would have been easy to make a mistake."

"Professionals don't usually make those kinds of mistakes."

"Snipers have an entirely different scope of training. But a civilian hit can still have professional qualities and human error."

"True. Which leaves me with a whole lot of nothing to move on."

I nodded. I knew all about the whole lot of nothing he was dealing with and I had more information than he did.

"Did you call Morrow yet?" Carter asked, changing the subject.

"I was about to. I wanted to do it before Ida Belle and Gertie got up."

I retrieved my cell phone from the living room and dialed

Morrow's number. It was early, but I knew he'd already be awake. He answered on the first ring and I leaned closer to Carter so he could hear.

"Good morning, Director Morrow," I said.

"Fortune," he said. "I was going to call you today."

"Do you have an update?"

"A small one. We know Dwight entered the country from Mexico but we lost his path in Houston. With Houston's proximity to Louisiana, I was concerned, but then we received word last night that he was spotted in DC. Have you had any trouble?"

Relief coursed through me when I realized that for once, my father had lived up to his word. He was on radar, and this conversation with Morrow would ensure anyone gunning for him knew the last place he'd been seen. The best part—it was nowhere near Sinful.

"I had to dispatch a couple of people yesterday," I said. "There's not going to be any way to identify them."

Translation—bad guys are dead and there's not enough left to run through databases.

"Do you need a cover story?" Morrow asked.

I looked at Carter, who shook his head.

"At this point, it's been handled locally. I'll let you know if that situation changes."

"Of course. Has there been any attempt at contact?"

"No. But then we never expected it, right?"

Morrow was silent for a couple seconds. "I know this has been hard on you. Are you doing all right?"

I smiled because I'd managed to direct the conversation exactly where I wanted it to go. This single exchange between Morrow and me had the potential to get the heat off me and move the entire bumbling contingent of terrorists to DC.

"That depends on your viewpoint, I guess," I said. "I went

to New Orleans this past weekend with some friends to check out the whole Mardi Gras thing, and I thought I saw my dad in the crowd. I ran after this guy like an idiot but given the celebration, probably fit right in."

"What made you think it was him?"

"The guy looked a little like him but in rethinking things, I'm sure it wasn't. He's just occupying so much of my mental space that I'm probably seeing things."

"Well, you were at Mardi Gras. I hear there's drinking involved."

"Oh yeah. And plenty of it."

"What about the nudity?"

"Saw it. Didn't participate in it. Mostly wishing I hadn't seen it, either."

"I hear it's quite the show. I'm sorry, Fortune, but I have to get to a meeting. If you see or hear anything, please let me know. And if you want backup, just say the word. The agency is working on this round the clock. I'm going to get answers for you, Fortune. I promise."

"Thanks."

I hung up and Carter raised one eyebrow. "That's it?" he asked. "How did you tip him off?"

I gave him a sad smile. "You didn't catch it? The key word was 'dad.' I never refer to my father that way."

Carter gave me a sympathetic look. "Did you and Morrow establish that tip after your father was spotted on that security camera?"

"No. Before that. We knew that under dire circumstances, I couldn't exactly call and mention the weather or my bad back or any other regular sort of conversation item because Morrow and I just don't talk that way. But given that he was my father and the CIA golden boy, mentioning him wouldn't set off alarms. I just didn't figure that I'd be using him as a pass code and he'd also be the reason for the usage."

He took my hand into his and squeezed. "You had the plan in place. That's what's important. And now Morrow will be looking for the information you sent. You've done everything you can do."

I nodded. But I still wasn't convinced.

"And this time, your father came through," Carter said.

"Too little, too late."

"It's never too late to do the right thing."

CHAPTER TWENTY-THREE

After my phone call with Morrow, Carter headed out with a thermos of coffee and a sandwich bag of cookies. It wasn't the best breakfast, and I'd even offered to cook him some eggs, but he'd said he'd grab something from the café later on. After he left, I knew I was in trouble. I wanted to clean something. I never wanted to clean anything unless I was avoiding something worse. In this case, thinking about the potential attack on world leaders and thinking about my father. I didn't even have space left to *not* dwell on the whole Katia situation.

I had emptied the contents of the refrigerator onto the counters and was scrubbing the shelves when Ida Belle and Gertie made their way into the kitchen. They took one look at me and Gertie shook her head.

"She's cleaning," Gertie said. "This isn't good."

"Or she's really, really hungry," Ida Belle said, sifting through the goodies on the counter.

"Eat anything you want," I said. "That was my plan. Then I have less to put back in the fridge."

Gertie frowned. "Yeah, but I'll be doing more laundry on all those new clothes I'd need if we ate all of this."

"Your pants have elastic waist, don't they?" Ida Belle asked.

"It's not only about fitting into pants," Gertie said. "It's also about how I look in the nude."

"God willing, no one is going to see you in the nude anytime soon," Ida Belle said. "Now, grab a fork and dig in."

"I guess it *is* months until bikini season," Gertie said.

"It's decades *past* bikini season for some of us," Ida Belle said.

I finished up with my cleaning session, grabbed a fork and a pan of blackberry cobbler, and sat at the table with Ida Belle and Gertie.

"Is Carter still sleeping?" Gertie asked.

"No," I said. "He came and went a little while ago. He's hoping to catch a nap later today, but with everything going on, who knows."

Ida Belle shook her head. "Between the car explosion and Godzilla's midnight snack, I'll bet he's used up all of his creativity brain cells."

"Are they going to drag the bayou for the bodies?" Gertie asked.

I nodded. "The game warden is coming in with some men to help. They'll do a surface search as well as a drag. What are the odds that they find anything?"

"Slim to none," Ida Belle said. "Godzilla took that guy off to store for later. The one Carter shot would have been swept into the lake. After that, who knows where he could wind up. But it won't take the critters long to pick the bones."

Gertie nodded. "This is a *really* good place to hide a body."

"Oh well," I said. "We probably couldn't have ID'd them anyway and ultimately, it doesn't really matter who they were. We already know why they were here."

"That's two down last night and we're not sure how many

on the highway," Ida Belle said. "You'd think they'd back off, right?"

"And they might," I said. "I talked with Morrow this morning. He said my father was spotted in DC."

"Do you think the right people heard the call?" Gertie asked, looking excited.

I nodded. "There's no doubt in my mind that information has filtered back to all interested parties, including my admonition that while I'd dispatched a couple of bad guys, I hadn't seen or heard from my father."

"Do you think it's enough to draw them off?" Ida Belle asked.

"I think it's enough for them to back off at least," I said. "If they revert back to observation only, then we only have to wait this out nine more days."

"Lord, it's like I'm five years old and waiting for Christmas Day," Gertie said. "Nine days can't pass soon enough."

"And in a complete turn of events, Carter divulged some information on the Katia case," I said. "Not much that we didn't already know—Larry being intel and Katia's company being under investigation—but he talked to some former neighbors and some of the women seemed to think things weren't right in the house. One suggested that perhaps it was a domestic abuse situation. She said she recognized the look on Natalia's face as she'd worn it herself for years."

"That is interesting," Ida Belle said. "And something we had already considered, but it holds more weight coming from others who probably had them under observation for longer than we have."

"So what do we do?" Gertie said.

"I honestly have no idea," I said. "I think this is the part where we have to do what the police do—sit and wait."

"I'm horrible at sitting and waiting," Gertie said.

"It's not my strength either," I agreed. "Unless, of course, I'm aiming."

My cell phone rang. Mannie.

"How are things there?" he asked as soon as I answered.

"We had a little excitement last night," I said, and gave him a summary of the Great Alligator Takedown.

"You know, just when I think things can't get any stranger, you manage to top yourself."

"Technically, that one's all on Godzilla."

"The fact that you've named an alligator is enough."

"Good point," I said.

"Please tell me your security camera captured all of it," he said.

"It did and it was quite the show, which we enjoyed one viewing of before deleting. Having evidence around that would conflict with whatever Carter files in his report isn't a good idea."

He sighed. "You're right, but I mourn the loss."

"What about you?" I asked. "Did you see anything while roving around Sinful last night?"

"Apparently not the good stuff," he said. "But I did see something odd. I went out to that motel to check in on our friend Fedorov. When I exited the highway, I saw a car getting on and I swear it looked like Larry Guillory driving."

"Older-model white Accord?" I asked.

"Yep."

"What time was that?"

"About nine thirty."

I frowned. Not long after we'd left Phyllis's house. But what would Larry want with Fedorov?

"Did you try out the laser?" Mannie asked.

"Yep. Used it on Larry and Natalia last night," I said, and filled him in on the conversation.

When I was done, he whistled. "Looks like our friend Larry is in this up to his neck."

"He's definitely up to something. Did you find out anything on Fedorov?"

"Very little. He's a Russian national and has worked for the company for fifteen years. Transferred to the New York office from Moscow ten years ago. Other than that, he's a blank slate."

"Amazing how many people who work for that company have an aversion to social media, right?"

"Any developments with your father?"

"According to Director Morrow, he's been spotted in DC."

"So maybe you're off the hook."

"I hope so. That alligator can only hold so many bad guys."

He chuckled. "I'll check in later. Tell Ida Belle her guest accommodations are excellent and I appreciate the loan."

I repeated Mannie's conversation and Gertie shook her head.

"We should have stuck around Larry's house last night and followed him," she said.

"Don't you think he would have noticed?" Ida Belle asked. "Not much traffic around here that time of night. And even less exiting the highway for that hotel. Heck, Larry already thinks we were spying on him and he didn't seem all that stable last night. If he caught sight of us following him, no telling what he'd do."

"She's right," I said. "Larry is hostile and a potential killer. We can't follow here like we can in a city."

"We need those trackers like what was on Ida Belle's car," Gertie said. "Then we could follow people."

"You need to know who you're following and the time and ability to get the tracker on the car," I said. "I doubt we could have managed the installation on Larry's vehicle. Not with that security camera up front."

"Then let's be proactive," Gertie said. "Let's just put a tracker on everyone in Sinful. That way, when someone is doing a dirty later on, we're ready."

Ida Belle and I stared at her.

"Yeah, that's a little too Cold War Russia for me," I said.

"It's too everything for me," Ida Belle said.

"Well, we have to do something about Larry," Gertie said. "Why would he be going to see Fedorov if they weren't in cahoots?"

I frowned. "That's a good question."

I grabbed my phone and called the motel, then asked for Fedorov.

"I've been calling him since yesterday and he doesn't answer, but I'm sure he was staying there. Can you call his room?"

The clerk did so and came back on the line.

"I'm sorry, but he's not answering," he said.

"Look, I know this is asking a lot, but could you send someone to check his room? He's a diabetic and he never remembers to take his meds. He missed a very important appointment this morning and I'm afraid something is wrong."

"Lady, I don't get paid to babysit."

"I guess I could send the police. They'll break down the door, of course, and sometimes they notice other things when they're on a call..."

"Let me get my keys. What's your number?"

I gave him my number and disconnected.

"I guess we're in the sitting and waiting mode again," Gertie said, and sighed. "This detective work isn't nearly as exciting as it looks on TV."

"Nothing is as exciting as it looks on TV," Ida Belle said. "That's why it's fiction."

Ten minutes later my cell phone rang and I could barely make out what the clerk was trying to say because of his breathing. Finally, he managed a coherent statement.

"Your friend is dead!"

"Oh no! Are you sure? Did you call for an ambulance?"

"Look, lady, I'm not doctor but there's a bullet hole right through the middle of his head. That's dead and no ambulance is going to fix it. What the hell do I do?"

"Call the police," I said. "Make sure no one else goes in the room and write down everything you touched when you went in."

"Yeah, yeah...I can do that."

The call disconnected and I looked at Ida Belle's and Gertie's shocked faces. They'd been able to hear everything.

"Dead?" Gertie said. "Larry must have killed him. But why?"

I shook my head. "Maybe because Fedorov knew Larry had killed Katia?"

"But if Katia had gone rogue and Fedorov was sent to deal with her, why would he care if Larry did the dirty work?"

"He wouldn't," I said. "And he wouldn't let on that he knew about it, either."

"Which means Larry must have seen Fedorov in Sinful sometime that night," Ida Belle said.

"And Fedorov saw him," I said. "If Larry thought there was any chance Fedorov knew he'd killed Katia, he couldn't afford to let him leave and tell what he saw."

It sounded right but felt wrong. But I couldn't figure out why.

Ida Belle's phone rang and she cringed. "It's Phyllis."

"Answer," I said. "You can ask her about Larry's movements

last night."

Ida Belle answered but couldn't even get a word past hello in before Phyllis started shouting.

"I could hear them screaming," she said. "Then there was a loud crash and she ran out of the house and tore out of here like a crazy woman. Then Larry comes out of the house a couple minutes later, blood all over his face! He got in his car and drove off after her. He's going to kill her! I knew it. She found out about—"

Ida Belle hung up and we all jumped up from the table.

"We have to find Natalia before Larry does," I said.

"But we have no idea where she's going," Gertie said.

"She's in a car," I said as we jumped into Ida Belle's SUV. "And there's only one way out of Sinful. Head for the highway."

Ida Belle tore through downtown, collecting a couple of dirty looks and the finger as she blew by, but as far as I was concerned, there were no casualties so no harm, no foul. We hit the highway and I grabbed the binoculars but couldn't spot Natalia's car anywhere.

"Keep driving," I said. "She can't be that far ahead."

I pulled out my cell phone and called Carter but it went to voice mail. I cursed and left a message but I couldn't give him any more information than what we had. I looked again and spotted a car that might be Natalia's several miles up the road.

"There!" I said.

Natalia was pushing her econobox to the limit but it was no match for warp speed on Ida Belle's SUV. I stopped looking when the speedometer passed 130 and just prayed that none of the local wildlife chose that moment to cross the road. I scanned the highway again for Larry's car but didn't see it.

"She's turning off," I said, and pointed as Natalia's car barreled off the highway and onto the service road, kicking up grass as she ran off the exit lane a bit.

"Where the heck is she going?" Gertie asked.

"I thought you could tell me," I said as I texted the exit number to Carter. "What's that way?"

"A couple of camps and an old marina," Ida Belle said.

"Escape by boat," I said. "That's the best bet in these parts. Hard to follow if you don't have one and hard to find if you don't know those channels like the back of your hand."

"You can bet Larry doesn't know them at all," Gertie said. "I've never even heard him mention fishing."

"Where is Larry?" Ida Belle asked as she took the exit. "I figured he would be right behind her."

A thought occurred to me and I turned around with my binoculars just in time to see Larry's car come over a rise in the highway.

"He doesn't have to keep up," I said. "He's got a tracker on her car. That's why he didn't go after her last night."

"You think so?" Gertie asked.

"If he takes this exit we'll know for sure," I said. "No way he had a visual on her when she left the highway."

"Well, he didn't count on us being in between," Ida Belle said. "At least we'll be able to get to her before he does."

"And then what?" Gertie said. "Do we hold him off until she gets away?"

"Seems like the best plan," I said.

Ida Belle turned onto the road Natalia had used and we bumped along the dirt and weed path.

"The turnoff for the marina is just ahead," Ida Belle said. "But I don't see Natalia's car anywhere. And everything's so dry I can't tell which way she went."

"Do the camps down here have docks?" I asked.

"Probably," Ida Belle said. "I haven't been down these channels in a while though. I have no idea what kind of shape they'd be in. For that matter, I don't know that the marina is functional either."

"I fish this way sometimes," Gertie said. "There's docks at all of them. They're rickety but they exist. All Natalia needs is deep enough water and a place to jump in from. It's not likely she has designer luggage to worry about."

"Take the turn for the marina," I said, praying that I was making the right decision.

Ida Belle hung a hard right and Gertie and I held on tight. A couple minutes later, she slid to a stop in a small clearing in front of the bayou. Several dilapidated piers stretched out along the bayou. But there was no sign of a boat or Natalia.

"She must be using one of the camps," Ida Belle said as she turned around and headed back for the road.

"I hope Larry hasn't caught up with us," Gertie said, echoing my thoughts.

My phone rang and I checked the display, hoping it was Carter, but it was the nurse who'd taken care of Natalia after her attack. I braced myself to keep from bouncing and answered the call.

"Ms. Redding, this is Gilda Jackson. You had some questions about Natalia Guillory?"

"Yes, Ms. Jackson. Thanks so much for calling me back."

"Is this a good time?" she asked. "You sound a little strained and it's a bit loud."

"This is fine," I said. "My friend's vehicle has a loud engine is all. But I'm not driving so I'm okay to talk."

"I'm not sure you're okay to ride," Gertie said as we hit a large hole in the road and both went flying off our seats.

"I just wanted to know if you observed anything odd while you were caring for Natalia," I said. "I'm a private detective and there's some question as to whether the attack on her and her sister was random or not."

"You think someone was after her?"

"Yeah, pretty sure." *Especially as we're hoping to keep him from killing her right now.*

"That's horrible," Gilda said. "I do remember the girls. Hard not to, such pretty young women and an awful tragedy like that. We lost the sister before we could even get her to surgery. There was so much blood we couldn't even tell how bad off they were until we removed the hair. But the sister's gash was so deep that she'd lost too much blood. That poor woman fell apart when she found out her sister hadn't made it. Then her memory being off—I really felt for her and her husband. I can't imagine waking up one day and not knowing my family or having one of my family wake up and not know me. It was hard all the way around."

When you're nearing the end, always go back to the beginning.

I sucked in a breath as Gilda's words registered and then everything lined up, just like a winning pull on a casino slot. But surely, that couldn't be? Could it? But it was the only thing that made sense.

"Gilda, I'm so sorry, but we're having some car trouble and I'm going to have to call you back."

I disconnected and made a mental note that I owed the poor woman a call and an explanation as soon as this was over. I hoped that explanation didn't include another body.

"How far away is the camp?" I asked.

"There are two down here," Ida Belle said. "The exit for the first is coming up soon. There!"

She slowed down and I studied the dirt but couldn't tell if anyone had just passed there. "Which one has deeper water?" I asked. No way Natalia was trying to escape on a bass boat.

"The next one," Gertie said. "The channel gets wider there."

"Are you sure?" Ida Belle asked.

"Positive," Gertie said. "I lost a new rod and reel there. It was too deep to fish it out."

"That one," I said. "The deep one."

Ida Belle pressed the accelerator a bit more and we continued straight. "What's wrong?" she asked as she glanced over at me.

"I'm afraid we might have been mistaken," I said.

"About what?" Gertie asked.

"Everything," I said.

All of a sudden, Ida Belle's SUV rounded a corner and burst into a clearing, almost on top of Larry's car. Gertie yelled and Ida Belle slammed on the brakes. We slid to a stop just inches from his back bumper and Gertie pointed and yelled.

"Over there!" she said.

I looked to the right and saw Natalia grab a backpack from her car. A speedboat was waiting at the dock, a man I didn't recognize behind the wheel.

"Where's Larry?" Ida Belle asked.

"There!" I pointed to a figure slumped on the ground in the brush just to the side of Natalia's car.

"We can't let her get away!" I yelled and jumped out of the SUV.

"What?"

I heard Ida Belle and Gertie yelling behind me but I couldn't stick around to explain. I dashed over to Larry and saw the gunshot wound in his stomach. He groaned and stared at me, disbelief filling his expression.

Ida Belle and Gertie rushed up behind me and dropped down next to Larry.

"Get pressure on that wound," I said as I jumped up.

"He doesn't even have a weapon," Gertie said. "Why would Natalia shoot him?"

"That's not Natalia!" I yelled as I took off for the dock.

CHAPTER TWENTY-FOUR

ANNIKA HEARD my decree and swung around. She sneered when she saw me and fired a couple shots. I dived behind a tree, rolling over, and popped up as she ran for the dock. The driver of the boat had ducked down when the shots began and now peered over the edge of the boat, his expression full of shock and fear. Clearly this was not what he'd signed up for, which gave me an idea.

I shot a single round over the boat, just inches from his head. He screamed and reached for the starter. A second later, the boat roared to life and in his desperation, he gunned it. The boat shot away from the dock, but the steering wheel must have gotten turned because the boat swung around in a tight circle, then came straight back at the dock.

Annika dived out of the way as the boat hit the old ramp and launched up the incline and onto the bank. The boat prevented me from seeing where Annika was but I assumed she would make a run for her car. Sure enough, a couple seconds later, I heard her car engine rev and she threw it in Reverse. The car shot backward for a couple feet, narrowly missing Ida Belle and Larry, then seemed to lag before moving forward.

I ran from behind the tree, ready to shoot out the tires, when I realized the tires were already flat and the car was barely able to move in the dirt and rocks that formed the driveway. Annika jumped out of the car, took another shot at me, and sped off for the woods. I leveled my gun but couldn't pull the trigger. She had fired at me, but she wasn't now. And given my credentials, I couldn't afford to shoot her in the back. That was a hole even Carter couldn't dig me out of.

I turned up the speed as I ran after her but just before she reached the tree line, her feet flew out from under her and she tumbled backward onto the ground. She scrambled up but her fall had given me time to close the gap. She spun around as I approached, her foot aimed firmly at my head. I ducked and moved in, punching her in the gut. She staggered back and lifted her pistol. But before she could fire, I delivered a blow with my foot directly onto her knee.

I heard the crack and her eyes widened before she screamed in pain. She dropped her gun as she fell on the ground, scattering Mardi Gras beads as she hit. I hurried to grab her pistol, then trained it on her as she writhed on the ground, clutching her knee.

"That's the problem with you Russian spies," I said. "You always think you're better than American spies. Checkmate."

Gertie ran up and handed me a set of handcuffs. I secured Annika, who was now sobbing silently into the dirt. I heard sirens in the distance as we hurried over to Ida Belle. Larry was scary pale when I dropped down next to him.

"His pulse is getting weaker," Ida Belle said. "I hope that's the ambulance because the sheriff's department isn't going to do us much good right now."

She'd no sooner finished speaking when the ambulance

rounded the corner and slid to a stop right in front of us. The paramedics rushed out and I explained the gunshot wound and approximate time. They secured Larry onto a gurney, shoved him into the ambulance and were gone in a matter of minutes.

As they disappeared around the brush, Carter's truck swung into view. He jumped out and ran over to us.

"Are you all right?" he asked. "What happened? Who was in the ambulance?"

"Larry," I said.

"His wife shot him," Gertie said, and pointed to Annika.

"What?"

"Not his wife," I said. "His sister-in-law."

All three of them stared at me.

"You really think that's Annika?" Gertie asked.

"I'd bet my grill on it," I said.

"Gertie shot a hole in your grill," Ida Belle said.

"Okay, then I'd bet Carter's grill on it," I said. "I broke her leg when I kicked her. It's not compounded so she won't bleed out but that has to hurt. You should probably arrest her and get her to a hospital to have that set. She's going to need to be able to walk when she goes on trial."

"Annika?" Carter said again, looking dumbfounded.

I nodded and he shook his head. "I'm going to secure her in my truck and call for another ambulance. Then the three of you are going to tell me what the heck is going on."

As he walked off, I heard a groan and we swung around as the boat driver struggled to stand.

"I'd completely forgotten about that guy," Ida Belle said as we hurried over.

We all had our weapons out but it was clear as we approached that he was still scared to death and no threat at all. We holstered our weapons and helped him out of the boat.

"Are you all right?" I asked.

He looked up and down his body, feeling his chest and head. "I think so. Maybe. I don't understand what happened."

"Join the party," Gertie said.

"Are you with a women's rescue?" I asked.

He nodded. "Natalia contacted our organization about six months ago, saying she had suffered years of abuse and needed to get away before he killed her. She had pictures from a hospital stay where she sustained a head injury and a broken arm. Neighbors we contacted at previous locations described a situation that mirrored most abusive homes. She called us last night to say she couldn't wait any longer and we pushed up her date."

"Why did you meet her here?"

"She was afraid her husband would follow her. And given only one road in and out of Sinful, it seemed safer to extract her by boat. I do it a lot." He glanced back at his boat and frowned. "Or I used to. When I saw that man show up and Natalia shoot at him, my first thought was getting her out of here. Then she shot at you and things got crazy. What happened here? Was she lying about the abuse?"

I laughed. "She was lying about everything."

"Then maybe it's time you explain," Carter said as he stepped up.

"Some of this is speculation on my part," I said. "You'll have to have Annika fill in the blanks, but this is what I think happened. Natalia, Annika, and Katia all worked for the same shady corporation, but when they'd been there long enough to be groomed into the shady parts, Natalia bailed, not wanting any part of it. Then she met Larry and turned on the charm, figuring marrying an American, especially one in intel, guaranteed her safe passage out of the country and protection for life."

"But something happened and she went to New Orleans to meet Annika," Ida Belle said.

I nodded. "Yes. I think Annika wanted out, which is why she came to the US when she never had before. The hit went out on Annika but Natalia was the one who was killed. Then when Annika awakened in the hospital, she heard her sister was dead and insisted on seeing her. That's when she realized both their heads had been shaved. Annika wore her hair shorter than Natalia but without the hair, they looked exactly the same."

"So she pretended to have a head injury so any differences would be attributed to that," Ida Belle said. "And she went home with Larry and became Natalia. Wow. That's seriously ballsy."

"But explains why Larry was saying she'd never been the same since the attack," Gertie said. "She wasn't the same person, so she couldn't possibly be."

Carter narrowed his eyes at me. "How do you know these things?"

"Later," Gertie said. "I want to hear the rest of the story. How did you figure out that it was Annika and not Natalia?"

"I didn't until the nurse called and made that comment about the shaved heads, then all the things that didn't quite fit suddenly did," I said. "And then there was her vocabulary. Natalia made a couple of comments that stood out. Like when she was talking to Larry she said maybe Katia needed to 'regroup.' And when he got mad at her, she said, 'the enemy is dead.' While on the phone with the rescue organization she said, 'I can't hold any longer.' The choice of words is more military than civilian."

"Oh, you're right," Gertie said.

"And then there were the fireworks," I said. "Remember at the Sinful Ladies booth, Lina got scared when the illegal fireworks went off, but Annika said immediately that it was just fireworks and they weren't close by. Only someone with a lot of ballistics experience could have made that determination in the split second she did."

"That also explains why she could make that shot in the first place," Ida Belle said. "Lina wasn't her child."

"Exactly," I said. "And think about this—if we'd known from the beginning that it was Natalia that had been killed three years ago and Annika was pretending to be her, then who is the most likely person to have killed Katia?"

Gertie's eyes widened. "Annika."

I nodded. "Because even though Larry was willing to accept the changes just to have his wife back, Katia, who'd known her their entire lives, would have seen right through her."

"So why was Katia there in the first place?" Ida Belle said.

"My guess is for the same reason Annika went to New Orleans three years ago, but we'll probably never know. Still, I think the fact that Fedorov was trailing Katia is a clear indication that she was in trouble with her superiors."

"So who killed Fedorov?" Gertie asked. "We know Larry was at the motel last night."

"You know what?" Carter asked.

I waved my hand. "Later. Yes, Larry was at the motel because he used the tracker on the car to follow Annika to the motel. He probably arrived shortly after Annika completed her mission."

"He assumed she was meeting a rescue organization," Gertie said.

"Or another man," Ida Belle said.

"Well, she sorta was," I said. "But she was there to put a bullet in his head. I'd bet money Fedorov wasn't going to leave Louisiana without knowing who beat him to the punch with

Katia and what she might have divulged before they did. And the longer he stayed, the more chance there was that he'd realize Natalia wasn't Natalia."

"That all makes perfect sense," Gertie said.

"But how much of it can be proven?" Ida Belle asked. "I don't see Annika breaking down over this. Someone who can pretend to be her dead sister, live with her husband, raise her daughter...that's a person with no conscience."

"I'm sure the Feds will be taking over with Annika," Carter said. "If everything you say is true, they have ways to make her talk."

"Once Larry gets over being depressed and mad, he'll be able to help," I said.

Gertie shook her head. "I don't think Larry will ever get over being depressed and mad. Right now, he thinks his wife tried to run away from her family and was willing to shoot him to do it, but that's not half as bad as the truth."

The second ambulance pulled up in the clearing, and Carter went over to help them load Annika, complete with handcuffs on the gurney.

"I'm going to follow them," Carter said. "Just in case she gets a second wind, then I'll have to come back and deal with whatever this is." He waved his arm at the collection of cars and boat. "But as soon as I get home, we have got some serious talking to do."

"Uh-oh," Gertie said as he headed off. "You're in trouble."

"That's sort of my default," I said. "Hey, who flattened Annika's tires?"

"I did," Gertie said. "I have a nail gun in my purse that I keep charged."

I grinned. "Of course you do. Throwing the beads on the ground was genius. If Annika hadn't tripped on them she might have gotten away."

"I think you would have caught her," Gertie said. "But I'm glad I could help, even though I had to sacrifice my best beads to do it."

I threw my arm around her shoulder and squeezed. "How about you let me buy you some more? Just this one time."

Gertie brightened. "Maybe just this once."

"Let's get out of here," Ida Belle said. "I need a drink and a shower. In that order."

"Uh, excuse me," the rescue driver interrupted, "but do you think I could get a ride?"

I looked at him. "You like things that go fast, right?"

CHAPTER TWENTY-FIVE

IT WAS a long night filling Carter in on everything, especially with all the interrupting he did to either ask where I'd gotten information or complain about the answer after I'd told him. But when everything was said and done, he finally admitted that without our help, Annika would have disappeared and Katia's murder would probably have gone unsolved. I suggested he suck up to the Heberts a little and maybe they'd give him inside information, but he didn't look excited about the idea. He was even more disconcerted over the laser but he knew he wasn't winning that argument.

The Feds gained custody of Annika the next day and it took them only twenty-four hours to convince her to turn state's evidence on the corporation in exchange for leniency and to be tried in the US rather than deported back to Russia, which would have been certain death. The Feds had given Carter enough information to know that my theory was pretty much how everything had played out, but all the questions about the nuances of the situation would have to remain unanswered.

Larry was touch-and-go for a bit but pulled through. Three

days after the big showdown, he was moved into a private room at the hospital and asked to see me. It was one of the hardest things I'd ever done, explaining my theory to Larry. When I saw his reaction, I knew that deep down, he'd known something was horribly wrong but either didn't want to face it or couldn't bring himself to believe it. He kept insisting that even though he knew Natalia had married him to get out of Russia, she'd softened after marriage and he was certain she cared for him.

I hadn't felt that sorry for someone in a very long time. I had no idea what he was going to tell Lina, and I could tell by his reaction to what I shared with him that he didn't either. The Feds and Carter had already picked his brain over everything but hearing it from me was somehow different, and I could see his previous denial had turned to resigned acceptance by the end of our conversation. Maybe because I was former CIA. Maybe because I was a Sinful resident. Or maybe because Ida Belle, Gertie, and I had saved his life.

Larry had admitted that he'd been in contact with Natalia's shrink she saw after the attack in NOLA. Her behavior had been so much more erratic since Katia's death, he'd been trying to get a psych hold to have her evaluated. I told him to contact any of us if we could help but I had a feeling that once Larry was better, that house would be for sale and he'd put Sinful in his rearview mirror. I wouldn't blame him. Why stay with all the reminders? It was better to take Lina somewhere completely different and start over.

We paid a special visit to Phyllis and filled her in on what we were allowed to repeat—basically that Natalia wasn't Natalia and Larry was as much a victim of Annika's actions as everyone else. Phyllis shifted from thinking Larry was the worst man in the world to cooking baked goods to deliver when he got home. Another reason I figured that For Sale sign would be going up soon.

We also visited Big and Little Hebert and Mannie and brought them up to speed on everything the Feds wouldn't let leak. They were shocked by the turn of events but happy that the role they played helped expose everything and save a decent man from certain death. Mannie had shown them the video of the ambulance theft and the car explosion, and Big had declared me to be the most interesting hurricane that had ever blown into Louisiana. I took it as a compliment. I'm pretty sure he meant it that way.

And finally, we made a short trip back to New Orleans so Gertie could meet with the casino manager and get her motorcycle on order. It was supposed to be delivered in a couple weeks. Gertie had already told Ida Belle she was giving it to her, but we were keeping that tidbit from Carter because his expressions when Gertie talked about it were priceless.

So life in Sinful sort of drifted back into normal, and every day that passed, we were one day closer to the coup. Morrow and I had exchanged conversations a couple times. He indicated my father was still in the DC area but had used the code word "dad," so I knew he'd received the magazines. He attempted to sound normal on our phone calls, and to anyone listening in, he would have. But I knew him better than anyone else at the CIA. After all, he'd helped raise me. I knew he was strained. And I worried about him every day, but there was nothing I could do but wait.

The only good thing was that I appeared to no longer be under surveillance. No one had tripped my cameras or attempted to run me off the road. No strangers had been spotted in Sinful, and with everyone buzzing about the Larry-Annika situation, they were all on high alert again, seeing bad guys behind every bush. The enemy wouldn't have been able to stop for gas near Sinful without someone calling the sheriff's department.

With the threat no longer hanging over us, Ida Belle and Gertie moved back to their houses. Carter insisted on riding it out until the allotted time had passed but he was so busy with sheriff's department business that I rarely saw him until night anyway. Ally was probably the most excited of all of us to get everyone back into their own home. That meant Francis went back home to Gertie. Ally reported that he'd been on a *Godfather* revival kick and had been quoting the movie, complete with gunshots, all day and night.

On *the* day, I sat in my backyard with Ida Belle, Gertie, and Carter, pretending to enjoy the beautiful weather but checking the display on my phone every second, silently willing it to ring. Carter grilled hamburgers and even Ronald dropped by with a casserole for Godzilla in case he turned up. I was seriously afraid Ronald was going to insist on us becoming neighborly and I wasn't ready for that kind of commitment. He'd gazed longingly at the burgers on the grill, but when it was obvious an invitation wasn't forthcoming, he'd finally headed back to his house, prom dress, silver slippers, tiara, and all.

We finished our burgers and were contemplating another round of beers and breaking out the cookies when my phone rang.

"It's Morrow," I said, almost frozen.

They all stared at me as the phone rang and finally, I managed to lift it and answer.

"All clear!" Morrow's words boomed through the phone and a cheer went up around me.

My shoulders slumped as a week and a half's worth of tension fled my body.

"I take it your crew is all there?" Morrow asked.

"Just waiting for your call so the celebration could begin," I said. "What can you tell me?"

"The coup was completely decimated," he said. "We coordinated with some handpicked operatives from the countries that would have been affected, and we picked up over thirty terrorists involved in the plan in our sweep and killed a few more. The equipment has been disarmed and dismantled and will be studied. We've identified all the terrorist cells participating and have already begun plans to counterattack, targeting leadership."

"If they're not organized within, they can't organize with others," I said. "What about the internal problem?"

"That was hard," Morrow said. "No one wanted to believe it, but when we started kicking over rocks, we got enough to indict everyone. It's going to be very ugly for them."

"Their choice," I said. "I have no sympathy."

"Neither do I," Morrow said. "You really came through on this one, Fortune. This country and several others owe you a huge debt of gratitude and it pains me that you won't be standing on a platform in DC when medals are handed out."

"That's okay. I get my thanks these days in baked goods, and I'm happy with that."

"I never thought I'd see the day that Fortune Redding was settled and happy in civilian life, but I believe you."

"What about my father?"

"Well, he's been cleared of any treason charges even though the military has elected not to officially claim him."

"Of course."

"But I'm afraid I have some bad news where he's concerned," Morrow said, his tone grim. "Operatives caught up with him on a boat off the coast of Cape Charles but before our guys could intercept, the boat exploded."

I shook my head and sighed.

"There was no body recovered," Morrow continued, "but the extent of the damage is such that no one could have survived the explosion. And we had visual confirmation of your father boarding the boat and then on deck just minutes before it blew. I'm really sorry, Fortune. This is not something a child should have to live through once, much less twice."

"Good thing I'm not a child anymore."

"To a parent, you're always a child. I'll let you get back to your friends. Please call me if you need anything."

I hung up and filled the rest of them in on the conversation. They cheered over the arrests, and Gertie, who might be even more mercenary than me, cheered over the ones who were killed. They all sobered when I got to the part about my father.

"Do you think he's really gone this time?" Gertie asked.

I shook my head. "I don't know. If anyone could have escaped that situation, it would have been my father. But Morrow seems certain, so..."

Carter took my hand and squeezed.

"I'm really sorry," Ida Belle said.

Gertie nodded. "Me too."

"Yeah, I am too," I said. "Does that mean I forgave him?"

"It means whatever you want it to," Ida Belle said. "There are no rules here. Only what's right for you."

"Well, what's right is that a coup to destroy world leaders didn't happen and the enemy is disbanded. I think it's time to break out whiskey shots and those cookies. This is a celebration, after all!"

Gertie jumped up from her chair and clapped. "I got beads for everyone...just in case it all went well. They're in my purse. Let me run get them."

She hurried into the house and returned with her purse, which she plopped into her chair and began to dig through.

"Found them," she said, and tugged on a set of beads. "Oh no!"

I heard a recognizable clink and jumped up from my chair as Gertie yanked the live grenade out of her purse and chunked it in the bayou. It barely hit the surface before it exploded, sending a spout of water a good twenty feet in the air. We all stared as fish began to float to the surface.

"Sorry," she said. "I must have depressed the striker lever, and then the beads got tangled in the pin and when I pulled..."

She looked at the three of us, staring at her in disbelief, then turned her hands up.

"Fish fry?" she asked.

A WEEK LATER, most everything had returned to normal. Carter and Tiny were back at his house doing the bachelor thing, except for the nights when I was there or he was at my place. Larry, as I expected, had wasted no time, and the For Sale sign was up. He'd packed everything and moved a couple days before. I never heard from him again after our conversation at the hospital, but I couldn't blame him. I wouldn't want to see or talk to anyone who reminded me that I was intel and got duped by a Russian spy pretending to be my wife. There were mitigating circumstances, of course, but I figured once Larry got over grieving the real Natalia, who'd died years ago, he would settle into angry pretty quickly.

It was a glorious Tuesday morning and I'd just finished putting on a load of laundry when UPS knocked on my door and left a package. It wasn't a rare occurrence, as I preferred to get everything I could delivered rather than do the whole shopping thing, but I couldn't remember ordering anything in a while.

I retrieved the package and headed to the kitchen for a break and a glass of sweet tea. After I sat, I opened the box and pulled out what appeared to be a picture of some sort. I pulled the wrapper away from the frame and gasped.

It was a picture of the Florence Cathedral. My mother's favorite structure.

I drew the picture close to my chest and smiled.

"Thanks, Dad."

More adventures with Fortune and the girls coming this summer!

For information on other series or to sign up for Jana's new release newsletter, please visit her website.

Made in the USA
Columbia, SC
10 September 2020

19945280R00176